Backfield in Motion

Jami Davenport

Copyright 2013 Pamela D. Bowerman

ALL YOU'LL EVER BE
IS A PRETTY FACE

Star running back Bruce "Bruiser" Mackey has heard those words his entire life, especially after his twin brother's tragic accident. He might use his surfer-boy good looks to land lucrative endorsements for his secret charity, but he hates books being judged by their covers. Which is why it's wrong that his friend Mackenzie Hernandez is intent on giving herself a makeover.

Sure, Mac and her father have been reeling financially since her brother disappeared three years ago, and Lumberjacks management gives an annual scholarship that might get her life back on track, but he can't imagine anyone smarter, sexier, or more beautiful than Mac already is. He can't keep his hands off her—and the more they spend time together, the less he wants to. She's perfect as is. One way or another, he'll make sure the team's tomboy groundskeeper gets a full ride. And between the two of them, they can learn to accept what's behind them and look downfield to a future full of win.

Backfield in Motion

Jami Davenport

www.BOROUGHSPUBLISHINGGROUP.com

PUBLISHER'S NOTE: This is a work of fiction. Names, characters, places and incidents either are the product of the author's imagination or are used fictitiously. Any resemblance to actual events, locales, business establishments or persons, living or dead, is coincidental. Boroughs Publishing Group does not have any control over and does not assume responsibility for author or third-party websites, blogs or critiques or their content.

BACKFIELD IN MOTION
Copyright © 2013 Pamela D. Bowerman

All rights reserved. Unless specifically noted, no part of this publication may be reproduced, scanned, stored in a retrieval system or transmitted in any form or by any means, electronic, mechanical, photocopying, recording, or otherwise, known or hereinafter invented, without the express written permission of Boroughs Publishing Group. The scanning, uploading and distribution of this book via the Internet or by any other means without the permission of Boroughs Publishing Group is illegal and punishable by law. Participation in the piracy of copyrighted materials violates the author's rights.

Digital edition created by Maureen Cutajar
www.gopublished.com

ISBN 978-1-938876-80-6

A big thank-you to Adrianne Lee, pie-baking queen, author-extraordinaire, Seahawks fan and Wilson defender. Even more importantly, a friend who is always there when I need her, even when she's in deadline hell.

ACKNOWLEDGMENTS

A big heartfelt thank-you to my noontime walking buddies, also fabulous authors:

Margaret Mallory, my partner-in-crime and fellow commiserator (is that a word?) for all things Amazon.

Anthea Lawson, for her steadfast practical advice on writing, publishing, and life in general.

Theresa Scott, for her infinite wisdom, her sense of fairness, and awesome listening skills.

CONTENTS

Title Page

Copyright

Dedication

Acknowledgments

Chapter 1 Pretty is as Pretty Does?

Chapter 2 Gridiron Cinderella

Chapter 3 The Play Fake

Chapter 4 Sisters in Crime

Chapter 5 You Ain't Seen Nothing Yet

Chapter 6 Tackled for a Loss

Chapter 7 Illegal Motion

Chapter 8 Double Date

Chapter 9 Rocking the Ferry

Chapter 10 Crossing the Line

Chapter 11 Running Touchdown

Chapter 12 Staying in Bounds

Chapter 13 Blindsided

Chapter 14 Out of the Huddle

Chapter 15 Free Agent

Chapter 16 Out of Downs

Chapter 17 Coaching Strategies

Chapter 18 Puzzled
Chapter 19 Back and Forth
Chapter 20 Stopping the Play
Chapter 21 Baggage Claim
Chapter 22 Zone Blitz
Chapter 23 Handoff
Chapter 24 Game Over
Author's Note
Author Bio

Chapter 1
Pretty is as Pretty Does?

"Yeah, yeah, Bruiser, all you'll ever be is just another pretty face."

"Never criticize the face that feeds you," Bruce Mackey, a.k.a. Bruiser, shot back as he gritted his teeth.

Nothing but a pretty face? Hell. That wasn't the type of thing a person tells a 230-pound premier running back for the Seattle Lumberjacks. Not that Bruiser hadn't worked his ass off to craft that very superficial image—then worked that much harder on the football field to show the world and the NFL that he was a football player first and pretty face second.

Football was his job and his passion. On a normal day, it took two linebackers and handful of defensive backs to bring him to his knees as he fought like a wild man for a few extra yards, hence the odd nickname Bruiser.

Playing the role of a pretty boy usually suited him just fine. Other than being one tough hombre on the football field, no one expected anything serious or profound from the league's "Hottest Hunk," which kept even the nosiest of reporters from diving deep enough to unearth the painful truth lurking behind his carefree mask. That was just fine with Bruiser. He let his play on the field speak for itself. The rest was no one's business but his.

Harold, the photographer, winked at him. "Hey, I'm not criticizing. That pretty face is certifiable money in the bank."

Bruiser didn't wink back.

Click. Click. Click.

He didn't move, just held his pose and stared over the head of the photographer at nothing.

"Look straight into the camera. Pretend I'm a beautiful woman across the room at a party. I'm beckoning you."

"You? I don't have that good of an imagination. No one does." Bruiser resisted the urge to roll his eyes. He really hated this stuff, but money was money. He had a debt to pay and an even bigger promise to keep.

"Relax. You're too stiff."

Stiff? Hell, his dick had shriveled to nothing on this unseasonably chilly forty-five-degree morning. It wasn't like he was acclimated to anything below sixty degrees after spending the last several months in Southern Cal, having traded the Seattle rainy season for warm sand, mega endorsement deals, movie cameos, and bikini-clad women. He'd only returned to the Emerald City a few short days ago.

"I'm freezing my ass off. Hurry up, will ya?"

"You're in a snit today." Harold sniffed as if Bruiser had hurt his feelings. Well, fuck, Harold wasn't the one standing around in a frigid horse barn wearing nothing but SportsJock underwear, a Stetson, and a pair of Tony Lamas. Harold's assistant flitted around like a pesky fly, messing with Bruiser's perfectly styled blond hair. He fought like hell not to bite the poor little guy's head off just for sport.

"Okay, tease us a little. Hook your thumb in the waistband and pull it down just so it stops short of your junk."

Bruiser knew the drill. He almost made more from modeling than he did football. Plus, he didn't have a modest bone in his body. If they'd asked him to strip, he'd have stripped and given them the full-meal deal. But the league frowned on all-out nudity, so Bruiser's nude modeling had to be tastefully done with the goods disguised in dark shadows.

Bruiser changed his pose, propping one foot on the hay bale.

"Turn slightly. Put your back to me. Good. Good."

Click. Click. Click.

"Now strip off your shorts, hold them with a finger, and cover your package with your hat."

"How does that sell underwear?" Despite Bruiser's immodesty, getting nude fucking irritated him today.

"Do I look like a marketing person? Just another pose they asked for."

Bruiser shrugged and shucked out of his briefs—not easy when wearing boots—and dangled them on one finger as he held his hat over his crotch area. Harold clicked away while Bruiser changed poses and forced himself to stay alert.

"I expected your dick to be so big you'd need a sombrero to cover it."

Bruiser dropped the hat and spun around to face the speaker. Mackenzie Hernandez, known as Mac to all the guys on the team, stood in the barn door. Small and fit, with a nice little body, Mac was kinda cute with her upturned nose, mischievous deep brown eyes, and long, wavy, dirty blond hair, but she downplayed her physical attributes as if she didn't give a shit about appearances.

Mac made a show of looking at his crotch and arching an eyebrow, not the least bit embarrassed. But then, not much embarrassed Mac.

Caught off-balance, Bruiser stared down at his dick. A sombrero? Of course it was big enough to need a sombrero. What the hell was she talking about? Even shriveled in the cold, damp Seattle morning, he didn't think it looked that small.

Did it?

He bent down to pick up his Stetson, not bothering to cover himself, and tamped down his annoyance while ramping up the charm.

Little dick, my ass.

"Now, honey, that cuts me to the quick." He held his Stetson over his heart and let out an exaggerated sigh.

"I sincerely doubt that. Your skin is as thick as your head is large."

"Ah, so you admit it. I am big. I knew you were just jerking my chain. I like that in a woman." A slow smile spread across Bruiser's face. She'd walked into that one.

Mac's mouth pulled into a firm, straight line, and her eyes glinted with what looked to Bruiser like murderous intent.

"You creeping up on me, honey? Just had to get a sneak peek? Don't blame you; all the ladies feel that way." Bruiser grinned. She deserved a little shit after the sombrero comment.

Bruiser was a flirt and tease, two of his many talents, and he didn't discriminate. All women were fair game, regardless of age, race, or religion. And Mac was one of his favorite targets because she didn't know the first thing about flirting. He loved to tease her, try to get beneath her tough-girl exterior. Today he'd hit pay dirt. Flustered yet clearly annoyed, Mac backed away. "I'm not stalking you. I promised Derek and Rachel I'd feed their horses while they're out of town."

His teammate, Derek Ramsey, and his wife, Rachel, owned the horse farm.

"Ma'am, you'll need to leave until we're done shooting," Harold said. He sniffed, his boxers all in a bunch over the interruption.

Well, damn. Bruiser was just starting to feel entertained.

"Mac won't bother me. She's almost like one of the guys—with boobs." Bruiser looked her up and down. "Nice boobs, though, hon." He waggled his eyebrows. "We'll catch up later. Once you recover from the sight of my incredible body."

"Overconfident ass," Mac shot back.

"Absolutely, sweetheart. You like me that way." He winked at her, and she glared back. He was winning points today.

"I don't like you any way but on the football field."

Bruiser opened his mouth to fire off an answering round when Harold interrupted him. "Hey, Bruiser, let's finish this."

Still grinning, Bruiser turned away from Mac and struck a pose. He had a job to do and giving her shit wouldn't get it done.

But later all bets were off.

* * * * *

Mac Hernandez stalked to the grain bins madder than a cat tossed in a swimming pool. Bruiser Mackey was a prick, a pretty-boy prick of the worst kind and as shallow as a dried-up mud puddle in the middle of a Seattle summer. And dammit, just thinking of the guy made her panties wet.

She should've flipped his shit right back in his pretty face instead of ogling his perfect abs, nice ass, and, well, his other assets.

Just one of the guys.

Usually she didn't give a shit about being one of the guys because it was the truth; only today it pissed her off for some reason. Maybe because he'd caught her gawking at his privates, something she never-effing-ever did. Heck, her maintenance and grounds position at the Lumberjacks practice facility put her in direct contact with several tons of muscular egos, many partially dressed or even naked. They never bothered to cover up around her, and she'd never cared because she was like one of the guys.

Until today.

Until the man she'd harbored a secret crush on for the past three years stated that fact out loud.

She shouldn't have a crush on a superficial guy like Bruiser, but tell that to her heart. He was everything she disliked in a man, a preening peacock who exploited his looks for money. But he was a damn good football player in spite of his preoccupation with his appearance.

Even worse, he continually flirted with her, making every attempt to embarrass the hell out of her with his outrageous comments. And he did embarrass her, though she thought she hid it well—usually.

Mac hazarded a glance back at him, his fine ass once again clad in tight underwear. His perfect eight-pack abs glistened with whatever crap they'd rubbed on his tanned skin, while his arm muscles bulged and flexed as he assumed different poses.

He looked over his shoulder, caught her staring and winked at her, setting her face on fire again. Mac never blushed. Absolutely fucking never. Except when Bruiser gave her shit or looked at her with those penetrating blue-gray eyes. Thank heavens the darkest corner of the barn concealed her face.

Damn, but the man had one fine body, and she'd witnessed some incredibly sculpted bodies in her time with the Lumberjacks—called the Jacks by just about everyone—but Bruiser's body was the finest of the finest.

Mac's Aunt Helen used to say never to date a man prettier than you. And Bruiser was way too pretty for a plain woman like her, with her dishwater blond hair, nondescript brown eyes and so-so figure.

Not to mention his—uh—equipment might be more than she could handle. Despite what she said to the glamour boy, he was—ahem—well endowed. Way too well. With her relative inexperience with men, she'd best stay away from said equipment and said pretty boy.

The guys would be shocked that she was sexually inexperienced, but then no one knew the real Mac. They only knew the tomboy Mac they saw every day mowing the practice field grass in perfect straight lines or pulling weeds in the flower beds or beating them at a game of pool at the sports bar near Jacks' HQ. They knew the Mac who didn't have a life, and while Mac may not have a life, she had a mission—a mission to figure out what the hell happened to her older brother, who'd gone missing three years ago. She spent all her off hours investigating new leads and going over old ones with her father.

Which was why she fantasized about an absolute fantasy guy like Bruiser. Harmless fun and a distraction from how screwed up her life really was.

Mac turned back to her chore of feeding the horses and forced herself to ignore the photo session several feet away. In fact, she ignored it so well she didn't even notice when they finished up for the day. Instead, she focused on the horses munching away at their grain and making the deep guttural noises horses make in greeting. Someday she'd have money and a stable full of horses and she'd get a life.

Yeah, that'd happen when hell froze over or Mac wore a dress.

"Hey, sweetheart, did you miss me?"

Mac jumped as Bruiser's hot breath teased her ear. She whirled around and swatted at his chest, now clad in a Jacks sweatshirt. "You scared the crap out of me, you asshole."

He chuckled. "I'm not the asshole. That's Harris's role." No one on the team could come close to dethroning Tyler Harris, the team's quarterback, from his self-proclaimed position as the team's resident asshole.

"You have a point there." Mac strode away from Bruiser, head held high, throwing flakes of hay into the stalls. Bruiser followed her. Instead of his usual brash smile, he appeared—worried? Bruiser?

"So do you really think I'm small?" He studied her with concern, as if her opinion regarding the length of his penis actually mattered. It wasn't like overconfident Bruiser would ever be concerned about what she thought.

He stepped closer to her—too close. His scent surrounded her, engulfed her. Oh, God, please. Just one night, just one night with the Jacks' pretty boy, and she'd never ask for another thing. Never.

His blue-gray eyes bored into her and his brow furrowed. Well, damn, the pretty boy was actually concerned. Mac shook her head, eager to dispel his insecurities, even as she battled with the reason why. "Too bad your brain isn't as big as your dick."

A big smile tugged at the corners of his mouth. "I knew it. You think I'm large."

"That wasn't a compliment, so don't let it go to your head."

"Too late, already has. Both of them." Then he met her frosty gaze with his steady blue-gray one and a slow, sexy smile crossed his face. "Hey, you're in luck. I'm at loose ends tonight. How about we get a burger at that place down the road?"

"You buying?" Mac slipped into her usual buddy mode, knowing that's all she was to Bruiser and being pathetic enough to play her part.

* * * * *

A few minutes later Bruiser slid into a booth seat across from Mac. He pulled a ball cap over his head to avoid being recognized, not that it helped. People still stared. He ignored their stares and took a long pull off his beer.

"So, little lady, how goes the battle?"

"Same old, same old," Mac muttered.

Something seemed to be stuck in her craw. Bruiser admired that about Mac. She never put on pretenses; what you saw was what you got. Sometimes he envied her ability to be who she was and not give a damn what others thought, while he spent way too much time worrying about others' expectations and how he measured up. Chalk up that particular issue to a father who made it clear Bruiser never measured up and a mother and sister who believed appearances weren't everything—they were the only thing.

He admired Mac. She didn't dress or behave to please anyone but herself—a rare trait in a woman. But Mac was no ordinary woman.

As if reading his mind, Mac stared across the table at him. "I don't think I've ever seen you in jeans."

"Pretty awesome, huh?" He glanced at her baggy sweatshirt with the horse snot on it. Mac never cared about that crap. She was who she was. She carried off this earthy sexiness that put other women to shame with their fake faces and fake boobs.

"You're an awesome pain in the butt."

Bruiser threw back his head and laughed. "Mac, you're a hoot."

"I don't see what's so funny."

"You should've been born a guy."

"You're not the first person who's said that." She shrugged and looked away, almost as if he'd hurt her feelings. He shook off that outrageous thought. Mac was the toughest woman he knew.

Bruiser leaned back in the booth and grinned. He liked Mac, really liked her. She was such an exact opposite of the other women in his life, and he found her straightforward honesty refreshing. Besides, he knew a kindred spirit when it tackled him to the ground.

Oh, yeah, Bruiser recognized it—that very pain that hid behind the false smile and the sparkling eyes. Yeah, he recognized it because he had the same dull pain himself, the one that never went away and at times became a sharp stab to the gut. No one saw it but his best buddy on the team, Brett Gunnels. Not his parents. Not his closest friends. Only kindred spirits saw the mutual burden of guilt carried by another.

Apparently Mac battled similar demons. Bruiser had heard things from the guys, but he didn't know the details. He could probably search for them but he kept his nose out of other people's business, expecting them to do the same.

"How're things going at work? Vince giving you any more shit?"

"I can handle that tool." She focused her full attention to the TV showing the Mariners game. Bruiser made a point not to pry and let it drop. When she glanced back at him, their gazes met. A strange little curling sensation tickled his stomach lining, almost like the first stage of desire. Yet even as he tried to drag his gaze away, he couldn't, like an elk caught in the crosshairs of a hunter's rifle, knowing he was going down but not able to save himself.

What the hell? Desire? *For Mac*? Fuck, he didn't even know if she dated guys or girls. He must be losing it. Yet some primal instinct insisted a passionate woman lurked beneath all those baggy clothes and that tough-girl facade. And he knew this how? He wasn't sure, but his mind flashed to a vivid vision of Mac, naked and straddling him, taking him deep, then pounding up and down on him until he damn near reached insanity.

Him and Mac? Hooking up like two sex-starved teenagers? *Crap.* Bruiser scrubbed his hands over his face.

"Are you okay?"

He glanced up with a guilty start. "I'm awesome. Remember?"

She smiled, and it changed her, made her look softer, more feminine. Funny how he'd never noticed what a knockout smile she had, but she didn't smile much. His dick noticed, too, and pressed against the fly of his jeans almost painfully. He shifted his ass but couldn't find a position that gave him any relief. Well, there was one position, but that wasn't going to happen.

Damn. He'd call one of his standbys tonight and get some. Maybe he'd call two. It'd been a while since he'd indulged. In theory, a threesome sounded like any man's dream, but in reality, not so much. Especially when the two women were narcissistic and competing for his attention. Screw that, maybe he'd stick with one woman.

Only for some reason, sex with an anonymous woman with big fake boobs and long muscular legs didn't excite him like it had a few weeks ago. Most of the women he dated worked out so much that they had these hard bodies, more like a guy than a woman. He glanced at Mac. She was muscled, too, but more from hard work than from working out in a gym.

He jumped when Mac's hand touched his. "Seriously? Are you all right?"

Her concern touched him. Rarely did anyone care about him or his feelings beyond how it could benefit them, including his family—especially his family.

He faked a devil-may-care smile and nodded. "Keep touching me like that, and I'll be more than fine." He drained the last of his beer.

"You'd flirt with an eighty-year-old grandmother."

"Try it sometime. You might like it."

"Flirting with an eighty-year-old grandmother?"

"No, flirting in general. It's harmless fun."

"You do it just to irritate me." Mac's brown eyes flashed fire.

Bruiser only grinned even more. He loved getting a rise out of her. "My flirting irritates you? Most women are flattered."

"Most women aren't me."

Bruiser got a chuckle out of that. "You're so right, Mac, but I wouldn't want you any other way. You're an original."

She pursed her lips as if his words tasted sour. Hell, he'd meant it to be a compliment. Time to hit the road before he fell all over himself trying to impress a woman he couldn't impress. Bruiser stood and dropped a couple twenties on the table.

"Gotta go. This should cover it." Then he got the hell out of there.

Whatever this weird preoccupation with Mac was, he needed to squash it flat. As he sped down the street in his badass SUV, he dialed a number and made a date with for the next night.

Chapter 2

Gridiron Cinderella

Mac's boss waved her down as she made a pass across the practice field with the riding lawn mower. She slowed and turned off the engine, annoyed at being interrupted but trying like hell not to show it. Jed Simms might be her boss and the fields and grounds manager for the Lumberjacks, but he was also a life-long family friend. His craggy face reminded her of one of those dried-up applehead dolls her grandma used to make. Too much time in the sun, but even so he seemed the picture of health.

Tapping her fingernails on the steering wheel, she waited for Jed to walk up to her. If she drove over, it'd ruin her perfectly straight lines. And no one did straight lines like Mac.

"We need to talk." Jed grimaced, and Mac immediately went on red alert.

"Am I gonna like this?" She frowned while the pessimist inside her braced for the worst. Jed never interrupted her when she was mowing.

"Uh, knowing you, probably not." He shook his head and looked everywhere but at Mac. This wasn't good at all.

"What is it?" Mac held her breath. Her intuition warned of bad news ahead.

"I need a head count for the Jacks' annual summer barbecue at the owner's Lake Washington mansion. Can I count you in?"

Mac scrunched up her face and shook her head so hard her ponytail slapped her in the cheek. "No way am I going to that bullshit barbecue." Every summer the daughter of the team's owner put on this huge barbecue though the name was a misnomer. It was a black-tie charity affair that made the society page of the newspaper, nothing like Mac's idea of a barbecue. But then Veronica never did anything small. Unfortunately, her position as the Jacks' personnel director gave her the power to dictate attendance.

"Vince is going."

"He is? That suck-ass." Mac swore under her breath. Dread filled her. Not Vince. Her nemesis. The guy whose life's mission was to make her look bad or get her ass fired.

"He's willing to play the political game to reach his goals." Jed stared her straight in the eyes, and Mac stared right back, her gaze unwavering, even though she wanted to look down.

"I'd rather be chosen on my merits, not how far my head is stuck up someone's ass."

So that's what this was about—the coveted scholarship. Every few years, the Lumberjacks awarded an employee a full-ride scholarship to the college of their choice, as long as their area of study benefitted the organization. Mac wanted that scholarship so badly she could taste it. Even more, she had her eye on the horticulturist position, which would be available in the next year or so due to the current horticulturist's impending retirement. Most NFL practice facilities didn't employ a horticulturist, but the Jacks' facility bordered Lake Washington and part of the property included wetlands and shoreline, which required careful management. Down the road, she'd work herself into turf management.

"This is Veronica—the owner's daughter—we're talking about." Jed looked across the field as if assessing the deep green grass, only he didn't fool Mac. His Adam's apple bobbed as he swallowed. "Mac, Vince is lobbying to make himself the frontrunner for the scholarship. He's been here longer, and he's trying to convince management he's a better fit."

"He's a lazy ass. He hides out half the day and lets the rest of us do his work for him."

"Management doesn't see that. *You* need to make an effort here if you want that scholarship. You need to be seen out of your normal work clothes in situations other than mowing the fields or weeding the front flower beds."

"Fine, I'll go to that damn barbecue, but I'm not wearing a dress." Heck, she couldn't remember the last time she'd worn a dress. Had she ever worn a dress? Maybe when she'd been a toddler at her mother's funeral.

Jed grinned, enjoying her annoyance all too much. "It's all part of the job. You'll need a date. Do you know someone you can ask?"

A date? As if on cue, Bruiser, dressed in nothing but a pair of shorts and running shoes, jogged by. Mac's eyes fastened onto the man's ripped body, and she licked her lips so she wouldn't embarrass herself by drooling. Sweat ran down his spine and disappeared beneath his waistband. She'd love to lick that sweat off his body, slide her hands under those shorts and grip that fine ass of his, and then she'd—

"I never would've guessed it." Jed snorted out a chuckle.

With a guilty start, Mac jerked her head back to her boss. "Guessed what?" Her face burned worse than it had on that summer day she'd fallen asleep at the beach.

"You have a thing for the team pretty boy." The teasing glint in his eyes terrified her.

"No, I don't. I appreciate a fine male body, that's all." Mac started the lawnmower to drown out Jed's amused laughter. As she put it in gear, she shot Jed one last irritated scowl and hollered over the engine. "Don't get any ideas. I'll get my own damn date."

"Make sure you do."

Mac groaned at the thought of what Jed would do if left to his own devices. She'd definitely dig up a date.

Somewhere.

* * * * *

A few hours later, Mac lined up a shot and dropped the eight ball into the corner pocket. With a long-suffering sigh, Derek Ramsey, the Jacks' all-pro wide receiver, shuffled back to his seat, ignoring the jeers of his teammates. Mac pumped her fist in the air, then swept her gaze around the room, seeking out her next victim. Not one of the chickenshits would even establish eye contact with her. Cowards, every last one of them.

Sprawled around a long table sat a dozen or so Seattle Lumberjacks who lived in Seattle year-round. They met almost every Monday night for beer and pool at O'Malley's Sports Bar a few miles from the Jacks' practice facility. Mac had been coming here with the team for the past three years. Sometimes the group dwindled to a few guys. Other times, during football season, the rowdy bunch took over the back room and watched Monday Night Football together for some raucous good times with Mac in the thick of it all.

She'd always been more comfortable with men than women. Hell, all her best friends growing up had been men. She'd never cultivated actual girlfriends or traded makeup secrets or talked about hot guys. Lately, she wished she had, because she was absolutely clueless about girl stuff. Sometimes even a tomboy wanted to be seen as a woman.

And why was she thinking this now?

This weird preoccupation lately with getting more girly better not have anything to do with seeing Bruiser bare-ass naked with all his equipment on display. Her gaze flicked to the object of her after-dark bedroom fantasies, and man, she'd had some hot ones. Bruiser leaned forward, a heart-stopping smile on his face, laughter in his sexy voice, and entertained the group with some outrageous tale about hang-gliding off California cliffs.

Mac sighed and plopped into a chair next to Brett, the Jacks' quiet backup quarterback and a bit of an enigma. He raised an eyebrow at her, and she looked away. Brett saw everything but never said much. She felt his eyes on her and knew he was reading her like a trashy novel. Squirming slightly, she finally met his gaze and prayed nothing on her face gave away her weakness.

"Take a picture, it'll last longer," she quipped.

Brett didn't back down, didn't even blink. "What's got your tail in a knot?"

Mac glanced around the table. Derek and Bruiser discussed the holes in the Mariners' pitching staff. Tyler and Zach engaged in a good-natured pissing contest over whether the offense or defense would win more games for the team in the upcoming season. No one paid Mac and Brett any attention.

"I have a problem." Mac scowled and drew rings on the table with her beer glass.

"Yeah?" Brett leaned forward.

"Yeah. I need to be more visible to management, especially Veronica, if I want a chance at the Jacks' employee scholarship."

"Makes sense. But how?"

"I need to be seen as more than the person who mows the grass."

"Hey, you keep all the plants healthy, too, even the finicky ones." Brett shot her a rare grin, his pale blue eyes twinkling. Mac smiled back at him. There were times when she almost suspected Brett had a crush on her, which seemed outrageous. Regardless, the reclusive backup quarterback never acted on his feelings.

"I need to be seen in a more professional light by Veronica."

"Good luck with that. She hates everybody but Bruiser. He's her poster boy for a football player." Brett snorted, as if he found this little fact highly amusing.

"I know."

"So what's your plan?"

"I need to go to that damn barbecue for starters."

"Well then, go." Brett always had a simple, direct answer for everything.

Mac felt her face heat up. How did a girl explain that she didn't know how to be a girl? In her typical Mac way, she just spit it out. "I don't know what to wear and all that crap."

"Lavender can help with that." Tyler inserted himself into the conversation. "She lives to shop. At least that's what my credit card says."

Mac jumped, unaware she'd caught the attention of the other guys at the table. Just fucking wonderful, as if this whole thing weren't humiliating enough. She turned to Tyler, unable to keep annoyance out of her voice. "We were having a private conversation."

"Yeah, Mac, whatever." Tyler rolled his eyes. "It's not like your voice doesn't carry."

"Great. So I'm not just an inept dresser, I'm a big mouth."

"You could tone it down a little," Zach added with an apologetic shrug.

Mac crossed her arms over her chest and gazed around the table. "This is as toned down as it gets."

"Like I said, I'll have Lavender call you."

"Rachel is great at shopping on budget," Derek offered.

"Kelsie can help, too. If she cleaned me up, she can do it for anyone." Zach ducked his head, as if realizing what he'd just said. "Not that you need cleaning up. You look great as you are."

Mac stared at her ragged fingernails. Maybe she did need a little help.

"Give me your number. We'll have the women get in touch with you." Tyler could be as bossy as Mac's cranky, geriatric cat.

With a heavy sigh, Mac wrote her number on a napkin and passed it to Tyler. Working to gather her courage for one final request, she chewed on her lower lip and stared at a framed painting of dogs playing poker hanging crookedly on the opposite wall. The bulldog was cheating.

Mac looked back at the guys and cleared her throat. "I need one more thing. An escort to this barbecue."

For a moment, silence reigned around the table. She caught the quick glances from one guy to another and wanted to crawl under the table.

"I'm taking my wife or I'd be glad to do it," Zach said.

"Me, too."

"I might as well have a wife. I'm taking Lavender."

"So when are you going to marry her?" Derek challenged Tyler, who also happened to be his cousin.

"I don't do marriage. We're a couple. She knows that." Tyler tipped his chair back on two legs and chewed on a straw. His attempt to look nonchalant didn't fool Mac. Marriage gave the guy claustrophobia.

"Oh, man, you're in deep shit, Harris. You'd better put a ring on that girl's finger before she kicks your dumbshit ass to the curb." Zach grinned at his friend, obviously enjoying the quarterback's discomfort.

"She knows a good thing when she sees it." Tyler's chair slammed to the ground, and he oozed complacent arrogance. Mac doubted Lavender was nearly as complacent about their situation.

"I bet she knows a hopeless cause when she sees one, too." Zach howled with laughter and the rest joined in.

"No way in fucking hell am I marrying. You guys can live with a ball and chain, but not this guy."

"Hey, we're talking about Mac here." Brett steered the conversation back to her. "I'd love to take you, but I'm out of town that weekend." Regret burrowed lines on his face, as if he really did want to take her.

A couple other single guys offered up their excuses. Mac gripped the edge of the table to stop herself from sinking under it while dying a slow death from embarrassment. None of them wanted to be seen with the woman who was plain as a bagel without cream cheese.

Mac smelled like fresh dirt and mowed grass, not expensive perfume. She cut her own hair when it got too long. She didn't own a dress or makeup beyond an old tube of pink lipstick and grocery store mascara. Yeah, guys like these didn't take out girls like her, even as a favor. Even worse, only one guy in this room interested her, and he'd never offer. Not the pretty boy who only did what benefitted Bruiser.

"Bruiser, Veronica thinks you're God's gift to the fucking NFL. It'd be a big advantage to Mac if you took her." Brett had read Mac's mind. Oh, lord, not Bruiser. *No, no, no.*

"Yeah, Bruise, that's perfect. Veronica salivates every time you get near her just thinking about the different ways she can use you to promote the team." Derek winked at Mac, but she didn't wink back. She was too busy resurrecting her pride, yet none of these assholes seemed to give a shit about her discomfort.

"Yeah, like the *Men of the NFL* Calendar. What were you, Mr. July?"

"August," Bruiser growled, as if irritated that he even remembered the month. "Just for the record, my relationship with Veronica is purely business."

"Nobody's saying it isn't," Zach pointed out.

"So it's a done deal. You'll take Mac." Tyler lifted his beer in a toast.

Bruiser hesitated for a brief moment, just long enough to telegraph to Mac that he didn't really want to take her. "I'd love to take you, honey." His mouth tipped up in that sexy smile of his. This was no big deal to him, while it was everything to Mac, on so many levels.

Mac slipped her hands under the table and clenched them together to cover up the shaking. Invisible fingers wrapped around her throat, rendering her unable to speak. Hell, breathing was a big enough chore.

Her and Bruiser? On a date? Even if it was a fake one. A pity date. She knew her mouth was opening and closing like a newscaster with a broken teleprompter. Tyler's mouth kicked up in a knowing smile. When the jerk nudged his cousin, she kicked her vocal cords into operation. "I—I don't think—"

"It's settled." Tyler smirked at her, as if she weren't fooling him one damn bit, and reached for the pitcher of beer, draining it. "Who's buying the next round?"

Mac sat back in her chair and resisted the urge to bite off what was left of her fingernails. Everything was far from settled, especially her wildly beating heart. She shot a glance at Bruiser, who wasn't even paying any attention to her. Taking her to the barbecue was the equivalent of a mercy date. Bruiser could flirt with her, but she didn't even register on his radar as a woman. Unless Kelsie and company could work a major miracle.

But did she want to register on his radar? Where the hell would that get her?

Most likely nowhere good.

* * * * *

Bruiser hated being played, and the guys had just played him. Big time. He waited until Mac and the rest of his jerk-off teammates left the bar then he turned on his former—as of a few minutes ago—best friend. "Why the fuck did you suggest I take Mac?"

"You didn't have to say yes."

"Yeah, you pricks backed me into a corner. I couldn't turn her down without hurting her feelings."

"Do you care? About her feelings, that is?"

"Yeah, I do. Surprised? I like Mac." Bruiser was pissed and out of sorts, which probably had something to do with his recurrent fantasies about Mac riding him for all he was worth into one mind-altering orgasm after another. Shit, he'd been trying to squelch those particular visions for the past week by dating a different woman every night. And each night, instead of taking Ms. Anonymous home and banging her brains out, he dropped them off and left. Visions of Mac's pretty brown eyes and toned, athletic body moving underneath his had driven away his desire for anyone else.

God, he needed to get a grip. Bruiser rubbed his eyes with his fists.

"Everyone likes Mac." Brett ground his teeth together, obviously misinterpreting Bruiser's attitude as not wanting to take Mac out.

Feeling oddly weary, Bruiser leaned his elbows on the table, rested his chin in his palms, and looked up. "Not as much as you do. Why don't you ask her out?" Maybe that'd solve his current preoccupation. He didn't mess with another man's woman. Ever. If he could get these two damaged souls together, he could go back to his normal life of meaningless, recreational sex and superficial friendships.

"I don't know. She probably wouldn't go." Brett took a big gulp of his beer.

"How the hell do you know? You've never asked her."

"I might."

Bruiser stared at his friend and shook his head. "You're a piece of work, Brett, you know that?"

"Takes one to know one."

"Sure does," Bruiser chuckled.

Brett stared at his beer as if it held the answers to world peace. "I wish I could take her."

"I wish you could, too. Cancel your plans."

"I can't. I'm in Portland judging a pet parade fundraiser to benefit to an animal shelter. Remember? I asked you, and you said no. Said you had commitments."

"Uh, yeah, that. My plans got cancelled." Bruiser had been outed. "I'm not good with animals." Pets reminded him too much of his own crappy upbringing with his barfly mother and crazy-wild sister and their unattended menagerie of dogs and cats. "Hey, I gave you a big check to help with expenses."

"You think money replaces people, Bruce?"

He didn't have an answer for that. His ex-wife, CeCe, would say money solved everything. She took half of his rookie-year signing bonus and hooked up with a New York quarterback so she could bask in the limelight of the Big Apple. Bruiser had really loved that woman. Adored her, actually. They'd been together since high school, dated all through college, and married as soon as the Jacks drafted him in the first round. Less than a year later, she left him with a broken heart and empty bank account. She'd been one in a handful of people in his life who'd deserted him, and after that Bruiser tore a page from his family's playbook and kept his relationships superficial. A guy didn't get fucked over that way.

He had one simple rule when it came to women: His one-week rule. Most didn't last one entire night, but none of them lasted a week. Not since CeCe. At least he hadn't confided his secret guilt to her. If she'd known the depth of his private pain, she'd have used it and turned it back around on him.

She'd been his biggest fucking mistake. Being betrayed by someone you loved and trusted sucked worse than losing the Super Bowl in the last second of the game.

He kept his relationships so superficial, he didn't even know much about Brett, his best friend, and he didn't ask, even though he suspected his buddy had similar scars from his own past. Brett had interrupted his college education to become a paratrooper. Sometimes Bruiser caught the tragic sadness in Brett's eyes and worried like hell about his friend, but he kept his concerns to himself, holding the world at arm's length and concentrating on football and his foundation.

Except lately he'd been concentrating on Mac, which was fucking weird. Hell, he didn't even know if she cleaned up well—or cleaned up at all. A new image crashed into his brain: Mac wrestling with him in a pit of warm, thick, gooey mud. Her body covered with wet, soft dirt and her nipples standing out against the material of a thin T-shirt and nothing else.

Oh, hell. He smacked the flat of his palm against his forehead.

"What is wrong with you?" Brett narrowed his eyes and studied Bruiser with a gaze that pierced way too deep.

"Nothing, just got a headache. I'll flip you for the next round of drinks."

"Nah, I'm done for the night. Gotta get back to the kids." Brett's kids consisted of a shitload of animal rejects, which was why Bruiser never went to Brett's place.

"Catch ya later then."

Brett sketched a salute and headed for the door, stiffing Bruiser for the bill. With a sigh, he took out his wallet and paid up. Across the room, an athletic, blonde woman chatted with her friends. She caught his eye and waved. She reminded him a lot of Mac. Bruiser got up from the table and made his way to her. Maybe he just needed a change in type.

Or maybe he needed something more, something he wouldn't get from a one-night stand with a stranger he picked up in a bar.

Smiling at the ladies, he walked past their table and out the door.

Chapter 3

The Play Fake

Mac plopped down in a plastic lawn chair on the concrete patio of her little house and kept her back to the house next door. Two years ago she'd planted arborvitae next to the fence dividing the two properties in hopes they'd block any view of the neighbors, but the shrubs weren't growing fast enough for her taste.

The old craftsman-style cottage had been her home for about four years. Previously, her grandmother had lived there. This property had been in her family for four generations.

After Mac made the decision to move into the long-vacant house, she'd worked side-by-side with her brother Will to make it livable. Since he'd lived next door, it'd been easy for him to drop by and work on stuff, even though it pissed off his selfish wife, Sonja. No one in the family ever understood why Will married the woman. Well, other than the obvious. She had big boobs and wasn't afraid to show them off. But a wedding ring hadn't guaranteed Will exclusive rights to that show.

Mac rubbed her eyes with her fists and let out a shuddering sigh. She glanced around her carefully landscaped yard with its flower gardens erupting in a riot of summer colors. Birds splashed in the birdbath and flitted to and from various birdfeeders. She loved her little house and was immensely proud of all the improvements she'd made over the years.

Shifting in her lawn chair, Mac's gaze swung toward her house. Beyond the open French doors on the opposite wall, an ornate, antique mantle surrounded the old brick fireplace. Will had found it on CraigsList and sanded, stained, and installed it as a surprise for her birthday.

God, she missed her brother with his dancing, mischievous eyes and zest for life. His absence left a huge hole in her heart that time didn't seem to heal.

Bart rubbed his black head against her leg, and she bent down to pick him up. The crotchety, old black cat with one good eye and a ripped ear purred his approval. He'd showed up at her back door one day and demanded in no uncertain terms that he upgrade his status to a house cat. She'd relented and been his loyal servant ever since. Mac hugged him close, burying her face in his soft fur, while his purring gave her a sliver of comfort.

"Mac? I thought I'd find you out here."

Mac turned and smiled as her father, Craig Hernandez, sank his lanky body into the chair next to her. "Hi, Dad."

He looked weary and old with his bloodshot eyes and rumpled shirt he'd most likely slept in, if he got any sleep. So much for a relaxing retirement.

"Hey, honey. I got a lead via the website yesterday. Someone thinks they may have spotted your brother in Port Townsend last weekend. What time do you want to head up there on Saturday?"

Try not at all. Mac cringed inwardly at her traitorous thoughts. "Dad, I can't go Saturday. I have plans."

Her father frowned. Nothing deterred him from his mission. "What could be more important than finding your brother?"

"What's the point, Dad? We aren't going to find him in Port Townsend because he's not there." She fought to keep the exasperation from her voice. The last thing she wanted to do was spend the three-hour drive cooped up in a car with her father as he went over all the evidence he'd collected for the trillionth time.

Guilt and duty tore her in half. He had no one else. After Will disappeared her dad had driven away his golfing and bowling buddies with his obsession to find his son. He'd alienated the only woman he'd dated since Mac's mother died when Mac was only three.

Only Mac remained. She couldn't abandon him. Or Will. Lately, she'd begun to fear her father might be losing it, on the verge of a breakdown or something.

"We can't pass up any leads. You never know which will be the one. What's wrong with you, Mac? We always reserve the weekends for Will."

"I know. I just need this Saturday for something else. How about Sunday?"

He brightened up, and she mentally kicked herself for caving once again. "Sunday's a deal." He stood, bent down to stroke the cat on her lap, and turned to leave.

"Want to stay for dinner?" She longed for just one normal dinner with her father where they'd talk about sports, fertilizer, and last's week's pool game. Only she knew they wouldn't.

"Can't. I'm meeting with Trudy."

Not Trudy again. "Dad, there's nothing more Trudy can tell you. She's milking you for a free dinner."

"There has to be something. She's Sonja's best friend and the last known person to see Will. She's hiding something." Her father's eyes gleamed with his rabid obsession, which unfortunately had become his norm.

Mac glanced at the seventies-style house next door, at one time her parents' house, then Will's, now Sonja's home with her second husband, Ben.

Resentment and anger over the injustice of it all flooded through her. Once part of the same family property, that house was where Mac grew up with her brothers, Will and Clint. It should still belong to her family, not to *that* woman.

"Eventually I'll wear her down. I have to." Craig's voice steered her attention back to him.

"I think *she's* wearing *you* down." She couldn't count how many times they'd had a similar conversation.

Craig shrugged. "He's my firstborn. I can't give up on him."

"Dad, at some point, you need to face facts and live your life. Will wouldn't want you dedicating every spare moment to finding him."

"What you're really saying is that you want to abandon your big brother, too?" The sadness in his eyes pierced right to her heart.

"No, Dad, I don't. I loved Will, but he's gone."

Her father sighed and stood up. "Bye, hon. I'll let you know what I find out."

"Bye, Dad." Mac watched her father walk out the gate, his shoulders slumped, his gait shuffling.

Maybe if he thought she was seriously dating someone he'd cut her some slack like he did Clint. Only that deception didn't sit well with her any more than abandoning her father did. Besides, she'd need a guy to play along, and what guy would volunteer for that duty?

Her mind quickly detoured to Bruiser, with those blue-gray eyes, perfect face, golden hair, and deep tan. Not to mention that ripped body. Oh, God, especially that body.

She shook her head and had to laugh. What an outrageous thought. Just because Bruiser had been backed into a corner with no way out and graciously accepted his fate didn't mean they had anything going other than a casual friendship and Mac's late-night, secret fantasies with a vibrator named Bruce.

* * * * *

The next morning, Bruiser walked into the Regional Burn Center in Seattle. He was a regular fixture at the center and showed up like clockwork every Tuesday morning when he was in the area, sometimes more often. The center served the entire Pacific Northwest. Burn patients came from all over to receive the critically acclaimed care and surgical procedures pioneered here. He'd seen it all as far as physical damage done by burns, but the mental and emotional scars were far worse.

Bruiser lived an illusion, one he'd perpetuated so long that the real Bruiser rarely came out to play. He was the team's poster boy, always saying the right thing, making news with his daredevil escapades, and being a damn good football player. Veronica Simms loved him, but not like that. Hell, no. Bruiser avoided women who emasculated men, and Veronica avoided men she couldn't pussy whip. Instead, they'd developed a business relationship. She did more for him than his agent when it came to finding lucrative endorsements, and he supported her favorite charities as she did his.

People claimed Bruiser had become the face of the Evergreen Burn Foundation because he was a publicity whore and liked the added attention that came from doing charity work with kids. They didn't realize he *was* the foundation, at least in part—a large part. His secret charity, The Brice Fund, made a generous donation every year to the foundation. In fact, pretty much everything Bruiser earned from modeling and endorsements went to that cause.

He owed Brice that much.

What people didn't know and Bruiser wouldn't tell them was that beyond the publicity photos taken of him visiting the hospital, there were countless more visits that were never documented. This morning was one such visit.

As soon as he walked off the elevator, Mary, the charge nurse, pulled him aside. "We have a patient we'd like you to work your magic on. He needs a little TLC."

"Giving you guys hell, is he?" They often steered him toward kids who were tough to handle.

Mary nodded and raised her gaze to the heavens. "Beyond hell. He's severely burned from a head-on car crash, which killed his mother and father. The firemen on the scene estimated he was trapped in the car for almost a minute before they could get to him. The only thing that saved him was his mother's body on top of his. The poor kid had second and third-degree burns over a majority of his body. He just turned eleven, and he's spent the last several months here in the hospital."

"Oh, man, that has to be tough for the kid." Stories like that reminded Bruiser that no matter how bad someone might think their life was, someone else always had it worse.

"His mother and father were professors at the UW. No brothers and sisters. His only living relatives are on a church mission in South America or somewhere. They won't return for another month or so."

Bruiser nodded. "So he's all alone?"

"He had some visitors at first, friends, teachers, but lately no one has come by. It's pretty tragic. We do what we can, and he tries, but it's really hard for him."

"Where is he?"

"Zero-four at the end of the hall. His name's Elliot."

"Got it." Bruiser leaned closer to her. "So, Mary, when are you going to leave your husband and run away with me?" He grinned, enjoying their usual banter, and winked at her, even though she was old enough to be his mother.

"I'll let you know." She winked back.

With a chuckle, Bruiser made his way to the end of the hall, stopping to talk to kids on the way before entering Elliot's room.

Lying on the bed was a small, scrawny little guy with thick glasses and a stubborn set to his jaw. A book was propped in a stand on his table, and he appeared to be lost in it. Bruiser hesitated for a moment, not because the kid's face set him back on his heels, but because something about this kid struck a chord deep inside him, sliding past carefully constructed walls into that place marked with an "Enter at your own risk" sign.

Bruiser adored every one of these brave kids with a fierce protectiveness. He often rented a suite at the ball park and took them to baseball games. As they healed, he helped them acclimate to a world that often couldn't help staring at them. He never once looked at these kids with repulsion like his parents once had. Never.

Stepping into the room, Bruiser plastered a smile on his face. He loved *his* kids, as he liked to think of them, loved how they put on such a courageous face to the world, how they opened up to him when they realized their outside appearance meant nothing to him but their internal beauty was everything. The kids understood him better than his closest friends—hell, better than he understood himself. But they saw a side of him no one else saw. The therapy worked both ways.

The kid glanced at him, his face wrinkled and red from the skin grafts, one eye partially closed, and only the remnants of a nose and ears.

"Hey, buddy. How's it going?" Bruiser walked over to the bed.

The kid squinted at him through the thickest pair of glasses Bruiser had ever seen. "I'm not your buddy." No animosity behind his words, just a factual statement.

Bruiser tried not to smile. "You could be if you gave me a chance."

"Who are you?" Elliot gripped the remote as if it were a weapon he could wield at any second.

"Not into sports, are you?"

Elliot shook his head. "Nope. I'd rather read than watch a bunch of men chase a ball around." He pointed to the pile of books on the table next to the bed.

Bruiser picked up one. Shakespeare. Damn. He looked at the stack. Classics, every one of them: Twain, Scott, Dickens, and Poe. At the same age, Bruiser was smuggling Playboy magazines into his bedroom. Elliot turned the page with a bandaged hand on a dog-eared Tom Sawyer hardcover—at least it was a kid's book.

"I'm Bruiser Mackey, running back for the Seattle Lumberjacks." Bruiser patted Elliot on the shoulder. "And you're Elliot."

The kid blinked a few times then nodded. "Yeah." He stared at his book. "I don't watch football. Mom said it was barbaric, and Dad said it was boring."

"It can be both at times." Bruiser grinned and sat on the edge of the bed.

Elliot met his gaze, his forehead wrinkled with worry. "Don't I bother you?"

Bruiser narrowed his eyes and made a show of studying the kid, looking past the angry red splotches on his face, missing right ear, and bare, scarred head. "Bother me? Hey, just because you're a bigger fan of Tom Sawyer than Tom Brady?"

"Who's Tom Brady?" The kid stared up at him with a quizzical expression. He really didn't know.

"Uh, Super Bowl-winning quarterback for the New England Patriots. Not my favorite team, but it is what it is."

Elliot gave him his full attention now. "Not mine either, but then, none of them are. I don't like football."

Bruiser held his hands over his heart in a dramatic display that would've made the Kardashians proud. "You're breakin' my heart here, Elliot."

"I am not." Elliot stared at him like he'd gone nuts.

"We're just gonna have to turn you into a football fan. I'll consider that my personal quest. I'll get you to some games." Bruiser leaned toward the kid, still smiling, daring Elliot to smile back.

Elliot's mouth turned down into a bigger frown. "I can't go to a game. Not like this. My face scares people."

"I think you're unique." Bruiser sobered and put on his serious face. "It's what's inside that matters, Elliot. Don't ever forget that."

Elliot swallowed and stared at his hands gripping the sheets.

Needing to lighten the mood, Bruiser spotted a checkers game sitting on a chair. "How about a game?"

Elliot perked up. Kids were like that, incredibly resilient. "I'm pretty awesome at checkers."

"More awesome than me? I'm the awesomest checker player around."

"Awesomest is not a word." Elliot stared at him through those thick glasses, so very serious. Too serious for an eleven-year-old.

"According to who?" Bruiser challenged, playing the dumb blond jock to the hilt.

"Merriam-Webster," Elliot shot right back. The kid had spunk after all he'd been through.

"Never met the guy."

"What do I get if I win?"

"What do you want?"

"To watch all the old *Star Trek* reruns, like a marathon." Elliot almost appeared excited.

Bruiser gagged as if the thought were making him sick. "Ah, man, anything but *Star Trek*. How about *Star Wars* or *Robocop*?" He actually liked Star Trek, but the kid seemed to be enjoying their banter.

"Star Trek was ahead of its time. Did you know that space warp is possible?"

"Uh, no, actually I never thought about it. Sure I can't talk you into a classic like *Planet of the Apes*?"

Elliot shook his head pretty vigorously. "Nope, that's my prize. I won't settle for less than Kirk and Spock. You'd like it. The women have really short, tight uniforms." Elliot actually laughed, a rusty, hoarse sound as if it'd been a long time since he'd used it.

"Well, now that you mention that, you're on, because I never lose a bet." Bruiser grinned and got a smile in return.

"Neither do I, not at checkers," Elliot shot back. "Don't you want something if you win?" Elliot scooted his little body higher up in the bed.

"Uh, sure, you have to watch a football game with me."

"Only one quarter. I'm too young for more with that level of violence." Elliot stared at him with no expression on his face.

It took Bruiser a full minute to realize the kid was jerking his chain. "A full half."

Elliot shook his head. "One quarter. That's my final offer."

"Okay, fine, but I get to call you buddy. Deal?"

"Deal—buddy." Elliot smiled at him, really smiled this time. Bruiser grinned back.

They setup the board game on Elliot's lap tray, and the kid thoroughly enjoyed kicking Bruiser's ass. Bruiser promised to come back over the weekend with a full DVD set of the original *Star Trek* series. Elliot gave him a hug when he left, as witnessed by a grateful set of nurses.

For all his Super Bowl rings and awards, nothing beat the satisfaction Bruiser got out of seeing these kids smile and hearing them laugh, ass-whooping or not.

Chapter 4

Sisters in Crime

Mac sat on a stool positioned in the middle of Zach and Kelsie's huge kitchen while three women circled her like she-wolves prowling around a wounded fawn. Kelsie Murphy rubbed her chin and stood back, as if she were a painter studying a blank canvas.

Lavender, Tyler's girlfriend, took a sip of her wine and hiccupped. Rachel, Derek's wife and an assistant football scout for the Lumberjacks, grabbed the counter to steady her very unsteady feet. She had a hard enough time with gravity without adding alcohol to the equation.

Mac was putting her future in the she-wolves' hands, and she was still sober. What did that say about her?

"Where do we start?" Lavender hiccupped again and topped off her glass, tossing the empty wine bottle in the garbage. With a clink, it nestled among the other wine bottles.

"Bruiser's sister volunteered to do her hair, add some highlights, take the dirty out of the dirty blonde. I'll teach her to do makeup." Kelsie wobbled around her, taking a big gulp from her wine glass.

Mac marveled at how someone could be so drunk and so graceful at the same time. When Mac drank too much, she got loud and lurched about like a three-legged hound dog.

Lavender leaned against the counter. "I have just the dress. I suspect we're about the same size. It's sexy as hell."

"She needs sexy. Who would have guessed you were hiding that figure under all those baggy clothes?" Kelsie said.

Rachel dropped into a chair. "I've worked quite a bit with Veronica. I'll give you the scoop on her so you can make small talk and impress her with your knowledge of things not related to plants."

"I don't have any knowledge other than plants and sports."

"You will," Rachel cackled with an evil laugh and her sisters in crime joined in.

"So," Kelsie ticked off on her ruby red fingertips, "clothes, hair, makeup, small talk. What else? What are we missing?"

"Wine. We're missing wine." Lavender snapped her fingers. "More wine, garçon."

The other two draped themselves across the stools and poured another drink. This time they coerced Mac into joining them. A few hours and way too many wine glasses and tequila shots later, Mac was certifiably drunk, having a great time, and refusing to be the first of the group to end the night, probably a bad move on her part.

Lavender leaned her elbows on the counter and grinned a wicked grin, obviously up to no fucking good. "Okay, ladies, truth or dare. If you were single, and you could sleep with any man in the world, who would it be?"

Mac rolled her eyes. Couldn't they just enjoy a good drunk without playing stupid games?

"Zach," Kelsie hiccupped and giggled.

"Derek," Rachel grinned, her eyes all glassy and unfocused.

"No, no, no," Lavender groaned and pounded her forehead with her fist. "Pretend Derek, Tyler, and Zach are out of the picture. Give me a name."

"It's your idea, Vin, you give us a name."

"Channing Tatum, but I still think Ty's hotter. Rachel, you're next."

"Christian Olsen. Kelsie?"

Kelsie giggled, scratched her head as if she'd forgotten the question, and finally answered. "Matt Bomer."

Three pairs of eyes turned to Mac. She belched, a very unladylike sound, but then no one had ever accused her of being a lady. Not one bit. Squinting, she tried to focus on the blurry faces swimming in front of her. At least she still had enough of her wits about her to keep her mouth shut, even as she felt her face getting redder. This was not the time for honesty.

Lavender narrowed her eyes and raised one eyebrow. "It's one of the guys, isn't it?"

"One of *our* guys?" Rachel held her hand up to her mouth and ripped off a hunk of fingernail.

"No. No." Mac shook her head. Big mistake, as it made the room spin. Or maybe her body was spinning and the room was stationary.

Lavender wasn't about to let her off easy, drunk or not. She narrowed her eyes and studied Mac. "Wait a minute." She started to smile. "It's Bruiser."

Wallowing in embarrassment and speechless with horror, Mac knew her face revealed her most carefully guarded secret.

"It *is* Bruiser." Lavender clapped her hands together, reveling in her discovery way too damn much.

"As in *our* Bruiser with the eight-pack abs," Lavender hiccupped again and giggled.

"Bruiser with the great hair," Kelsie smiled dreamily.

"Bruiser with those smoky blue eyes." Rachel leaned forward, resting her chin on her knuckles, and sighed a deep sigh.

"Well, I mean, you know, who wouldn't think he was hot?" Mac backpedaled, but even in their inebriated state the women weren't buying it.

"You have a crush on Bruiser."

"How long have you felt this way?"

"I —I don't feel that way, I really don't."

"Bullshit." Lavender obviously knew crap when she heard it, which probably came from living with Tyler for the past year.

"Wait till we're done with you; we're gonna knock his cleats off. You'll have him begging for mercy." Kelsie eyed her with the certainty of the beauty pageant star she'd once been.

"I don't want him begging. So I think he's hot. That doesn't mean I want to screw his brains out."

"Of course, you do. What single woman wouldn't want a big bite of what he's selling?"

On that note, the women ignored her. Lavender raised her wine glass. "Hey, girls, now we're really on a mission, not just to help Mac's career but to cast a line and get that big fish to bite." The she-wolves clinked their glasses together.

Mac didn't know whether to be horrified or encouraged.

* * * * *

Bruiser dried off his wet body and wrapped the towel around his waist. He dropped down on the bench in front of his locker and checked his messages. Nothing unexpected. He was meeting Chelsea and Sondra for drinks and entertainment tonight. A slow smile spread across his face at the thought of the two BFFs and the fun they'd had together last time. Those crazy-assed women just about sent him to an early grave with a big smile on his face. And here he'd thought he'd been in shape. After they'd finished with him, he'd slept for twelve hours.

Bruiser stared in the mirror hanging in his locker and ran a comb through his blond hair, wishing he had dark hair like Harris, or a mean look like Zach, or even a guy-next-door face like Derek. Hell no, he looked like a fucking movie star, and he fucking hated it.

Well, mostly. He did appreciate the perks, especially the female ones.

He sighed and pushed a wayward lock of hair off his forehead, making sure his hair was perfect. He couldn't help it; he did care how he looked. He had a brand to maintain.

He glanced around to find Brett staring at him. Last year they'd accidentally discovered a mutual love of fishing after which they spent hours together on Puget Sound and area lakes fishing for whatever happened to be biting. As a result, Bruiser became close friends with the quiet backup quarterback, and Bruiser didn't have many close friends by his own choice. Neither did Brett.

Brett had the locker next to him and sat down, pulling on his shoes. "Looking forward to the barbecue?"

"What do you think?" Bruiser shrugged it off.

"You're a prick, Mackey. You wouldn't know a good woman if she landed in your lap."

"Hey, I'm not looking for a good woman—just the opposite. Good women expect commitments, and I'm not that guy."

Brett ran his fingers though his wet hair. "I wish I were taking her."

"So do I. Remind me again how I got roped into this?"

Brett ignored the question. "I bet she'll look great."

"Hope so." Bruiser frowned. "My future depends on my ability to market myself, and Mac isn't, well, exactly my normal date." He rubbed his chin for a moment. "Think she's gay?"

"No more than you are."

"You have a point." Bruiser had battled that label himself, just because he took care of his appearance and dressed in the most expensive of clothes. Truthfully, he hated shopping, but it was all part of his persona. He played the part. The ladies loved how he looked, and men wanted to be him, which put money in his endorsers' pockets and in turn in Bruiser's pockets.

"Besides, you got the hots for her, not me." Well, except for some recurring erotic fantasies, and he didn't have a clue where they were coming from. Maybe he'd grown as weary of his Barbie doll dates as he had of modeling.

Brett cleared his throat, suddenly looking nervous. "I have to warn you."

"Warn me? About Mac?" Bruiser snorted out a laugh.

"Uh. Not exactly. I saw your mom a few days ago."

Bruiser stiffened. "Did you get your hair cut?" Brett was the only teammate who'd ever met his family. Bruiser's mother and sister owned a hair salon on the peninsula. Brett had been going there for a year. Bruiser wouldn't let them touch his hair. He preferred to get it cut at a trendy salon in Bellevue rather than in his mother's pink and purple monument to poor taste.

"Yup. Eunice and Shanna said they haven't seen you in a while."

"I know," Bruiser swallowed back the guilt. He sent them money once a month to help pay for the salon expenses rather than visiting them, as if that replaced him. His mother, Eunice, had left five messages on his phone this week. Instead of calling her, he'd sent a text message.

Yeah, he was a crappy son, one who pretended he didn't have a family, which made him a crappy person, too.

Bruiser hated dishonesty for a multitude of reasons. His father had figured truth was useless when you can spin a whole web of lies. And Bruiser's ex-wife had used lies and guilt in equal doses to get what she wanted. Then his last three girlfriends hadn't been an improvement, except he hadn't been stupid enough to marry any of them. Forget that Bruiser practiced his own brand of deception every waking hour of his day, pretending to be someone he wasn't, rather than embracing who he was. But at least he was only hurting himself. This thing with keeping his family hidden was another thing altogether.

"Then why don't you go see them?"

"Why don't you go see your family?" Bruiser shot back.

Brett almost smiled. "Touché." He looked down at his watch. "Uh, but that's not exactly what I'm warning you about."

"What is it then?"

"You know how you told me your mother and sister like to chat?"

"Uh, yeah." Brett was the only person he ever talked to about Eunice and Shanna.

"Well, I told them about Mac and the barbecue. They volunteered to style her hair, do all that beauty stuff, the whole works on the house."

"Oh, no. No way."

"She doesn't have much money. They'd do it for free." Brett seemed to be trying hard not to smile, the dumbass.

"No. I don't want my mother and sister filling her full of embarrassing stories about my childhood." Or even worse, telling her the entire tragic truth of his childhood, a truth he fought tooth and nail to hide. Embarrassment he could handle, pity and blame he couldn't.

"You know that's not what you're worried about. They embarrass you. You're a real asshole."

If Brett only knew. "Yeah, so what?" Bruiser played along. He hated the guilt that burrowed a little deeper into his heart every day, which had a lot to do with why he avoided his family.

"Well, it's a done deal. I told Zach, and Kelsie set up an appointment for Mac."

"Ah, fuck. I thought we were friends. My mother's been trying to marry me off to a nice girl for years. She'll latch onto Mac like a burr on my ass."

Brett, the rat bastard, actually grinned a very rare grin. "Good luck with that." He stood, grabbed his jacket, and chuckled as he went out the door, leaving Bruiser alone with his thoughts.

"Well, shit." Bruiser spoke out loud. He worked damn hard to keep his personal and professional lives apart and his buddy just mashed them all up together.

With friends like Brett, who needed enemies?

Bruiser shrugged into his jacket and got the hell out of there.

Mac was kneeling down in the flower-beds at the front door of the practice facility as he walked out. He hesitated, his gaze dropping to her nicely rounded ass in those tight jeans. A ponytail tangle of dark-blonde hair fell across one shoulder and a thin sheen of sweat covered the bare skin above the back of her tank top. Bruiser licked his lips. His dick hardened instantly. Odd, since thinking about Chelsea and Sondra didn't get the slightest rise out of it.

Bruiser held his duffle bag in front of his crotch and plastered his charming smile on his face, a smile he'd never used before on Mac. Why he was using it now, he hadn't a fucking clue. This was just Mac, tomboy extraordinaire and good buddy to the majority of the team. If he were lucky, she'd say she'd changed her mind, and he'd be off the hook. Oddly enough, that possibility actually disappointed him.

One way or another, he'd convince her to get her hair done elsewhere. His mother and sister talked too much, way too much, and he didn't need Mac or anyone else knowing his entire sorry past.

"Hey, beautiful." He came to stop a few feet from her, careful to keep his expensive shoes on the sidewalk and out of the fresh soil.

Mac glanced over her shoulder, dirt smeared under one cheek. She rolled her eyes. "Beautiful? Seriously." She glanced away and wiped a strand of dull-blonde hair off her forehead with chipped and ragged fingernails. His mother would be appalled at the state of Mac's fingernails, which almost made him smile. Almost.

"Absolutely. In an au-naturel sort of way." Bruiser gave her his sexiest smile, the one that usually had women unzipping his pants. Not so Mac.

"Are you on drugs?" Mac snorted and sat back on her haunches, stretching the fabric of her jeans tighter around her ass. Bruiser's throat went dry, and he coughed.

She studied him with narrowed eyes.

Taking a deep breath, Bruiser jumped in the deep end, grateful he could swim with the best of them, and dialed up the charm. "The only drug I need is your smile."

"Let me get my boots on. It's getting pretty deep out here."

Bruiser leaned against the nearby building. "Have I got a deal for you, Mac. I'm going to save you the time of going all the way over to the peninsula to get your hair done. I'm setting you up with my stylist, Armand. The man's a regular miracle worker."

Mac frowned. "So you're saying I need a miracle?"

"Uh, no, no," Bruiser backtracked—great time for his legendary silver tongue to turn to scrap metal. What an idiot thing to say to a woman. "I'm just thinking you don't want to spend an hour one way on the Bremerton ferry."

"Maybe I enjoy a good ferry ride." She narrowed her eyes in a look that was pure badass Mac. "Are you ashamed of having your mother meet me?"

He was really fucking this up. "It's not you, it's them. They're a little tough to handle."

She didn't look like she believed him.

Bruiser dropped the charming act. "Oh, come on, Mac. I like you. I'm trying to save you here. You don't want to be around my mom and sister. Trust me."

"I don't?" She tempered her response with a smile, her eyes sparkling with mischief. Her face softened, making her look almost—pretty? Mac? Damn, his weird attraction to her needed to stop.

"You seriously don't."

"You just blew it, buster. Now I'm more committed than ever to meet them."

"Please, Mac. Let me make an appointment with Armand. He's one of the best stylists in Seattle. My treat."

"And miss meeting Shanna and Eunice? Not on your fucking life."

Shaking his head, he grinned at her in spite of himself. "You're a firecracker, Mac."

"You ain't seen nothing yet."

He was pretty sure of that.

Chapter 5

You Ain't Seen Nothing Yet

Hands with fingernails like bear claws shoved Mac into a salon chair while the She-Wolf Pack, as she'd come to think of Kelsie, Lavender, and Rachel, hovered nearby, as if they didn't totally trust Bruiser's sister and mother to do a good job.

Mac had her own reservations. Judging by the appearance of the place, she'd be lucky to escape without pink hair and fluorescent fingernails. She'd expected a classy salon because Bruiser was the ultimate in class. This place celebrated tacky beyond belief with hot pink and purple wallpaper, purple sinks, pink countertops, and cotton-candy pink chairs. Even the outside was a nasty Pepto-Bismol pink. All in all, it looked like a Barbie hair salon gone wild.

Shanna, Bruiser's sister, went for gaudy-chic with bleached blond hair, a tight purple tank top, and tons of tats, while his mother, Eunice, showed a little less of her wrinkled skin—thank God —but reminded Mac of one of those dancehall girls with red hair on the old Westerns her dad loved to watch—*had* loved to watch—until everything changed.

Mac swallowed the apple-sized lump lodged in her throat. Now was not the time to think about Will. Now was the time to think about doing all she needed to impress Veronica, even if that meant subjecting herself to a Eunice-Shanna makeover overseen by the Pack.

The She-Wolves had swept Mac along like a leaf in a flash flood. Once they'd discovered her crush on Bruiser, they jumped in with reckless abandon to transform her into something she wasn't. She prayed they didn't tell their men everything, or Mac would never be able to face the team again, especially Bruiser.

Even worse, she hoped like hell they hadn't told Eunice or Shanna.

Mac forced a smile as Eunice pulled up a small stool and bent over Mac's feet, making tsking noises and shaking her head. Mac squirmed a little and got sharp tug on her hair from Shanna.

"Hold still."

No wonder Bruiser never brought them around or mentioned them. And here she thought he'd been raised with a platinum spoon in his mouth and a trust fund to go with it, not by these two polar opposites. She almost smiled. So Bruiser was common folk, just like her family. Who'd have guessed?

She glanced up to find Kelsie hovering over her. The former beauty queen took over, giving Shanna specific instructions and ignoring Shanna's annoyance. Shanna slathered some smelly crap on her hair, wrapped strands in aluminum foil, and stuck her under a 500-degree hair dryer, leaving her to sweat a gallon while Eunice painted her toes a deep shade of hot pink complete with tiny Lumberjack logos on her big toe nails. Nice touch, she had to admit.

A half hour later, she sat at Shanna's station with her back to the mirror. The Pack wouldn't let her see until Shanna was done. Judging by the smug expression on Kelsie's face, she liked what she saw. Eunice painted her fingernails to match her toenails. Mac drew the line at acrylic nails. She did gardening for both a living and a hobby for God's sake.

Her hair fell to the floor at an alarming rate as Shanna snipped away. Mac tried not to watch.

Finally, as everyone in the salon oohed and aahed, Shanna spun her around. Mac gaped at the stranger looking back at her in the mirror. This person could not be her. No more split ends. No more dishwater. Her golden hair framed her face and fell a few inches below her shoulders. Wispy bangs feathered across her forehead.

"What do you think?" Shanna grinned.

"I think I don't look like me."

"Of course you do. We just brought the woman inside out into the light. We gave you a sassy haircut to match your sassy personality." Eunice preened like a proud mama who'd just given birth. In a way, she had.

"You look beautiful, Mac." Rachel gushed.

"You're gonna knock Bruiser on his nice ass. He'll never know what hit him. The boy will be begging for a little of your special kind of magic." Lavender winked at her co-conspirators.

"I'm not doing this to knock Bruiser on his ass. I'm doing this to be taken seriously by Veronica to earn that scholarship."

"Yeah, sure, whatever." Lavender rolled her eyes. "Bruiser will be all over you."

Mac allowed her wayward, sex-starved imagination to conjure up an image of Bruiser fucking her brains out. Not a bad idea, really. She glanced up guiltily to find Shanna and Eunice reading her as if she'd written those dirty thoughts on her forehead.

"*Our* Bruce and this Mackenzie?" Eunice narrowed her eyes and studied her, while Mac squirmed.

"We're just friends."

"Bullshit." Lavender turned to Eunice. "She's got the hots for him."

"I do not," Mac protested, mortified. Heat spread across her cheeks. She'd muzzle Kelsie and Co., or, even better, send them on a one-way trip to anywhere she wasn't.

Eunice's predatory smirk struck fear in Mac's heart. "You're just the type Bruce needs, much better than those shallow, emaciated little bitches he parades around for photo ops."

"Bruce is an opportunist. He likes his money," Shanna added without a bit of resentment.

"When my Bruce gets a look at you, he'll drop to his knees and give you the world. We're that good, aren't we, Shanna?"

"We are. She's going to be his game changer."

Game changer? Her? Mac? The woman all the guys considered just one of the boys?

Shanna nodded and smiled smugly. "The selfish bastard has met his match."

Mac hoped like hell she hadn't met hers.

* * * * *

Bruiser walked into the burn unit carrying a box of decadent chocolates, handmade at a little store in the Fremont district. He grinned at Elliot sitting up in the bed, bandages covering most of his body after his recent surgery. "Hey, buddy, you're up. How ya feeling?"

The boy genius and ass-kicker in checkers frowned and shrugged his bony shoulders.

Bruiser sat on the edge of Elliot's bed. He took the lid off the box and held it out to Elliot. "Check this out. Best chocolates in Seattle."

Elliot stared in the box and took out one chocolate. "Thanks." No smile. No reaction.

"Try it."

"Later." Elliot set the foil-wrapped chocolate on the nightstand. He stared past Bruiser and out the window.

"You need to start moving around. Stretch out your new skin so it doesn't shrink too much. How about you and I walk up and down the hall a few times."

Elliot sighed, as if he carried the burdens of the world on his thin shoulders. Finally he met Bruiser's gaze. "Do you think I'll ever have a girlfriend?"

Bruiser choked and blinked a few times. Damn, he hadn't seen that one coming. "You're a little young to be worrying about that now."

"I'm eleven. Girls think I look like a monster. They're actually afraid of me, like I'm not human." He held up a gnarled and twisted hand. His mouth turned down in a bigger frown.

Bruiser considered Elliot's words. "The only woman worth having is one who sees beyond what's on the outside to the great person on the inside." Bruiser mentally patted himself on the back for his good answer, even if it made him the world's biggest hypocrite. After all, he rarely looked deeper than a woman's bare skin.

"What would you know about that?" The kid's perceptiveness set Bruiser back on his heels for a moment.

"Uh, because I've been there. When she didn't get what she wanted out of me, she found someone else who could give her the money and fame she craved." Bruiser laughed. "The joke's on her. That next year I started in the NFL, and she ended up with a third-string quarterback who's been cut time and again."

"Now you can have any woman you want."

"Sometimes that's a curse."

"No way." Elliot squinted at him through the thick lenses of his glasses, as if not really buying Bruiser's bullshit. Only it wasn't bullshit. It was the honest-to-God truth, and Bruiser lived with it every day. Women didn't look beyond Bruiser's football fame and outward appearance, didn't give a shit about what was inside. Not that he didn't do the same thing, because he did. Yet, here he was counseling this kid on looking beneath the surface. Who the hell was he to talk?

"It can be. People take you at face value and don't think you have anything else to offer."

"If they take me at face value, they'll think I'm a monster."

"You're not a monster. You're going to recover and surgery will take care of the rest."

Elliot didn't look convinced. Not one damn bit. Bruiser didn't blame him. Not only did Elliot struggle with physical scars, he struggled with the deep emotional scars of losing his entire family.

"I understand you drove your friends away. You were really mean to them."

"They either stared at me or couldn't look at me." Elliot crossed his skinny arms over his chest and set his jaw.

Bruiser changed tactics to tough love. "Get used to it. Be strong and stare right back. Don't let anyone keep you from living your life. Give people a chance to get to know you. In fact, give them a reason to want to look deeper."

The kid studied him with an intensity that was unnerving. "Is that what you do?"

Well, crap. Honesty would complete destroy the point Bruiser was trying to make, while dishonesty would confuse the kid because obviously Bruiser did superficial really well. "Hey, we're not talking about me."

"Cop out." Elliot threw Bruiser's own words back in his face. "You don't like talking about stuff, letting people see you beyond football and all those underwear ads."

Out of the mouths of babes. Bruiser searched for one of his usual quick-witted answers to deflect personal questions. Standing, he leaned against the windowsill and put on his casual face."You don't think I'm a good example?" Bruiser asked. No one had ever been that bluntly honest to Bruiser before, not like this sixty-year-old in an eleven-year-old body. Hell, Bruiser didn't break the law, do drugs, or cause any kind of scandal to the team. He just did his thing and did it well. Sure, he lent his face and body to more endorsements than he could recall, but all the money went to a good cause, along with a good portion of his salary

"Do you think you are? You're physically perfect, and you don't let anyone see inside. Why should I? I'd trade my brains for your looks any day. It's easy for you to spout this crap when you don't have to deal with people staring at you in horror or hugging their kids close as if you're a danger to them."

Bruiser sucked in a sharp breath like someone had punched him in the gut. Unwelcome memories of another time slammed into him. How the hell did this kid who'd only known him a few weeks see him more clearly than family and friends who'd known him for years?

Thank God Elliot's nurse walked in and interrupted the conversation. Bruiser excused himself and got the hell out of there.

The truth hurt like a hammer to the head, and he damn well didn't want to face it.

Chapter 6

Tackled for a Loss

A sexy angel answered the door of the little bungalow, and Bruiser's tongue rooted itself to the roof of his mouth while his brain forgot his name. Holy shit, Mac never mentioned a sister, and a really freaking hot sister at that.

Shoving his shock out of the way, he lowered his voice and slipped into full seduction mode. "Hey, gorgeous." Skipping her face, his gaze ran down the woman's elegant neck and nestled in the ample cleavage of a tight, sequined pink dress, right where he wished his hands could settle on two healthy mounds of incredible tits. Bruiser swallowed and tried to force a few clever words out of his mouth. None came. Not a one. This never happened to him. So much for seduction mode. Try dumbshit mode instead.

"Hey," she said right back in a sexy, breathy voice.

Bruiser just stared. Damn, it wasn't like he hadn't been around tons of hot women, but there was something about this one. She seemed so guileless, so innocent, almost like she didn't have a fucking clue what a knockout she was. In his world, that was damn near incredible. An angel with the heart of a seductress. His type of woman.

The babe turned around and grabbed a frothy pink shawl type thing, giving Bruiser an incredible view of a nicely rounded ass. He cleared his throat and swallowed. His fingers itched to stroke that ass then give it a firm smack.

"Okay, I'm ready, but I feel seriously overdressed for the middle of the afternoon." She turned back around.

"You're ready?" He blinked and tried to process this hunk of information.

She smiled, a big, bad, sassy Mac smile.

Bruiser did a double take. His jaw dropped open so far it almost came unhinged. "Mac? Is that you?"

"Hard to believe?" Her megawatt smile lit this side of the earth and gave a new reason for global warming. In fact, this particular corner of his world was experiencing a heat wave.

Bruiser nodded. "Like fucking *hard* to believe. Seriously, that's you?" Even though his dick liked what it saw, part of Bruiser was weirdly disappointed.

Mac had been the only woman he knew who was not hung up on her appearance. Now she was like all the rest. He couldn't explain how he could be so turned on and disillusioned at the same time, but he was. His cock wanted to get her naked and his heart wanted the real, no-pretenses Mac, which was fucking dysfunctional on so many levels.

In a split second, her expression changed as if a cloud blocked out the sun. "Yes, really. It's me. Who did you think it would be?"

"I thought you had a sister or something."

"Nope, I'm the only female in my immediate family." Mac picked up a little purse and took small, mincing steps toward him on some pretty damn sexy high heels.

He had to grin. Yup, this vision of loveliness was Mac after all. "Ever been in heels before?"

"Not if I could help it."

"Hang on to me, baby. I'll take you for a ride." Bruiser held out his arm, and she grabbed hold as she attempted to walk in those shoes. This was going to be a good night; he could feel it in his bones *and* his dick.

Okay, dumbshit, that's no way to think about Mac. Hell, for all you know she could be gay. Most of the guys on the team speculated she was, and Bruiser never really gave it much thought one way or another. He sure as hell was giving it a lot of thought right now, hoping like hell Mac didn't play for the home team. What the hell, he'd take Brett's word for it.

Thinking of Brett gave him a stab of guilt. Bruiser really was a selfish bastard. Brett had a thing for Mac. A good buddy would further that relationship along, not think about himself. *Besides, the last thing Mac needs is a guy like me.* A nice, kind stable guy like Brett fit her like a comfortable pair of slippers, while Bruiser fit as well as those heels she wore—great for appearances but not the least bit practical in the long run.

He walked her out to his red and white 1958 Corvette, his baby. He only pulled her out of the garage for special occasions.

Mac gripped his arm tight as she stared at the car with greedy eyes. "This car is fucking incredible. You never told me you had a car like this."

Bruiser shrugged, enjoying her pleasure in the car.

"I wanna see the engine." *Oh, yeah, pure Mac.*

"Later. I'll be fed to the steelhead in Lake Washington if you show up with grease on that dress. Your girlfriends are a formidable bunch."

"We can't let that happen—to the fish."

He chuckled. "Kelsie scares the crap out of me. She can be all kinds of serious scary."

"She scares me, too." He felt her gaze on his face. "You know about fish?"

He shrugged one shoulder. Only Brett knew that he liked to fish. "You'd be surprised what I know about."

She didn't look convinced as Bruiser helped her in the car. She pulled lipstick from her purse and carefully applied it, dabbing at a smear on one corner of her mouth. Bruiser stared at her full red lips and forgot to drive. His pants felt two sizes too small and his cock two sizes too big. He swerved just in time to miss a street sign.

"Been driving long?"

He let out a long breath and stared straight ahead, embarrassed as hell. "You think?"

"I think you're behaving strangely. I don't look that different."

He snorted, unable to come up with any other response.

* * * * *

Mac forced her eyes straight ahead when all she wanted to do was stare at Bruiser in that tux. His broad shoulders filled it out just right. There couldn't be another man on earth who did justice to a tux like Bruiser did. But then Bruiser did justice to just about anything, including a well-worn pair of jeans.

He glanced at her, catching her ogling him. "Amazed by my raw sexuality?"

Mac bit back an unladylike response and distracted him with the first thing that came to mind. "Your family isn't quite what I expected."

By the way Bruiser's face hardened, she'd picked the wrong subject and stepped into a big pile of shit and, so typical of her, she trudged right on through it. *Yeah, don't heed the warning signs, just dig yourself a grave-sized hole.* "I mean, they're nice enough."

"You don't have to explain yourself. Everyone says that." Bruiser's smile idled on his face, motor running but no power behind it. His eyes had turned a cold stone gray.

"How come this is the first time I've met them? In fact, I thought your parents didn't live anywhere around here."

"My father doesn't. He's in LA." Bruiser's jaw tightened, and he stared straight ahead.

"They're divorced?" She just didn't know when to shut up. Never been one of her special skills.

"Like a dozen times between the two of them."

"Oh, wow." Mac shook her head in surprise.

"Yeah, wow. You can see why I have no respect for marriage. It's a crock."

"I understand why you'd see it that way. Do you only have a sister?"

"I had a brother, too," he said in an emotionless voice, his closed expression not inviting further questions. A muscle jerked in his strong jaw. She'd inadvertently hit another sore subject, actually beyond sore—an open, gaping wound.

A brother? She'd never heard that before. Yet he'd said *had*, as if his brother no longer existed. Maybe they were estranged. Or something happened to him. Something Bruiser very obviously didn't want to discuss. Tons of questions raced through her mind, but for once she curbed her nosiness. Everyone had private pain. She should know that better than anyone.

Mac cranked up the Mariners game, but she couldn't have stated the score if her life depended on it. Bruiser didn't speak again, seeming to be lost in his own thoughts, and thanks to her big mouth, they didn't appear to be pleasant ones.

Time ground to a turtle's pace as they made the short trip to the Simms family's Lake Washington home. Bruiser maneuvered his 'Vette around dozens of parked cars along the long driveway and pulled up to the grand front entry, tossed his keys to a valet, and strode around the car to the passenger door. Mac waited patiently while he swept the door open, not because she was trying to be a lady but because she didn't dare walk without clinging to his arm. He held out his hand, and she took it. The heat from his large, warm palm rocketed through her body like a missile finding its mark and detonating, engulfing everything in its path, including her heart and her common sense as she shuddered in reaction.

"Cold?" He angled his head at her, looking damned irresistible from the cleft in his chin to the way a lock of golden hair fell across his forehead. His expression softened and his mouth tipped up at the corners in one of his signature smiles.

"Just caught a cool breeze for a second," she lied.

He looked skeptical but said nothing. After all, it was at least eighty degrees. Instead, he tucked her hand in his forearm and led her to the huge front porch, which looked like it should be the entrance to a five-star hotel, not a single-family dwelling. Mac took a moment to appreciate the landscaping and rare plants flanking the entry. The place was a regular arboretum. The Simms had to employ a full-time gardener.

Mac glanced up at Bruiser and put on a brave face. He grinned and winked at her, the familiar, charming Bruiser taking over. "You're gonna knock 'em dead, Mac. Just smile and let me do the talking. Veronica will know exactly who you are by the night's end."

"I hope that's a good thing."

"Of course, it is. Trust me."

She wanted to trust him, wanted to believe he could wave his magic wand and transform her into Veronica's idea of a scholarship-worthy employee, but she wasn't convinced even Bruiser was that good.

Mac clung to him as they entered the house, taking in the sights and smells of the party. They paused in the doorway, and she closed her eyes for a moment, willing herself to play the part she looked, a part she oddly somewhat liked—except for the heels. A stranger had invaded her body, a stranger who liked pink, ordered a double-macchiato with caramel, and haunted downtown Seattle in search of her next pair of Jimmy Choos. Not that any of those things were true about her, but hey, she almost felt as if they could be. In some really weird way, she wanted to be that girl once in a while and do girly things. Was that too much to ask?

Mac placed one foot in front of the other with careful precision, attempting to walk like a girl and not a gorilla, but it wasn't easy. Drill Sergeant Kelsie's words played through her brain: *Stand up straight, shoulders back, head up, and smile, smile, smile like you're on the red carpet at a world premiere.*

A servant in a black suit with an English accent ushered them to the back of the house, where a tiered deck ran the entire length of the mansion. An emerald green lawn sloped down to a pebbly, low-bank beach where the lazy waters of Lake Washington lapped at the shore. The late afternoon sun warmed the breeze coming in from the water. A yacht large enough to house its own football stadium was tied at the end of a long dock. Over to one side a slate path led through a garden awash with flowers and shrubs, complete with a bubbling waterfall. And roses, lots of roses in a rainbow of colors lined the meandering path.

Bruiser nudged her. "Hey, what's going on in that head of yours?"

"I've never seen such gorgeous gardens."

"Well, Simms is worth billions. He can afford it. They probably have an entire crew of gardeners."

"Yeah, I'm sure they do."

Mac glanced over at the She-Wolves, who stood sharpening their claws and sipping wine with their men, the poor bastards. They gave her the thumbs-up, causing Derek, Tyler, and Zach to turn and look. Zach saluted her and Tyler shot her a cocky grin, while Derek gave her an approving smile. Mac relaxed a little. Obviously she'd passed muster.

Veronica glided up to them as smoothly as a figure skater and hugged Bruiser with more warmth than Mac ever thought she could possess. Then she turned to Mac. Her brow furrowed, her frown deepened, bringing out wrinkles around the corners of her perfect lips. "I think we've met before, but I can't place you." She looked Mac up and down, as if she were looking over a piece of horseflesh at an auction.

"I'm Mackenzie Hernandez." Mac held out her hand hoping a handshake would be appropriate.

Veronica shook her hand and continued to study her. "Mackenzie Hernandez?"

"I'm a groundskeeper at Jacks' headquarters."

"Oh, that's where I've seen you. You didn't look quite the same." She peered at Mac again, then dismissed her and turned her attention on Bruiser. He tried to steer the conversation back to Mac several times, but Veronica wasn't having any of it. She had great plans for a promo spot with Bruiser, and Mac was just an inconvenience she chose to ignore. The more Veronica drank, the more she hung on Bruiser's arm.

"Veronica, Mackenzie was admiring your landscaping." Bruiser subtly extracted himself from the woman's grip and tucked Mac's hand in his. His big hand felt warm and comforting surrounding her smaller hand and gave her confidence.

Mac jumped at the lead-in Bruiser gave her. "I love your wisteria arbor. That color isn't one I've seen before."

Veronica looked at her as if she were a moron. "We have people who handle those things. I don't concern myself with them."

Mac didn't quite know how to respond to that, but Bruiser came to the rescue. "Of course, you do, and it's up to you to hire just the right people."

"That's my mother's job. She's in charge of the gardens. I have no interest in them."

Strike two.

Bruiser gave Mac one of those looks that she interpreted as *This woman is a bitch.* "Well, Mac has two years toward her horticulture degree at the UW."

For the first time Veronica perked up. "What house were you in?"

"House?"

"Sorority."

"Oh, I wasn't in one." *Strike three.* Mac didn't even go down swinging.

"I see." Veronica looked over her head and waved at someone. "I must be off to my guests. Bruce, do think about what we've discussed and get back to me within a few days."

"Yeah, sure."

With that she flitted off.

"I tried." He gave her a shrug. His blue-gray eyes were apologetic.

"I know. Thanks for the effort." She leaned into him slightly as he stared down at her. Her heart pitter-patted with gratitude. Bruiser Mackey wasn't such a bad guy after all.

"She's a self-centered bitch." Bruiser flicked his gaze to Veronica and back to Mac.

"Try entitled, self-centered bitch."

He smiled. "That, too. We aren't done with her yet." His crooked smile gave him a boyish look. The man was so outrageously handsome. No guy should be that good-looking. She was going to enjoy this night while it lasted. Cinderella at the ball with Prince Charming and all that.

Only there was no glass slipper and her Prince Charming wasn't looking for a happily ever after. Or anything beyond a one-night stand, and not with Mac. She'd fallen for the most impossible guy in the world.

That's what made him safe.

* * * * *

Tyler finished his joke with his usual asshole panache, sending the crowd of people into raucous laughter. Bruiser faked it, even though he had no flipping clue what the punch line had been. The attention-whore quarterback had been entertaining the troops for about a half hour, thoroughly enjoying himself. Usually Bruiser vied for the center of attention along with Harris, but not tonight. He had a—uh—distraction.

Mac stood with Kelsie, Rachel, and Lavender, looking like a woman plotting her escape from tyrants. He would know; he'd hardly taken his eyes off her the entire evening. Something about this version of Mac did it for his dick. Or had he been in denial for a while now? After all, he'd been having these erotic daydreams about her for the past couple weeks way before this makeover. He couldn't quite put his finger on when he started seeing her as a woman, not just a buddy. But he had and now he couldn't let the images go.

Shit.

He didn't date women he worked with. The added complication made the inevitable breakup way too messy. Bruiser liked to keep his breakups quick, tidy, and amicable. Not only did this weird attraction to Mac not work for him on so many levels, it wouldn't work for her. Brett was interested in her. Brett, the only true friend he really had.

Dammit.

Even so...

What harm could one little dance do?

A band started playing as a deep red sun set to the west. Colored lights lit up as darkness settled, the alcohol flowed freely, and the party showed no signs of stopping.

Despite his best intentions, Bruiser found himself drawn to Mac's side. At five-foot-eleven Bruiser wasn't tall, but Mac was only five-three or -four. She made him feel like a big guy. He liked that a lot more than all those models he dated. A guy's ego could take a hit when he had to look up at a woman.

Mac glanced up at him through lowered lashes as he stepped up beside her, in an oddly feminine display of shyness. The relief in her brown eyes sent satisfaction surging through him. She'd missed him at her side, or those three friends of hers were just that scary. Either way, he'd take it.

He smiled down at her, and she smiled back. His stomach did a triple axel with a twist, leaving him fighting to breathe. Women did not affect him this way unless it had to do with sex. He couldn't quantify his feelings for Mac; they were different and not going in a direction he intended to travel. It would be smart to fake some sudden illness and get the hell out of here, but he wasn't that smart.

Next thing he knew, his mouth took over for his brain, while his heart and his dick applauded. "Excuse me ladies, but I'd like to take a whirl on the dance floor with the most beautiful woman in the room." Before her friends reacted and Mac could shoot him down, he grabbed her hand and pulled her onto the dance floor.

"You do dance?" A little late now to be asking that, but what the hell. She could step on his feet all night, and he doubted he'd notice. Not with that nice little body close to his, and those brown eyes holding him captive.

"Only a little, but I'm athletic and a quick learner." Her eyes twinkled brighter than stars in the night sky.

"So let's give it a try."

"Can I take off my shoes?"

"Sure, other women have."

It was a two-step to a country song, and Mac had no problem keeping up with him. She twirled and wiggled that cute little body all around him, anticipating his every move until he was panting after her like horny old dog. Bruiser was having a damn good time, which surprised him. In fact, it'd been a while since he'd had this much fun off the field or out of the sack and been this relaxed at a party. It'd been even longer since a woman intrigued him. This insane attraction to Mac blindsided him and pretty much knocked his denial on its butt, even though he should've seen it coming given his recent obsession with her.

The fast dance ended and Mac raced for the edge of dance floor, but Bruiser caught her hand and tugged her back into his arms. Bad idea, but he'd been full of bad ideas all evening. He couldn't explain why, but he had to have that fit little body pressed against his in a slow dance. Okay, hell, he probably could explain why if he really thought about it.

Mac didn't resist; instead she leaned into him, wrapping her arms around his neck. Despite muscles honed from her hours of physical labor, she felt like a woman, all woman, and he liked that. A lot.

She gazed up at him with a slight smile. Her perfume floated around him, leaving him in a haze as if he'd just drunk a tumbler of fine whiskey on an empty stomach. Her size fit him well. Everything about her fit him, from her soft breasts rubbing against his chest to her fine thighs brushing against his. And her eyes were the type of eyes made a strong man weak—eyes that haunted a man's dreams and took hold of a man and never let him go.

He grinned down at her like a damn fool, just happy to be him and enjoying life.

Sliding his hands down her back, he grabbed a handful of ass just to get a rise out of her and break the spell she'd so easily woven. She glared at him and smacked his arm. "Next time it'll be a knee to the groin, buster."

"I think you mean that," Bruiser said.

"You *know* I mean that. You sure know how to take advantage of a situation."

"Hey, I might be pretty, but I'm not stupid. Gorgeous night, great company, sexy little body plastered against me. What more could I want even if I'm concerned for the safety of my manhood?" No truer words were ever spoken.

"I am not plastered against you. You're holding me there." Her brown eyes flashed fire. Damn, he liked when she was all indignant and wallowing in denial.

He raised one eyebrow. She tried to pull away but he wouldn't give her the satisfaction. He owed her for all those times she kicked his ass at pool and took his money. Instead, he pulled her closer until their bodies meshed together.

He maneuvered her to a darker part of the patio, away from most of the dancers. She clung to him. Her incredible lips parted slightly, and she sighed the most provocative sigh he'd ever heard. He doubted she meant for it to be provocative, but pretty much any sound coming from those lips right now turned him on.

Their gazes locked, and Bruiser forgot everything he'd ever learned, including the ability to form simple words. Mac looked as dazed as he felt. He couldn't look away, even as the alarm sounded in his head to get out and get out fast. He'd always paid heed to that alarm, but not tonight. Not with Mac. To hell with it. He silenced all his inner thoughts except the ones that swore this was a good idea.

Yeah, a very good idea.

His gaze slipped lower to those luscious lips of hers. Big, full, and absolutely feminine. Bruiser lowered his head. Her warm, minty breath feathered his lips. He wanted to kiss her, and she wanted him to. He knew the signs. Only an inch separated them. So close. So very close. Her pink tongue darted out, and she wet her lips. Heat rolled off him in waves, like a hot sidewalk on a hundred-degree day. Oh, God, his knees almost buckled. He tilted his head, just one more inch. One little inch between his lips and the Promised Land.

Then he remembered Brett.

Brett, his buddy. His fishing partner. The only guy who truly understood him. Loyal to a fault and always there when needed. And Bruiser, the asshole, was about to kiss the hell out of Brett's love interest.

Friends were more important than a casual fuck. He could get a casual fuck anywhere. Right now, his actions affected two friends—Mac and Brett. He loosened his hold on Mac, allowing her to put a few inches between them. She stared at him, her lips still parted, and blinked several times, as if she couldn't believe her bad luck. Neither could he. What a fine time for his sense of honor and decency to assert itself.

"Sorry. I didn't mean to overstep my boundaries."

Mac's disappointment was written all over her flushed face, which was out of character. She usually had a better poker face than that. She crossed her arms over her chest and looked beyond him. "You're not, really. It's fine."

"No, it's not. We're friends, and I'm not the right guy for you." Bruiser managed a half smile in an attempt to downplay what had just *not* happened. "Now, Brett—there's a guy who could make a nice girl like you happy."

"Brett?" She squinted at him, as if trying to process his words.

"Yeah, Brett's kinda interested." His statement had the desired effect of driving a wedge between them. Bruiser stepped back, putting more distance between them physically and emotionally.

His arms dropped to his sides, feeling empty and aching for her. He shoved his hands in his pockets.

"In me?" She pointed at her chest, right at her cleavage, and he bit back a groan.

"Sure is," he managed, though he sounded strangled. "Has been for a long time."

"Isn't he your best buddy on the team?" She perched her cute ass on a rock wall and put her shoes back on, He gaped at her shapely legs until she gazed up at him. Oh, God, he wanted to bend her over the wall and kiss the hell out of her.

"Pretty much."

"I know you can't help but be your usual jackass self, but if Brett's interested, why were you hitting on me?" Her accusation punched him below the belt, but his selfish dick refused to give up its quest.

"Because I'm truly an ass. I apologize. It won't happen again. So will you?"

She stared up at him, hugging herself with her arms, as if she were cold. "Will I what?"

"Go out with Brett?"

"I can't answer that, since he's never asked me."

An unexpected stab of jealousy caught Bruiser completely off guard. Jealous? He hadn't been jealous since he caught CeCe flirting with the quarterback on his old college team. *Damn.* He needed to screw his head on straight, abandon his odd attraction to Mac, and go back to being a player, a role he'd starred in since puberty. Only hooking up with anonymous women didn't hold its usual appeal.

And despite all his inner bullshit, he knew the exact reason why.

* * * * *

Mac pushed herself off the stone wall and ran for the bathroom in the pool house as fast as her killer shoes would carry her without breaking an ankle. She didn't look back until she reached the bathroom door. A glance over her shoulder revealed Bruiser standing alone near the dance floor staring at her. Dang, uber-confident Bruiser looked adorably confused and uncertain—a lethal combination.

Pushing the bathroom door open, Mac shut and locked it. She rested her forehead against the cool tile wall until her breathing returned to somewhat normal and her heart ceased racing down the homestretch. Moving to the sink, she started to splash some cold water on her face, then remembered her eyeliner and mascara. Damn, but it sucked being a woman.

She stared at the stranger in the mirror and had to admit she did look pretty damn good, which explained Bruiser's insane temporary infatuation with her. Kelsie and Co. were miracle workers, not to mention Shanna and Eunice. She might even ask Kelsie to show her how she applied Mac's makeup earlier in the day. Not that Mac could duplicate the finesse of a master, but maybe she could manage without doing too much damage.

She was stalling. Applying makeup was the least of her problems.

Mac's head pounded harder than a drummer in a hard-rock band.

Bruiser?

Brett?

First, Bruiser's attention knocked her on her ass, then Brett wanted to ask her out? She'd suspected that the quiet backup quarterback might actually be interested in her even though he never showed any outward signs. Brett was a nice guy, a good-looking guy, the type of guy any decent woman with half a brain would love to date. So why wasn't she excited? This stupid-assed crush she had on Bruiser would never amount to anything. Hell, she so didn't even want it to go anywhere. It was just a safe, harmless crush.

Tonight something had changed between them, and she was afraid they'd never go back to being casual friends. Not that she had much time for even casual friends, not with her brother missing and her father on the verge of a breakdown.

Why did things have to be so complicated?

Steeling herself, Mac stood up straight and strolled out of the bathroom as if she hadn't a care in the world, then stopped dead when she heard voices and her name was mentioned. Holding her breath for fear of being caught, she stood there, exposed to anyone who rounded the corner. Backpedalling, she plastered herself against the wall behind a large potted plant.

"Really, Bruce, a gardener?" Veronica's bitchy voice dripped with disgust.

"She's a groundskeeper and a damn good one. Plus she knows her plants." Her heart warmed at Bruiser's defense of her.

"If you needed a date for tonight, you could've asked me. I would've set you up with any number of appropriate females. She's not in keeping with the image the team expects you to portray."

"Not the team, the image *you* expect me to portray. Besides, I think she looks damn good."

"That much was obvious. You were salivating after her like a teenage boy at the prom with the head cheerleader." Veronica snickered. "She mows grass for a living."

"Seriously, Veronica, I can't believe you're being such a bitch about this."

"Bruce, you're the face of our team. Women worship you. Guys want to be you. You need to keep up that image."

Bruiser snorted. "First of all, who I choose to spend time with is none of your business. Mac and I are friends. She wanted to come here to show you another side of herself."

"Oh, now I understand. This is pity date."

"I wanted to do this. Take some time to get to know Mac better. She's a hard worker and dedicated her job."

"What are you, her campaign manager?"

Mac closed her eyes. This was so not going well.

"She's applying for the staff scholarship. I want you to consider her."

"The facilities director is endorsing Vince. If he's not convinced she's the right choice, why would I override his decision?"

"Mac's the best person for that scholarship. Her continued education would be a great benefit to the team."

"And you know this how? It's not like you've mowed one blade of grass in your life."

"Maybe I have."

"Bruce, drop it. Forget doing her any favors and go back to taking care of yourself. It's what you do best." Veronica's laugh taunted Mac, and Mac flexed her fingers, engaging in a temporary fantasy involving wrapping them around Veronica's blue-blood throat.

"Veronica, just give her a chance. She's only a few years from her horticulture degree."

"It might as well be light years. She's too young and not a good risk for the investment. I think she's a typical young woman looking to snag a rich, hot football player, have babies, and…" Veronica's voice faded away.

Holding her breath, Mac waited until their voices blended with all the others. She rubbed a hand across her queasy stomach. The tantalizing smell of salmon and prime rib did nothing for her appetite. She was *not* a typical young woman, which should have been blatantly obvious to Veronica if she'd ever noticed Mac working at the facility. Obviously, she hadn't.

Mac called for a taxi and started walking, meeting the driver a few blocks away. Once she was safely in the backseat, she tapped out a text message to Bruiser: *Not feeling well. Didn't want to ruin your night. I got a ride home. Please enjoy the evening.*

Somebody should.

Chapter 7

Illegal Motion

Despite it being a very bad idea, Bruiser left the barbecue just before midnight and drove to Mac's house. Probably a little late to be paying a visit, but good sense had deserted him for some damn reason.

Bruiser stepped out of his car and was on the front porch in six long strides. He pounded on the thick wooden door. "Come on, Mac, open the damn door."

A few minutes later, Mac threw the door open, looking more than little pissed and sexily rumpled, reminding him of a woman who'd spent the night with her lover. Only she hadn't. At least he didn't think so. He looked over her shoulder but didn't see anyone inside. Relief swept through him.

He liked her like this—not that he didn't like her all dressed up, too. This was *his* Mac. The real Mac. Her face scrubbed free of makeup. Her flawless skin au naturel. Her golden hair in a haphazard ponytail. Unlike the beauty of earlier in the evening, he could handle this Mac. At least, he hoped he could.

"What the hell do you want?" She rubbed her eyes and glared at him.

He squinted into the bright porch light. "I came to see if you're okay." *Lame, Mackey, really lame.*

"Of course I'm okay. Now, good night." She tried to push the door shut.

He stuck his foot in it. "If you're okay, why did you leave the barbecue before dinner?"

"I wasn't hungry." She wouldn't meet his gaze.

Bruiser rolled his eyes, pushed his way inside, and plopped down the couch. He glanced around the cozy little living room and liked what he saw. Definitely a homey place, the kind a guy would look forward to coming home to after a long day at work. Neat and tidy without being overly so; the room didn't fit his image of Mac. In fact, he saw a woman's touch reflected in the attention to detail and the placement of the country-style accessories. But then Mac *was* a woman, a fact of which he'd been painfully reminded tonight.

Grabbing the remote, he switched to ESPN and made himself at home, even though he hadn't a clue why he was doing it. He grinned, goaded by Mac's annoyed expression. "Nice house." He gave her the once over and his gaze stalled out in the vicinity of her tits. Holy fuck, she had a nice rack on her. Not that he hadn't noticed earlier, but hell, she'd traded in her party clothes for a long, form-fitting tank top with no bra. Her nipples stood out against the thin material, like they were happy to see him. He sure as hell was happy to see them.

Catching him gawking, Mac quickly crossed her arms over her chest, which hiked up the bottom of her shirt. A nice pair of red lace panties peeked out from her jeans. Lace? Mac? Well, he'd be damned. Bruiser tried not to smirk but failed miserably, which seemed to piss her off even more. Pissed-off women possessed a lot of passion when channeled in the right direction, and a pissed-off Mac turned him on. Way too much.

Coming here had been a bad idea. He should just leave. A black cat that looked like a refugee from a losing battle sat on the arm of the couch and sized him up, cocking his head to see him out of his one good eye. Bruiser was pretty sure the cat found him lacking. He didn't much like cats. His mother had had cats when he was growing up. The little shits made it their job to torture him every chance they got. He leveled the cat with a leave-me-the-fuck-alone glare. The cat glared back, as if to say, *My house, buddy. Not yours.*

Mac stood nearby, not seeming to care that she wasn't exactly dressed for company. She propped her hands on her hips. Bruiser licked his lips as her chest rose and fell, mesmerizing him. He loved the challenge of a pissy woman, loved to cajole them into bed and turn them into putty in his experienced hands.

"You need to go."

He shrugged one shoulder and smiled. "How about a pizza?" The cat crawled across the back of the couch and sat near his shoulder, switching its tail and swatting him on the cheek with each stroke. He scowled at the cat. The cat scowled right back.

"You don't much like cats, do you?"

"What's to like about them?"

She almost smiled but not quite. Instead she turned her belligerence up a notch, which only served to nudge his interest up a notch higher.

"How about you leave? Now." Seeming to realize she might be showing a little too much, she tugged on her top, which off course pulled the material tight against her breasts. Bruiser drew in a sharp breath and cursed the powers that be, while at the same time thanking them for his good luck.

"Ah, come on, Mac. It's Saturday night. I left the party early because you ran out on me. The least you could do is be a charming hostess." He turned his practiced hundred-gigawatt smile on Mac, the one guaranteed to make a woman drop her panties.

Mac didn't drop anything, least of all her annoyance. "If you hadn't noticed, charming is not in my job description."

He chuckled. Oh, yeah, he'd noticed.

"Bruise, I have to get up early, okay? So see ya."

"Hey, it's Sunday tomorrow. I never would've pegged you for the church-going type."

"I'm not, but I have plans."

A smart guy would take the hint and leave. Not Bruiser. Actually, he should've never come here in the first place. No good could come from him being in the company of a half-dressed Mac. Especially considering how much she'd turned him on earlier.

Remember Brett. His repressed conscience demanded to be heard, and he looked away from Mac, battling with himself. He should walk out this door. Right now.

Mac helped him out and walked to the door, yanking it open. "Thanks for dropping by." She gestured toward the porch.

Bruiser balked, about to argue. With a heavy sigh, he stood and walked to the door, feeling a bit like a whipped puppy with his tail between his legs.

He made the dumb-assed mistake of hesitating just a few feet from her. He should've kept going, but his feet wouldn't move. His gaze met hers, and his world stood still. It was just like Bogie and Bacall—Bruiser was a sucker for old classic movies. He'd never had *his* world stand still. He'd always thought the romantic crap in those movies he loved was just a fantasy, especially when it came from a simple glance. But then his brain went into deep freeze, while his heart slipped out of its cage and sprouted wings.

The part of his brain that did function wanted to recite poetry.

Poetry? What the fuck?

He'd never been one to wax poetic unless said poetry got a woman naked. While his body definitely wanted Mac naked, surprisingly sex wasn't his priority. His stomach did these weird-assed somersaults like it did before running onto the football field for the first play of each game. Only Mac's house wasn't a football field and Mac didn't look a damn thing like his teammates.

The urge to taste her overwhelmed him, robbing him off his little remaining sense. He stepped closer, expecting her to retreat. But she stood her ground, neither of them apparently having the wherewithal to abandon ship.

Instead, this ship was gonna sail those rocky seas.

Bruiser raised his hand and cupped the back of her head, capturing the silky strands of her ponytail in his fingers. Angling his head, he lowered his mouth to hers. She looked up at him and the longing in her eyes drove him forward. He had to taste those lips, just once, just a sample, had to know if the effect she had on him extended to kissing. She parted her lips and a soft sigh escaped. That was the last invitation he needed.

His mouth touched hers, setting off a spark and igniting a fire that laid waste to his entire body. He forgot his name, rank, and jersey number.

God, she tasted good. So fucking good.

Bruiser applied more pressure and she met him halfway. Her lips sealed to his, and he slipped his tongue inside that sweet, wet cavern of pleasure. He pushed her against the open door, pressing his hips against her, while his rigid dick rubbed against her stomach. She groaned into his mouth and dug her fingers into his shoulders. Her left leg wrapped around his thigh. Holy crap. He'd be taking her up against this wall any minute for all her neighbors to see.

Her tongue danced with his, thrusting, parrying, retreating like a fencer. She made little mewing sounds, driving him into a mindless fever. He slid his hands under her shirt and upward to heaven. The swell of those fine breasts tickled his fingertips, creamy skin beckoned to him, dared him to cup her in his hands. His dick ached to be buried deep inside her.

Breathing hard, Mac pulled her mouth away from his and sucked on his neck. He liked that, liked that she marked him. Liked it way too much. Liked the feel of her warm body. She was addicting, and the last time he'd allowed himself to become addicted to one woman, it'd ended in disaster and the second-worst pain of his life when she left him. That simple thought wedged in his brain, interrupting his passion with a stab of reality. Pain. Hurt. Betrayal.

This woman was dangerous.

Then there was Brett. His buddy. His trusting friend. And Brett didn't trust many people.

With a superhuman effort born of a well-concealed conscience, he pushed her away, holding her at arm's length. His head reeled from the effects of a drunken stupor, even though he wasn't drunk. Or maybe he was, from her kisses.

Shit, this stuff didn't happen to him. He was always in control when it came to sex and sex play. Not that he didn't enjoy sex. He did, but he liked to be on top, even when he wasn't on top.

Mac leaned against the wall and blinked at him, confusion in her eyes, her lips swollen, her breathing coming in short gasps. Blonde strands of hair framed her face, her ponytail in wild disarray.

Bruiser dropped his hands to his sides and started backing out the door. "I'm sorry, I— I— That was stupid. It won't happen again."

Without waiting for her response, he sprinted out the door to his car and got the hell out of there. Way to fuck up a friendship, not just with Mac but with Brett. The sooner he convinced Brett to ask her out, the sooner this screwball attraction would be a thing of the past. He never messed with other men's women.

Bruiser gunned the car and shot away from the curb, but he couldn't run away from his biggest problem.

Himself.

* * * * *

Morning came too early after a sleepless night. Before Mac knew it, she was staring out the window of her father's old pickup as it wound its way along Hood Canal on Highway 101. Her father didn't seem to be much for talking, thank God. He cranked the Mariners game and grunted a few times, but that was it. Good thing, because between tossing and turning all night and thinking of Bruiser, she couldn't muster enough brain power to carry on the most rudimentary of conversations.

He'd kissed her. Mac brought a finger up to her lips and touched them.

She felt his lips as if they were still pressing against hers, demanding she return the passion. And she had—big-time—for a brief moment that lasted both a lifetime and not nearly long enough. The tingle on her lips spread down to her thighs and parts in between. She glanced at her father, who was still gratefully oblivious to her aroused state. Thank God. This had to stop. *Especially* in the company of her father.

Mac blew out a breath and stared at the sparkling, blue waters of Hood Canal. She needed to concentrate on yet another day of searching, not fret about Bruiser and his momentary lapse. The guy flirted at random with any woman still drawing a breath and most likely kissed every woman with the same reckless abandon. Not that she'd been breathing. One look in those stormy eyes, one flashback of him naked in that barn, and she'd lost the ability to breathe, to think, to function.

How the heck would she survive with that man crowding her thoughts every day and night? While he, oblivious, worked out in full view of her hungry eyes wearing little more than a pair of shorts, sweat dripping off his pecs and drizzling down that trail of blond hair that ran under his waistband.

Oh, Lord. She bit back a moan and chomped down on her knuckles.

This was ridiculous. Utterly ridiculous. She had more serious concerns than her juvenile crush on a guy who was the male equivalent of a slut. Not that she minded man-sluts. They did have their uses but she hadn't been with a guy for pure recreation since her college days. She almost smiled at the thought. Frat boys and pretty-boy running backs probably had a lot in common in and out of the sack.

"I feel good about this lead."

Mac jumped, so deep in her own thoughts that she hadn't even noticed her father had flipped off the radio. "Uh, yeah, Dad. Me, too."

Liar.

Her father swore every lead would be the *one*. She couldn't decide if he earned points for being positive or being in denial. She turned in the seat to face him and banished Bruiser from her mind. Well, she at least pushed him out of the way a little.

"We'll find the clue we need this time. I can feel it." Her dad had felt every one of those clues.

Mac wanted to talk about something else, like the future, her plans, her hopes, her dreams. Her dad used to listen to her and encourage her. She missed that.

"Dad, I may not have as much time to devote to the search." She gathered her resolve and plunged onward. "I'm going to try for the team scholarship. I want to finish my degree in horticulture." She'd dropped out of college when Will disappeared. "I only have a few years left, and the scholarship includes an internship with the team."

Instead of being happy for her, Craig's mouth turned down in a scowl. "How are you going to work full time, go to school, and help me find Will?"

Mac sighed, knowing this had been coming. "Dad, I really need to do this and do it now. Working for the Jacks is my dream job. The current horticulturist retires in the next few years. I need to get my degree, need to prove my worth because I want that job."

Her father didn't look one damn bit convinced. "So you're planning to abandon your brother?"

"Dad, it's not like that. I can't live the rest of my life in limbo. We may never find out what happened to Will. Besides, I'm not abandoning you. I'll still help out. I'm as committed to seeing this through as you are."

Craig ground his jaws together and stared straight ahead. "I know the answer is right around the corner, just out of reach if we could only get that least piece of the puzzle." With those words, her father was off and running. He forgot about Mac in his obsessive quest for the truth. Starting with the day Will disappeared, Craig went through everything they knew, step by step, detail by detail, even though Mac had heard it all a hundred times before. Hell, she'd dissected every aspect of Will's disappearance herself.

As her father ticked off the facts, he sucked her into that all-too-familiar vortex. Her mind fixated on the solving the puzzle. They discussed each tip, turning it every which way, hoping to find that one clue that'd so far eluded them. They were like crackheads needing their next fix. As soon as Mac tried to break free and get a life, some new information would surface and drag both of them back down.

Two facts they both agreed on: *Will was dead and his widow knew what happened to him.* Mac knew it. Her father knew it. And so did the investigators. They had no body, no evidence, but plenty of motive. At least Mac and her dad thought it was motive: a business missing large sums of money, a wife who happened to be the bookkeeper, and an affair with Will's best friend. The entire sordid mess had guilty written all over it.

Craig pulled off the pavement onto a seldom-travelled dirt logging road. The truck bounced along as Mac's stomach clenched with apprehension. She knew this road, and she hated this place. Firs and hemlocks crowded both sides of the truck, blocking out the sky and what little light there happened to be on this dreary day. A branch scraped the side of the door, making an eerie screech.

No one could hear a person scream in a remote place like this.

"Dad, why are driving down this road again?" Mac swallowed hard, willing herself not to give in to the metallic taste in her mouth. "I thought we were going to Port Townsend."

"I just want to take one more look around." Her father's determined expression resigned Mac to their side trip, as much as she dreaded their destination. She gripped the armrests, digging her still-painted fingernails into the cracked vinyl. "We've looked a hundred times. So have the cops. We didn't miss anything."

"Please. Since we're in the area, let's check it out." Her father smiled his sad smile that made her heart bleed for him. What she would give to see a real smile on his face once again, hear his hearty laugh, and listen to his teasing when she lost yet another poker round to him and her brothers. Card games were not her forte.

Craig pulled his truck off the logging road into a small clearing. Moss hung from huge cedars and hemlock trees. A slight breeze ruffled the boughs. The sound should've been comforting, but it wasn't. Not in this place—the very place hikers found Will's truck three years ago almost to the day, three months after he went missing.

Mac sighed, feeling like shit for being such a selfish bitch. She knew why this area drew her father back time and again. It was the only connection they had to Will's disappearance, at least the only one they would explore. Sonja had never let them back in the house after Will disappeared.

Mac watched as her father wandered around the clearing, then disappeared down the same trail they'd walked dozens of times before. With a heavy sigh, she got out of the truck and poked around the area. Nothing seemed out of place; nothing had changed except the grass was taller and the blackberry vines weaved their thorny arms into the clearing, claiming more and more territory as their own.

"Mac! Mac!" Her father's urgent, frantic tone slammed into her.

Mac's head jerked up. She spun in the direction of her father's voice and broke into a run, crashing through the woods. Tree limbs slapped her face as her feet hit the narrow trail. Her heart pounded in her ears at the frantic sound of her father's voice. Lord, she wished she'd learned to shoot a gun. She'd carry it on these trips. She slid to a stop, her chest heaving.

Her father stood several feet ahead, pointing at the ground, his face chalky white.

"Dad, you scared the crap out of me. I thought you were in danger or something."

Craig ignored her alarm, his entire attention focused on a small pile of garbage on the ground. "Look at this." Agitated, his whole body vibrated.

She bent down to get a closer look but saw nothing but a couple plastic garbage bags, empty tin cans, discarded junk mail, and a broken child's toy.

"Don't touch it. It's evidence."

"Dad, it's nothing. Someone dumped their trash here. Happens all the time in the woods, unfortunately." Mac stood up and shook her head.

"Are you sure?"

"I'm positive. Let's get back in the truck. It's going to rain." She started down the path then half-turned and waited for her father. He stared at the pile of garbage as if willing it to turn into the clue he so desperately sought.

But it wasn't a clue, and no amount of wishing could transform it into something it wasn't.

Chapter 8

Double Date

Bruiser cast his line and leaned back in the seat of Brett's fishing boat, a twenty-five-foot C-Dory Tomcat built locally in Ferndale. The two friends often sat for hours on the lake or Puget Sound in this boat, rain or shine, sometimes talking, sometimes not, and often not catching a thing. Regardless, Bruiser enjoyed it.

Eighty-degree warmth soaked into his T-shirt as rays of sun bounced off Lake Washington like a million tiny diamonds riding the waves of the large freshwater lake.

"So how'd it go with Mac the other night?" Brett never took his eyes off the end of his pole, waiting for that telltale tug that announced a fish on the line.

Bruiser gave a guilty start and sat up straight. He forced his face into what he hoped was his best innocent expression, even as he felt his ears getting hot. "Fine. You know Mac."

"Yeah, but the guys said she didn't look like Mac, she looked damn hot."

"I guess." Bruiser shrugged one shoulder, even as he recalled how hot Mac had looked. Really fucking hot. Throw-her-on-the-bed-and-bang-her-brains-out hot. He bet the sassy blonde would be one wild lady in bed. Those mental pictures were worth a million words. *Oh, yeah, baby, give it to me like only you can.*

"Did you get a pic?"

Bruiser jumped, almost dropping his pole. "Uh, yeah. On my cell." Like he hadn't looked at it dozens of times since last Saturday night. Putting his pole in the rod holder, he fished his phone out of his pocket, flipped to the photo, and handed it to Brett.

"Wow. That's Mac?" The asshole practically salivated as he stared at the picture.

Bruiser's stomach clenched with something that felt like jealousy. "Yeah, that's her."

"Damn."

Bruiser snatched the phone from him. When Brett cast a strange look his way, Bruiser fought to come up with a plausible explanation. "Hey, she's like my sister, and you're drooling all over her."

Liar.

He'd sure as hell not treated her like a sister Saturday night. And this morning she'd been spreading bark near the practice field and he'd stopped to admire her fine ass in those tight Wranglers. Since when did he lust over a woman in Wranglers of all things? Only he sure was now.

"Sorry. I didn't mean to disrespect her." Brett had the common decency to appear embarrassed, which made Bruiser an even bigger jerk. "You always get the girls."

Bruiser shrugged. "Not Mac, we're not like that." Oh, but part of him wanted to be like that in so many dishonorable ways.

"I'd love to go out with her. I'm every woman's second choice, you know? Sometimes it gets damn old being number two all the time, being the backup, even when it comes to women."

"I know, it sucks." Bruiser shot a wry smile at his buddy.

"What would you know about being number two? I bet you've never taken a backseat in any situation. Top draft pick. Starter from the beginning. All the ladies want you."

Bruiser studied his pole and wondered how to rouse Brett from his pity party. Rarely did Brett complain about his position, so

Bruiser figured he deserved a little wallowing once in a while. "I was always second choice, up until I turned thirteen."

Brett met his gaze, honestly surprised. "You? Second to who? I find that hard to swallow."

Hesitating, Bruiser weighed his options. He never talked about his past, even with his ex-wife, and his family avoided any mention as if broaching the subject would be enough to detonate a nuclear bomb and lay waste to the planet. So no one knew. The press never unearthed it thanks to an incredibly good agent with scary-good spin-doctors.

Brett waited patiently. His friend had never one tried to force information, content to let Bruiser talk or not talk. Yet today, he wanted to tell Brett about the most painful part of his past. After all, he'd heard a few of Brett's stories.

Releasing his held breath, Bruiser fingered his pole. "I had a twin brother."

Brett sat back as if hit by a strong right hook. His mouth dropped open in shock. For a moment, he couldn't seem to find the words. "You had a twin?"

"Yeah. Brice. He was everything I wasn't. Or wasn't at the time." It felt better to talk than he'd expected. "We were both athletic, but he was better. I was a good student; he was a perfect student. I had a lot of friends, but *everyone* wanted to be his best friend. My parents favored Brice, especially my father, a two-bit movie producer who craved fame. My sister and I were afterthoughts, sometimes annoyances. You see, Brice was going places, and they spent all their time grooming him to go those places."

"Like the Kennedys groomed their oldest son, Joe, to be president?" Brett loved history so it figured he'd make that comparison.

"Yeah, until he died." Bruiser watched Brett digest that bit of information.

"After he died, the Kennedy patriarch turned to his next oldest son to be the president."

Bruiser nodded, the vise gripping his chest making it impossible to speak. He clenched his jaw and stared at his line dangling in the water and bobbing with each wave. Water slapped against the boat's fiberglass hull—usually a soothing sound, but right now it grated on his nerves.

"And Brice is gone, too?"

Bruiser couldn't say the words. Even after all the years, he couldn't describe his complete devastation when he found Brice with a bullet hole in his head. Brice—the perfect brother, son, friend, athlete—couldn't live with his imperfections after the accident. A selfish way to go, leaving his friends and family to blame themselves—they hadn't done enough, hadn't seen his depression, hadn't been able to prevent his suicide.

The guilt lived inside Bruiser like a vital organ.

"I'm sorry. I guess you do know what it's like to be second-string."

Bruiser bit his lower lip and said nothing. He reeled in his line, re-baited it, and cast it back out. Yeah, he did, and he still played second string—to a ghost. Shaking off his melancholy, he raised his head, changing the focus back to his friend. "You need to get together with Mac."

"I guess." Brett's reluctance didn't surprise Bruiser. After all, the guy seemed pretty shy around women, which bordered on next to incredible for an NFL player, but Bruiser had seen Brett in action —or maybe inaction was a better word.

Brett and Mac. Any dating site would pair those two up in an instant. No one in their right mind would pair Bruiser with Mac. On so many levels his attraction to her was so wrong. First of all,

Bruiser was too damaged. He hid it all behind his fake smile and party-boy persona. Secondly, Brett was better suited for Mac. He'd be loyal, faithful, devoted, and he'd love her like—

Shit. Bruiser didn't deal in love, he dealt in lust, and Mac deserved a man who'd treat her like she was special. And Brett deserved a woman who'd do the same. If Bruiser was smart and a decent guy, he'd fix Brett and Mac up, call it good, and move on.

Perfect idea.

Now where to start—even if part of him didn't want to?

* * * * *

Mac looked up as Bruiser stopped in front of the picnic table where she was eating her lunch. "Hi."

"Hey, beautiful, what's up?" He pointed at the stack of papers in front of her.

Mac rolled her eyes. "These are the forms for the scholarship."

"Paper? Who does paper anymore?"

"I think it's a test of our commitment. We have to do it all from scratch, no cutting and pasting from similar forms we've filled out."

"Leave it to Veronica. So you're going for it?" Bruiser smiled that lopsided smile that made his blue-gray eyes twinkle and her heart thump a little harder. His perfect white teeth contrasted with his dark tan and blond hair. Mac swore he looked better every time she saw him, maybe because as she got to know the man inside, she liked him even more. It'd be so much better for her if she didn't.

"I'm going to try."

"Good luck. You deserve it. If I got a vote, you'd be in." He put one foot on the bench and re-tied his shoe. Even his ankles and feet were sexy.

Mac looked down, oddly embarrassed. When she glanced up again, he was studying her.

"Did you change something?" he asked.

"No, nothing," she blushed, surprised he noticed. She'd applied makeup this morning, put her hair in a tidy ponytail, tucked in her polo shirt, and wore a clean new pair of jeans. Stupid, because she'd just get everything dirty, but hopefully the decision-makers would notice. Vince always looked neat and tidy because he barely did a stitch of work, but she didn't expect Veronica to be astute enough to figure that one out.

Bruiser continued to stare at her like he'd never seen her before. She knew she looked better than usual for work, but not as good as Saturday night. Her clothes did fit better, the highlights his sister put in her hair made the strands glow like bars of gold, and the subtle makeup Kelsie taught her to apply made her eyes bigger and cheekbones higher—or so Kelsie claimed. Yet Bruiser looked at her almost as if he didn't like what he saw.

"Is something wrong?"

He shook his head as if coming out of a trance, but Mac wasn't the type of woman who put men into trances, even momentary ones. Her lovesick imagination must be playing games with her.

"So I was wondering..." He hesitated, as if the words didn't come easy.

"Yes?" Her heart leapt to conclusions and her head followed.

"I have tickets to the Mariners behind home plate tomorrow night."

"I'd love to see the Mariners." She spoke too fast, sounding way too much like a desperate woman. Even if she was one.

Bruiser frowned, the action wrinkling his forehead. Damn, if even his forehead wasn't sexy. "Oh, good. I, uh, I wondered if you'd be interested in a double date."

"A double date?" Mac frowned and looked down at her sandwich.

"Uh, yes. I'm taking Veronica's cousin as a favor to her, and you'd be going with Brett."

Brett? This was about Brett? Not her and Bruiser? Mac swallowed and forced a smile. "I'd love to go with Brett." Fighting her disappointment, she met those smoky eyes with her own steady gaze.

"You would?" He seemed incredulous.

"Sure, but why doesn't he ask me himself?"

"Brett's a little shy around women."

"That's a shame. A nice guy like him." Inside, her heart sank to her toes. She should be excited about the opportunity to date Brett. Her crush on Bruiser had gotten worse and Brett might be just what she needed to squash her ridiculous fantasy—nice, good-looking guy and all. Any woman would be thrilled to date him.

"So, what do you think?"

"I'd love to." She smiled widely even though it pained her to do so.

A date. Her first in a few years.

Only with the wrong man.

* * * * *

After the game, the two couples went to a trendy waterfront restaurant. Bruiser's attempts to enjoy the evening crashed and burned in a mushroom cloud of smoke and debris. Holly, his date of the evening, kept yawning and casting glares around the table while rubbing Bruiser's thigh. Any other time, he'd be sporting a large boner, but tonight he couldn't get beyond several misaligned thoughts banging in his head.

Mac looked damn good—not fake, model good, but real, genuine female good. Like a woman a man could get dirty with and love every minute. A woman who wouldn't empty his bank account buying shoes but would actually fight him over who mowed the lawn. Her blonde hair was loose around her shoulders in golden waves. He wanted to bury his fingers in that thick mane while he lost himself deep inside her.

Fuck.

She tilted her head in the cutest damn way and smiled at Brett, while his buddy grinned back at her, looking happier than Bruiser had ever seen him. That made Bruiser feel like an even bigger bastard for coveting Mac and envying Brett.

The happy couple put their heads together, giggling like school kids. Hell, they'd been doing that all night. Bruiser couldn't hear what they were saying, but their secrecy pissed him off until he couldn't see beyond the red haze in front of his eyes.

Not being the center of Bruiser's attention, Holly stuck out her Botoxed lower lip and pouted. Bruiser forced a smile in her direction. She glared back at him. Funny how the woman didn't look the least bit attractive with a scowl on her face. Pure bitch, even though attitude had never bothered him before. After all, who cared about personality when a woman was hot in and out of bed? Only right now, like an idiot, he was caring.

"Let's go, Bruiser. I'm bored." Holly tugged on his arm.

Bruiser didn't even glance at her. "I'll call you a cab." Okay, now he *was* being an inattentive, rude bastard, Sometimes he didn't like himself very much. He hated superficial people, yet he was the most superficial person he knew. Or at least he walked the walk.

"Fine." Now his date slipped into full-assed pout, and there was no reclaiming the evening. She got up in a huff and stomped off. Bruiser trotted after her, full of hollow apologies.

They waited in silence for her cab. He paid the cabbie then leaned in to where she sat in the backseat. "I'll call you."

"Don't bother, you fuckhead. Obviously, you've lost your eyesight, but I haven't. I can't believe you'd prefer someone like *that* over me."

Bruiser opened his mouth to rip her a new one and defend Mac, then shut it. Shit, was it that obvious? He needed to get a grip. "Well then, goodbye." He watched the cab drive off into the night.

Good riddance.

He really was a shallow asshole.

Head down, Bruiser slipped back into the restaurant. Mac and Brett looked in his direction as if they'd just noticed he'd left, which made him feel even more miserable. He should be happy for Mac and for his buddy, but he wasn't, not one damn, selfish bit.

"Where'd you go?" Brett looked beyond him. "Where's Holly?"

"Not feeling well. I got her a cab home." Bruiser slid into the booth across from them.

"Oh." Brett and Mac exchanged glances like two co-conspirators.

The silence settled over them, and Bruiser squirmed. He was the odd man out. With a grim smile, he stood. "I guess I'll be going, too."

They both nodded. No arguments from either one of them.

Bruiser threw a hundred on the table to cover dinner and drinks, nodded at his two friends, and left, skulking out the door like a hound with his tail between his legs.

He jumped in his car and screamed out of the parking garage, hopping onto I-5, then I-90, across Lake Washington to his townhouse. Minutes later, he sat on his deck and stared out across the water, sipping on a beer.

His cell rang, and he grabbed for it, half-expecting it to be Mac or Brett. Maybe they'd gotten in a fight, and Mac needed a ride home. He jabbed the Answer button with his thumb, ignoring the caller ID. "Yeah?"

"Well, if it isn't my absentee son."

Bruiser cringed. "Uh, hi, Mom."

"Oh, so you do remember that you have a mother."

"Yeah, sure." He didn't quite know what else to say. "Sorry. I've been busy."

"With the sweet little blonde we prettied up a few weeks ago?" His mother sounded hopeful, way too hopeful. Depending on his next words, she'd be picking out silverware patterns, a china set, and knitting pink and purple baby booties—if she had a clue how to knit.

"No, she's, uh, seeing someone else." Or she would be after tonight, thanks to him. The thought of Mac naked and sweaty in bed with Brett tied his stomach in bigger knots than his first play on Monday Night Football as a rookie.

"What'd you do to screw it up this time, Bruce?"

"I didn't do anything. We're just friends, that's all."

"Humph. It's time you settled down with some nice girl like her, not all these plastic bitches you date." His mother's disappointment came through the cellular airspace loud and clear, but he couldn't make her happy any more than he had his father. Well, at least not for long, though she'd certainly loved it when he'd bought her and Shanna that beauty salon, setting them up across Puget Sound from Seattle. Unfortunately, an hour's ferry ride hadn't been far enough away. At least they didn't insist on attending his games.

"I'm never settling down, not ever. I don't need marriage, and I sure as hell don't want kids."

"You're being stubborn just to piss off an old woman."

"You're hardly old. And I'm not doing it to piss you off. But you haven't exactly given me a reason to see marriage in a good light."

"Well." She huffed. He pictured her crossing her arms over her ample chest and glaring at the phone. "I hardly think that's necessary. What's happened to you, Bruce? Fame has gone to your head."

"Yeah, Mom, it sure has." His fame and obsession with earning money was what kept her and Shanna in hair dye and fingernail polish and allowed them to work only three days a week.

"I want you to come to dinner on Sunday."

"I can't, I have to—" He hesitated, searching for an excuse.

His mother jumped on his hesitation before he could get another word in. "Two o'clock sharp. And I've invited Mackenzie, too, so you might as well offer her a ride like a gentleman."

"But, Mom."

No one was on the other end to hear his protests.

Chapter 9

Rocking the Ferry

Once Bruiser left, Mac and Brett's easy banter became stilted. With chaperones present, she'd talked with Brett like a co-conspirator, a brother-in-arms. Once alone, her tongue climbed to the roof of her mouth and refused to come down. Her brain sputtered to a stop and their fun night ground to a screeching halt. Nothing like the night she'd been with Bruiser.

Finally, the two of them left the restaurant.

Brett drove Mac home and got out of the car and walked her to her door. Mac tried to see the place through his eyes, with its wisteria arbor over the picket-fence gate, cute little red shutters, and a welcoming porch with hanging baskets of healthy, happy flowers, courtesy of her green thumb.

"I love your place. It's really homey." He smiled nervously, his hands clasped in front of him.

"Thank you." She managed a half-smile.

Brett stared at her. His intent expression telegraphed his desire to take this relationship to the next level. Turning her back on Brett, Mac fumbled with the key in the lock. Finally, she managed to unlock the door and push it open. Brett's hands gently gripped her shoulders, and he turned her around to face him. His pale blue eyes shone with hope and uncertainty, and her heart went out to him.

"I had a good time tonight." He smiled at her, a nice-guy smile, not a naughty-boy smile like Bruiser's.

"So did I." She did have a good time, sorta, but not in the way Brett intended. She liked Brett. Once he came out of his shell he had a quick, wry humor and sharp intellect which she found fun but not exactly exciting.

He tilted his head, lowering it toward her face. His gaze settled on her lips. Mac backed up across the threshold. "I'm really tired, Brett."

His face fell, the corners of his mouth tipped down, and his arms dropped to his sides. She was the worst kind of bitch for rejecting his kiss, but she'd be a bigger bitch if she led him on. The chemistry just wasn't there.

Why was the heart so fickle? Well, maybe not the heart; it might actually be lower than that. Whatever it was, though her head insisted Brett would be an excellent catch, her body wasn't in the game. In fact, it'd gone back to the locker room and was taking a cold shower.

"Okay, well, good night then." He shuffled backward a few steps.

"Brett, you're a great guy."

"Would you like to do something again?" He perked up slightly.

"Uh, sure." Now why the hell did she say yes when she didn't see this going anywhere? Because she was a sucker for a sad smile, and Brett had the saddest smile she'd ever seen.

"Great. I'll call you."

"Sounds good." Mac shut the door and leaned against it, hating herself for wanting Bruiser and giving Brett false hope. She rubbed her hands over her face, weary and tired yet wide awake.

She wanted a life. A normal life. Mac never stood up for herself and her needs and wants. She'd spent three years living in the past, hunting for answers she might never get. What if she went missing tomorrow? Could she say she'd lived her life to the fullest like Will had?

Would Will applaud her choices or chastise her for not following her dreams?

The answer to that question hit way too close to the heart of the matter.

* * * * *

Bruiser dreaded his mother's dinners. Not only was Eunice a barely passable cook, but his sister craved drama more than a reality show producer. Add to that an hour ferry ride both ways alone in a car with Mac, and it was a recipe for pure torture.

He needed to make something happen before training camp because images of Mac really fucked with his sleep. Running it off every morning and evening didn't help either. If anything, the exercise honed his edge instead of filing it down. Pulling into Mac's driveway, he hadn't even put his SUV in park when Mac bounded out the door, blonde hair streaming behind her and a purse slung over her shoulder. She was settled in the seat before he could get out to open the car door for her. God, she looked like heaven with a heavy dose of sin on top.

"Thanks for giving me a ride." She smiled at him, one of those pure heart-warming smiles. He found himself smiling back. She'd turned him into a sorry-assed sap eager for any crumb of her attention.

"It'd be pointless for both of us to drive." Bruiser took in her little top and skirt, along with the makeup. She looked damn cute. Sexy as hell.

"My, aren't we grumpy this afternoon. What's got your boxers in a wad?"

"I'm always like this when I'm about to visit my family." Which was the truth.

"I like your family. They're a hoot."

"Yeah, well, that's because they aren't related to you." Bruiser headed for downtown Seattle across the floating bridge.

"What's your problem with them?" Talk about getting to the point. He liked and hated that about Mac.

"They're just pains in my ass. They bitch at me all the time, try to control me, make demands of me."

"Are you the baby?"

"Yeah, what was your first clue? Other than they treat me like one." Except when they wanted his money. "Sometimes I wish they'd just go away and leave me alone."

"Don't ever say that. You never know when you won't have them around anymore." Mac swallowed and made this little hiccupping sound. Bruiser felt like a shit because he was one.

"Hey, that was an asshole thing for me to say, and I'm sorry. I don't want them to go away; I just want them to lay off."

"It's okay, you don't need to walk on eggshells around me regarding that subject. It is what it is."

Bruiser looked over at her and felt helpless at the pain on her face. He reached over and took her hand. "Then tell me. I'd like to hear. Maybe a pair of fresh eyes and ears would help."

As they drove she told him the whole story, about her brother and how he left work one Friday afternoon and was never seen again, and about her father, who seemed to lose his grip with reality a little more each day. The pain in her voice went right through his heart like a javelin. Finally, her voice trailed off and she looked at him with such a sad expression he just wanted to hold her and tell her it would be all right. But he knew it wouldn't, just like it would never be okay with Brice.

He cleared his throat. "If I can do anything just say the word. I don't have any experience with detective work, but I'm tenacious and stubborn."

Bruiser didn't let go of her hand, and she didn't pull away. He liked her hand in his, even if it wasn't as soft and smooth as most women's hands.

And he liked the idea that she trusted him enough to reveal something so painfully personal. Yeah, he liked that.

A lot.

* * * * *

A few hours later, Mac sat in the passenger seat as Bruiser drove his SUV back onto the ferry, where it was wedged between a semi-truck and the interior wall. Mac couldn't see a thing beyond the vehicles crammed on three sides of them. Washington State Ferry workers were known for their ability to fill every square inch of car deck space. If they had to abandon ship, Mac wasn't sure she could squeeze out the door.

Dinner had proven to be, well, uh, interesting to say the least, between Eunice's pink and purple décor, Shanna's biker boyfriend, and the family's constant badgering of Bruiser. She'd been fascinated by the screwed-up dynamics. Bruiser didn't have it any better than the rest of the world; he just hid it well.

"Thank God that's over." Bruiser stretched in the seat. He spread his arms wide in an arc, his fingers grazing her cheek. Mac suppressed a shiver even as she warned herself against taking such an accidental touch seriously.

"Want to go up top? Enjoy the salt air?" He grinned at her, one of those full-on grins that punched her in the stomach with a heavy dose of desire garnished with hard-to-deny chemistry.

Like she could get out if she wanted. "I'm fine. It's dark and rainy anyway. Not much to see."

She half expected him to head upstairs without her, but he didn't. Instead, his gaze travelled lazily up and down her body, coming to rest on her face.

"I like the view here better."

"You're so full of shit," Mac snorted, her voice extra loud after one too many margaritas. "Your family is a hoot. And the cats. I love the cats."

"Glad someone does," Bruiser muttered.

"They sure have your number."

"The cats or the family?"

"Both."

"They've always had my number and no insult is off limits." He pushed his seat back and tilted the steering wheel upward.

"I could see that. You must have pretty thick skin."

It was Bruiser's turn to snort. "Try elephant-hide thick." He turned to her, and his frowned deepened. "How'd it go with Brett?"

"Nice move deflecting the conversation from your family. He didn't fill you in?"

"A little, but tell me your take." He stared intently at her like a hungry restaurant reviewer eyeing a delectable menu, only she couldn't be on that menu. Tonight or any other night. Even if a naughty part of her wanted to be.

"We had a nice time."

"You don't sound particularly enthused." Bruiser almost looked happy at the thought.

"I like Brett, but—" Mac didn't know how to articulate what she wanted to say. Brett's a great catch, and she was an idiot for lusting after the wrong guy? Yeah, that about summed it up. Idiot. Wrong guy. Lusting. Definitely all three.

"He doesn't do it for you." Bruiser read her mind. He'd done a lot of that lately, and his perceptiveness threw her off kilter.

"Not really," she heard herself admit.

"Not like I do, but then who could blame you?" He shot her another lopsided, teasing grin, which didn't conceal an underlying layer of pure male heat. If he kept that up, she'd be divested of her pride and her panties.

Mac smacked him on the arm. He didn't even flinch. "That's pretty arrogant of you."

Bruiser shrugged. "Just telling it like it is. We've been dancing around each other ever since the barbecue."

It'd been a helluva lot longer than that, but originally she'd been dancing solo. "Looking for another notch on your dick?"

"Nah, quit notching it long ago. I prefer the bedpost." His storm-cloud eyes tempted her, drew her in, promised her all sorts of naughty things, the kinds of naughty things a nice girl secretly lusted after.

"Ran out of room, did you?"

"I'd take you for a test drive if you were sitting on the lot."

"Maybe I am." Mac couldn't believe she'd said that to him, but she had, and dammit she was going to own it, margaritas be blamed or not.

"Is that Mac or the tequila talking?" He didn't take the bait even though he'd thrown the first punch.

"Both. I'm not drunk. Just a little tipsy." Mac tugged on her skirt, which had hiked up to give Bruiser a good view of her bare mid-thighs. The seductress thing was new to her. Most women would've bared more thigh, but she figured less was more. Bruiser seemed to think so, too, if his scorching-hot gaze raking her legs was any indication.

"You sure you're a consenting adult in your close-to-right mind?" His slow, sexy smile said it all. Bruiser, pretty boy of the NFL, wanted to jump her bones. Damn. She sure as hell had fantasized long enough about jumping his.

Mac lifted her head and met Bruiser's steady gaze. "Oh, yeah, I'm consenting. I need to start living my life."

"So you want to live it now? In my Chevy?" Bruiser's stormy eyes held her hostage.

"Yes." She licked her lips and swallowed.

"Seriously?" He frowned, as if he wasn't quite sure if he understood her.

"I thought—I mean, I, oh, never mind. I read you wrong." Mac's face fell. She felt all kinds of stupid.

"It's not that I'm not interested, Mac. I am. Damn, but I am. In fact, I haven't been able to get you out of my mind for a few weeks now."

"Since when? The party?" Mac blinked a few times, unable to imagine Bruiser Mackey lusting over her while he ran his morning miles.

"Actually, before that. I was lusting over the real Mac. The one pre-makeover."

"Maybe this *is* the real Mac, but I've been hiding."

"You looked great before. You look great now. Either one works for me, as long as you're who you want to be—but you don't need that crap to make yourself pretty." He shrugged with a frown on his handsome face, even as his gaze did a slow journey down her body and up again.

"Pretty? You think I'm pretty?" God, she sounded so pathetic, like an orphan puppy begging for a little love.

There came that sexy, lopsided smile again. "Yeah, I do." His eyes glinted like the sun bouncing off silver dollars in a fountain.

"You want me?"

"Is that so hard to believe?" He sobered for a moment. "But what about Brett?"

"There is no Brett. I wish he interested me, but he doesn't. He's a great guy, and he deserves a woman who doesn't have her mind on other—pursuits." Not as long as Bruiser lived in every one of her sexual fantasies. Fuck, she wanted those fantasies to come true.

"Still, he won't be happy about this."

"I wasn't going to announce it to the whole team."

A shadow crossed his face in a brief cameo appearance. "You sure this isn't tequila talking?" Bruiser's tight laugh betrayed the amount of restraint he currently exercised.

"Do you want me or not, buster?" Well, maybe the tequila did talk—somewhat—but Mac knew what she was doing.

"Fuck, yeah." He leaned toward her, his scent filled her nostrils, intoxicating her more than any alcohol ever could. His warm breath tickled her neck, sending a shiver through her body. He trailed little kisses up her neck to her ear and along her jawline. Mac gripped the seat as if she'd rocket out of it any second.

In moment of tequila-fueled boldness, she slid her hand up his thigh to his crotch to that impressive bulge in his pants. She stroked up and down, and he groaned, deep and guttural like an animal in dire need of doing the nasty. With a trembling hand, Mac put a hand on his fly, unbuttoned and unzipped his pants.

"Bruiser?"

"Yeah?" Bruiser lifted his head and watched her with heavy-lidded eyes.

"What I said about your size during the photo shoot in the barn…I was just toying with you. Even limp, you were impressive."

"I know." He pressed his lips against the hollow behind her ear. She tilted her head to expose more of the sensitive skin to his lips. "Honey, I can show you impressive all night long."

"I bet you could."

Bruiser reached for her and toyed with the tiny buttons on her top.

"Here?" A thin layer of panic crept into her voice, and she attempted to squelch it. Be bold, be daring. Just do it. Live life on the edge. Just this once.

"No one can see in the windows. Too dark."

When Mac offered no protest, Bruiser bent his head, concentrating on the task before him—getting her naked in an SUV on a ferry. They might both be fucking nuts, but Mac had turned the corner on caring and entered the realm of careless. Obviously, Bruiser's vast experience undressing women paid off, as he unbuttoned every last button in record time. Pushing the thin material off her shoulders, he stared at her black lace bra, licked his lips, and groaned, deep and guttural.

"I'm sorta small." She couldn't help apologizing.

"Not to me. You're perfect." He stared at her boobs like a running back seeing open field to the end zone. She wanted him in her end zone. Bad. Fucking bad. Crazy-assed, need-you-more-than-I-need-my-sanity bad.

Bruiser hesitated, his eyes still on her chest. "Mac, I don't want to ruin a good friendship."

"It's okay, I don't expect anything afterward."

His brows knit together, almost as if that weren't the answer he wanted. "What do you expect, sweetheart?" He leaned in, his low, husky voice in her ear and his expensive cologne mingled with hardcore masculinity.

"I expect you—" Mac hesitated, drew in a deep breath and took a chance. "I don't expect a tomorrow. I don't expect a relationship. I just want you with me tonight."

Mac slipped her hand under his waistband and lowered her head toward his crotch, committing her words to action. She slipped into insanity, ready to give Bruiser a blow job on ferry so packed the ferry workers couldn't have squeezed in a kid's tricycle.

And damn, did she not give a shit.

Chapter 10

Crossing the Line

Bruiser held his breath and sent up a prayer of thanks to whatever saints listened to a man thanking them for getting him laid. He wanted Mac so much his hands shook and his heart slammed against his rib cage, while his dick begged for sweet mercy. He buried his fingers in her hair so she wouldn't notice what a pathetic, needy mess he was.

Mac was about to give new meaning to a ferry ride. He'd never see these white and green travelling highways the same again. Mac gave a satisfied sigh as she studied the bulge in his shorts. Then she lowered her head, her silky hair trailing across his belly and hips. Bruiser laid his head against the headrest, his breath coming in short gasps, and his heart hammering in his chest.

He lifted his hips—ever helpful—and Mac pulled down his pants, easing some of the pressure, but not nearly enough. Lowering her head once again, Mac fastened her teeth onto the elastic waistband of his underwear, yanking downward until his cock sprang free. Her warm breath feathered his bare skin, and his dick throbbed, a painful, need-wrenching throb. He damn well needed a little recreation between the sheets—or was that *seats?*—with this particular woman.

Hell, this woman had ruined his appetite for other women for the past few weeks, as if this thing between them might be more than mere recreation. Intentional or not, she'd teased him all afternoon in that sexy skirt with those shapely legs of hers and that form-fitting little top. Despite his insistence that he liked the old

Mac better, he sure as hell appreciated this Mac. In fact, he was so worked up, all he could think of was getting her horizontal in his bed. This damn SUV with its big-assed console didn't leave room for anything but a good blow job. Not that he was complaining.

Her soft, heavenly lips touched the tip of his penis, and she fisted her hand around his shaft. All rational thought dived into the dumpster in his mind—better than a gutter, he guessed, but pretty much the same difference because all he could think were dirty thoughts of how good her mouth felt going down on him and how good it'd feel to reciprocate.

She licked the length of his penis, then swirled her tongue around it as she made a circuit back to the soft, bulbous head. When she sucked a drop of pre-cum from the tip, the top of his head just about blew off. Then she went down on him. Talk about blowing off, and only not his head. He groaned and writhed on the seat, pushing his hips upward to meet the thrusts of her hand. Nothing had ever felt this good. At least nothing he could recall in his current state of mind. Not that he had a mind or even a state. She'd melted him down to raw hormones and lust.

Oh, God. He rolled his head back and forth and closed his eyes, massaging her silky blonde hair with his fingers while applying pressure to lower her head further down. If she deep-throated him, he'd have a heart attack.

Mac lifted her head upward and gazed at him, her eyes half-lidded and burning with lust. "I don't know how to take you deep," she admitted, her face coloring at her words.

"Just do what feels right. Because anything you do feels good to me." He grinned, happy she wasn't an expert. The thought struck a possessive chord as foreign to him as shopping in a thrift store.

She lowered her head again and took him a little deeper, bobbing her head up and down on his shaft while he shook like an unbalanced washing machine. Any second he'd empty his load.

"I'm going to come," he warned, grinding his teeth until his jaw ached.

"I want to taste you." She licked him again and sucked on him.

He gripped the steering wheel. His body spasmed while she drove him into temporary oblivion. He emptied himself into her sweet, hot mouth. Mac swallowed, then licked up the rest.

Bruiser leaned his head against the headrest, pretty sure he'd just died from sheer fucking pleasure because he couldn't remember how to breathe, and he was pretty certain his heart had stopped beating. Mac might have done all the physical work, but he was exhausted from the ride.

"*The ferry will dock in Seattle in ten minutes. Please return to the car deck,*" the captain alerted them over the ferry's loudspeakers.

Mac blinked several times and slowly sat up. She wiped her face with a tissue and glanced around, as if disoriented. Hell, he knew that feeling.

With a sigh, Bruiser pulled up his briefs and pants.

For several long minutes, neither of them said a word.

"It's your turn." Bruiser believed in giving as good as he got.

"But we're almost at the dock." Mac's eyes were glassy and unfocused. Pretty much how he felt.

"This isn't finished yet. Not by a long shot. Your house or mine?" Oh, yeah, baby. They'd take this well into the night. Sleep was greatly overrated.

"Mine. I have to feed the cat."

Bruiser burst out laughing. "That's my job."

She stared at him as if he'd gone mad. "Your job? You don't like cats."

"Oh, honey, I like pussies just fine. And yours definitely needs to be fed."

Her slow smile was his reward. "Is that a promise?"

"You betcha."

Not only was it a promise, it was a pledge.

* * * * *

Brain malfunction was an acceptable reason for what Mac had just done and was about to do—all night long.

She glanced at Bruiser, who gripped the steering wheel with white-knuckled concentration and stared straight ahead. He hadn't said a word since they'd left the ferry terminal. Sunday evening traffic worked in their favor and in matter of minutes they were speeding down the freeway.

The silence wasn't uncomfortable. In fact, it seemed to fit both their moods. Mac stared out the window, hypnotized by the white line as it sped past. A quick glance at the dash clock told her the night was young. It was only about six thirty, which left plenty of sheet time with a hot man and sexually starved woman. Oh, yeah. Stupid or not, it was going to be a good night all night long.

She glanced at Bruiser's face. His strong profile with that oh-so-sexy cleft in his chin accentuated by his more-than-a-five-o'clock shadow brought forth all kinds of naughty fantasies, starting with his beard scraping across her face, her nipples, her thighs. Damn, she was so wet between the legs she was glad she wasn't wearing slacks or there'd be visible evidence of her arousal.

Bruiser exited the freeway and slipped one hand off the steering wheel and up her thigh, then he rubbed her crotch in a circular motion.

"You're driving," she gasped.

"Honey, it's my turn to torture you a little and pretty soon I'll be driving more than this car."

"But right now you're driving this car—or should be."

"I can take care of that." He wrenched the wheel, sending her sprawling across his lap. "Now, that's much better."

Pulling into a parking garage, he drove to top floor, past a smattering of parked cars to a dark corner between a concrete pillar and the wall. "So whaddya think, honey? Will this do?"

Oh, God, would it ever. *Just get me naked now.* "I never knew you had a thing for public sex."

"I have a thing for all kinds of sex, and I can't make it home without tasting you first." Bruiser shot her his panty-dropping smile, and she melted all over him like chocolate left on a dashboard on a sunny day. Taking a quick glance around, he leaned over the console and hiked her skirt up to her waist in front.

"Nice," he said as he gazed down at her lacy pink underwear. "Do you wear panties like this under your work clothes? 'Cause if you do I'll never be able to work out when you're in the vicinity without imagining a more horizontal workout."

She nodded, mute but fired up for action. Bruiser put a gentle hand on her chin. She parted her lips and waited. He didn't let her down. He kissed one corner of her mouth and licked his way to the other corner before he took her mouth with a full-on frontal assault. His lips pressed against hers, and his glorious blond stubble rubbed across her face. His kiss was hot, hard, and demanding, full of promise and full of expectations. She so wanted to meet those expectations. The pretty boy and the plain girl. What a weird pair. What a perfect pair. Chemistry worked in mysterious ways.

Bruiser cupped the back of her head as he deepened the kiss like he wanted to eat her up. His other hand didn't stay idle. He slipped it under the crotch of her panties and found her wet and willing. Pulling back for a moment, Bruiser offered a slow, knowing smile.

"You're wet for me."

Mac nodded and pulled his face back to hers, marauding his mouth like a female conqueror. Bruiser didn't protest, not one damn bit. His finger slipped deep inside her, and he moved it in and out while his tongue made love to her mouth.

Just when she was certain she'd die, the tease stopped kissing her. Mac moaned in protest until he pulled her legs across the console, grasped her waist and lifted her hips into the air. With her legs draped across his shoulders, he held her crotch to his face and began to feast.

And oh my God, did he *feast*. Mac turned into a limp rag doll, not caring that the console pressed into her back and her toes were hitting the driver's-side window. Nothing mattered, and any amount of discomfort made it all worth it to have Bruiser's face buried between her legs.

He slipped his tongue between her folds and plunged it deep while sucking her juices. Reinserting his finger, Bruiser used it along with his tongue to drive her to the brink of insanity, up, up, up, until she swore she'd die because no mortal female could survive such heavenly torture.

And he wasn't done yet. He added another finger, while his tongue circled then sucked on her clit, over and over. Circle. Suck. Circle. Suck.

Despite her discomfort, Mac squeezed her eyes shut and clung to the seat, as waves of pleasure rolled through her body like an ocean tide on a stormy day.

Mac's body convulsed with senseless pleasure. Bruiser was unrelenting, he kept up the pressure and drove her deep into an abyss of desire she didn't know was possible. The pressure built up until she had to release it or die. Mac cried out and wrapped her legs around his neck while the most mind-blowing, incredible orgasm slammed into her with a fierce intensity.

Bruiser repositioned her, holding her to him, until the shudders subsided and she floated safely back to the rational world. When she finally met his gaze, he kissed her and she tasted herself on him.

"Wow." That was all she could manage to say.

"There's more to come. Halftime entertainment is over. Let's finish this game." Bruiser helped her lower her shaky body back into her seat. She fumbled with the seatbelt and closed her eyes as he drove out of the parking garage into the waning daylight.

Mac couldn't wait to get home to a more conventional place to do the real thing, but she suspected there would be nothing conventional about sex with Bruiser, even if it was in a bed after dark, just as there was nothing conventional about the man himself. All day she'd seen glimpses of the real man under the shallow persona, revealing more than Mac wanted to know about him. Knowing more might make her fall deeper, might make her crush more real, might do some irreparable damage—damage she couldn't afford.

* * * * *

Bruiser turned down Mac's street, ready for round three, the round where he buried himself inside her willing body, and Mac delivered a knockout punch that rendered them both winners. He'd sat on his annoying conscience and kept it muffled so it was only a slight nagging presence. With his mother and sister, he'd become a pro at shutting out nagging—but then most men with women in their lives could most likely say the same damn thing.

Right now his cock has assumed command, and none of his other body parts, including his brain, had any interest in an uprising. Yeah, the only thing rising would be his dick. Bruiser couldn't wipe the stupid-assed grin from his face. He'd waited too long for Mac, and he rarely waited for any woman.

Only—crap. Double crap. Fuck. Damn.

Bruiser couldn't believe his eyes. He pounded his fist on the dashboard in frustration. A pickup was parked in Mac's driveway. "What the fuck?" The words slipped out before he could stop them.

Mac's hand went to her mouth and she glanced guiltily at him, disappointment dulling her brown eyes. "I completely forgot that I'd promised my dad that I'd go with him tonight."

"Well, hell." That just about said it all. "How long do you think he's been waiting for you?"

"He's probably been here all day stalking the neighbors."

"Stalking your neighbors?"

Mac sighed as if she didn't want to go there, but Bruiser did, dammit. If his night was going to be abruptly cut short, he wanted the details—every damn last one of them.

"Mac, why would he stalk your neighbors?"

"Because that was Will's house, and Sonja and Ben live there now."

"Your brother's ex-wife—the woman you suspect murdered him—lives next door to you? You never told me that part."

"Twisted, isn't it?"

"A little," he admitted.

"I'm not moving. These two properties belonged to my great-grandparents, and I'll be damned if I'm going to let Sonja drive me off my birthright. She goes before I do."

"I get it." Bruiser really did, yet living with that constant reminder might make family ties not worth it. Talk about overwhelming drama the average person didn't need.

"So your father expects you to go with him tonight? This late?" Bruiser shook his head, attempting to clear out the haze.

"He won't care how late it is as long as Trudy is still at the bar."

"Is she his girlfriend?" Bruiser felt like he'd missed the most important episode of a TV series and had no frame of reference as to what the hell was going on.

"I wish it were that simple." Mac rubbed her temple as if she had a raging headache. "He thinks Trudy, Sonja's former best friend, knows something and is ready to spill the beans. I don't buy it. She's just milking him for money."

"So I guess our night it over then." Bruiser let out a disappointed sigh and parked in the driveway behind her father's pickup. Disappointment didn't quite cover it. Sure, he was damn disappointed about not getting any more action tonight, but deeper down in that place he never went, especially with women, he enjoyed her company and wasn't ready to go home to his lonely condo.

"Probably. Here comes Dad now." Small consolation, but at least Mac sounded as miserable as he felt.

Mac's father strode across the yard and rushed to the passenger door and flung it open. "Mac, have you been following up on something? Did you find out anything new?" Mac's dad didn't acknowledge Bruiser. The man's bloodshot eyes gleamed with a fierce intensity. Not a competitive intensity like Bruiser was accustomed to seeing, more like a guy on the verge of a one-way trip to the nuthouse. His unkempt hair and wrinkled clothes only punctuated Bruiser's initial assessment.

"I went to brunch at Bruiser's mother's house. I forgot about our plans." Mac glanced nervously at Bruiser, as if she wished he'd leave rather than bear witness to her family failings. Well, she'd had her shot with his dysfunctional family, and Bruiser wasn't going anywhere. Fair was fair.

"We always have plans on weekends. You know that." Her father glanced at Bruiser as if he'd just noticed him, then turned back to Mac, obviously disinterested in anything that didn't have to do with his lost son. "We still have plenty of time. Trudy's caving; I can just feel it. We're on the verge of something."

With a heavy sigh, Mac interrupted her father's ramblings. "Bruiser, this is my dad, Craig Hernandez. Dad, this is Bruiser Mackey."

Craig blinked a few times, scratched his cheek, and squinted at Bruiser. "I know you. You were Will's favorite player. He liked how you play balls to the wall with no concern for your own safety. Will was like that, too, you know."

Bruiser nodded, casting Mac a look that said *Is this guy okay?* She lifted one shoulder and said nothing. Mac got out of the car, and Bruiser debated whether or not to beat cleats or stay for the long haul.

"Bruiser, thanks for the ride." Mac dismissed him, just like that, like she hadn't been sucking his dick into a oblivion a few short hours ago or he hadn't been enjoying her pussy. After all they'd just done together in his SUV, she apparently still wanted him gone. Bruiser didn't like that. He wasn't sure why it bugged him, but it did.

"Come with us. A fresh set of eyes is always welcome. You might catch something we've missed," Craig said.

"Dad, Bruiser has better things to do." Mac shot him a look that said *Just leave.*

"I, uh, I doubt I'd be much help." Bruiser hesitated, torn between a stubborn inclination to stick around and his don't-get-involved mantra.

"Of course, you will." Craig wasn't taking no for an answer, that was pretty obvious.

Tossing a tough-shit grin at Mac, Bruiser nodded and followed her father to the pickup. Reluctantly, Mac followed and got in the backseat. Bruiser settled in the passenger seat, hoping like hell they didn't smell too much like sex. Not that it mattered. Craig seemed completely oblivious to anything that didn't have to do with Will.

Several minutes later, they walked into a greasy spoon with an equally dreary bar. Mac and Bruiser both headed straight for the bathrooms to wash their hands. When Bruiser came out, Craig was seated at a table in the bar, along with Mac. Bruiser ordered a whiskey. Since he wasn't driving, he might as well see if drinking would relieve some of the sexual frustrations currently hammering his body.

Trudy turned out to be a stereotypical waitress, right down the bleached blonde hair, gum chewing, and tight clothes. She latched onto Bruiser like a woman who'd won the Mega Millions. Bruiser didn't much like being anyone's lottery prize, but the irritation flashing in Mac's eyes goaded him on. She didn't want him here, and that hurt for reasons he couldn't explain.

When Trudy left to fill their drink order, Craig nudged Bruiser. "She's interested in you. Play along and see if you can get any info out of her."

"Dad, please, don't get Bruiser involved in this." Mac pursed her lips together, her narrowed gaze sliding from her father to Bruiser.

"He doesn't mind, do you, son?" Craig stared at him with such desperation, Bruiser couldn't say no, even though Craig's suggestion had Mac almost gnashing her teeth.

"I'll see what I can do." Bruiser smiled innocently at Mac. Maybe next time she'd think twice before she attempted to ditch him. Even better, they might finish up and get back to her house in time for a continuation of their car sex.

With renewed enthusiasm, Bruiser strolled over to the bar, dialed up the charm, and chatted up Trudy. The woman all but climbed into his pants. Her cloying perfume choked him and her cat-like claws dug into his arm, but Bruiser stuck with it, bullshitting her until he could get past the garbage to the good stuff, whatever the fuck that might be.

Trudy lowered her voice and glanced over her shoulder. "You naughty boy, coming on to me in front of them. You can't be dating Mac?" She said it as if it were an inconceivable possibility.

Bruiser clenched his jaw, unreasonably pissed at the scorn this fake bitch directed at Mac, but he forced himself to play along. "Uh, no, just hanging with them. She works at the Jacks' practice facility. I lost a bet and had to take her to dinner, so here we are."

Trudy nodded, shooting a glance at Mac's table then back to Bruiser. "I understand. I figured it had to be something like that. She's not your type."

Irritation rolled through Bruiser. Mac out-scored this woman any day of the week. Yet obviously, Trudy assumed she was more Bruiser's type. God, maybe she was, based on past girlfriends and hook-ups. The realization made him sick to his stomach.

"What are you doing later tonight?" Trudy pressed her hips against his, and Bruiser juked to the side with a smooth move that put a barstool between them.

"I have a commitment. Wish I didn't, but I do." What a lying sack of shit he was, but he reminded himself it was all for a greater cause.

"Maybe some other time." She ran a fire-engine red fingernail across the stubble on his chin. Instead of turning him on, he suppressed a shudder. He swore he could feel Mac's eyes burning a heart-sized hole in his back.

"Yeah, give me your number." Mac and Craig owed him. Big time.

Trudy scratched her number on the back of a paper coaster and handed it to him. "Don't lose this."

"Wouldn't dream of it." He folded it neatly and tucked it in his jeans pocket, then struck a casual pose leaning against the bar while keeping a strategic barstool between them. "So how do you know Mac and Craig?"

"Oh, my former best friend used to be married to her brother." Trudy stepped back a little, biting at her lower lip. On Mac the act would've been sexy, on Trudy it read like a guilty verdict. This woman did know something.

"Really? The one who disappeared?"

"Yes. Will." Her short, clipped tone didn't invite more questions, but Bruiser didn't give a shit.

"So you're not friends with her anymore?"

"No, she's a selfish bitch." Trudy wouldn't meet his gaze. Instead she ripped a paper coaster into little pieces.

"Do you think she did something to Will?" Bruiser sipped his beer and feigned casual disinterest, as if it were of no consequence to him.

Trudy's eyes narrowed and her expression turned guarded. She glanced at Mac and Craig then back to Bruiser. Her fake smile dropped off her face to be replaced with a suspicious frown. Before he could react, she reached a hand in his pocket and snatched the coaster with her phone number. "I might be a blonde, but I'm not dumb. Try some other sucker." She turned away from him and stalked off to bus tables. Bruiser closed his eyes for a moment, disappointed he'd come so close only to fail.

"What happened?" Craig asked when Bruiser returned to the table.

"I pushed too hard, too fast. She's already suspicious of you two. I should've come in alone."

"You tried. You don't need to do any more." Mac jumped in quickly, shoving a hand through her thick mane of blonde hair. If Bruiser didn't know better, he'd swear she was jealous, and he kind of liked that.

"She knows something. Somehow she's involved. There's no way someone like her would keep a secret unless it was to her benefit." Craig's eyes burned with an unbalanced intensity that made Bruiser uncomfortable. The guy needed emotional help.

"Dad, it was a long shot at best. Trudy isn't talking." She turned to Bruiser. "So what are the Jacks' chances at a Super Bowl this year?" Mac stared pointedly at him, her knee bumping his.

Bruiser blinked a few times, trying to focus on this abrupt change in topic. "I think we can do it. Last year was a bit of a rebuilding year, lots of new, young players and—"

"What do you think she knows?" Craig interrupted, as he kept his eyes on Trudy, like he'd suddenly see the truth by staring at her.

"What? Who knows? Veronica?" Bruiser didn't understand the question. Mac shot him a look that he couldn't interpret.

"Trudy, of course. She has to know something. I bet she helped dispose of the body, or maybe she lured Will somewhere under a false pretense, and they killed him there."

Bruiser didn't quite know how to answer that. He was used to dysfunctional families, but he felt sorry for Mac all the same. As annoying as his mother and sister were, they had lives. Craig didn't appear to have or want one. He expected the same from his daughter, and he was holding her hostage with guilt as his weapon.

Throughout the remainder of a crappy evening, Mac steered the conversation to one topic after another, only to have Craig steer it back to Will. Craig didn't have any interest in hearing about Mac's attempt to get a scholarship or become a sports turf manager. When they finally got back to her house, Craig followed her inside, still rambling about what Trudy must know. Mac cast an apologetic look in Bruiser's direction. He took the hint, said goodnight, and drove back to his townhouse.

Sexually frustrated, Bruiser chose a cold shower for company. Sure, there were other women he could call, but he didn't want other women right now. He wanted Mac, wanted her vertical, horizontal, upside down—hell, anyway he could get her.

He stood under the showerhead as the frigid water sluiced down his body, shriveling his dick, but not his desire. This thing with Mac was just about sex.

It had to be.

Bruiser's damaged heart and brittle soul couldn't handle anything more.

Chapter 11

Running Touchdown

Mac couldn't decide if her father had done her a favor or a disservice by barging past Bruiser into her house a few nights ago, essentially ruining Mac's plans for a little playtime with the league heartthrob. Scowling, Bruiser had just shrugged one shoulder, turned to his car, and driven away.

Instead off an all-night romp, Mac's evening consisted of the deadly dull boredom of listening to her father obsess over Bruiser going back to the diner by himself to weasel info out of Trudy.

Speaking of the Bruiser, Mac hadn't seen him at Jacks' HQ for a couple days. Probably on some modeling stint or endorsement. Bruiser endorsed everything from condoms to underwear to heartburn medicine. As long as someone slapped cash into his palm, he'd endorse their product. The man was an endorsement slut, along with his other vices, which made him *so* not the man for Mac. He was too preoccupied with his appearance, and she was not. Well, maybe that wasn't totally true. She'd grown fond of her new look, liked how guys gave her a second glance, how people listened to her, and how it made her feel more confident.

Despite her every argument to the contrary, Bruiser stayed at the top of her fantasy list, day and night.

That evening as Mac left work, her cell chirped. She snatched it up and speed-read the screen. A slow smile slid across her face and her panties went from dry to wet in under five seconds.

That had to be a personal best.

O'Malley's? Unless your Dad has plans for you.

Bruiser with those laughing storm-cloud eyes kicked every other priority in her life to the procrastination basement, and she got hot all over.

Mac tapped out: *On my way.*

Me, too.

Then she remembered. Her father wanted to spend the evening going over the clues one more time. She didn't even hesitate; she texted her father and cancelled. It was time for her to do something for herself, and she wouldn't say no to Bruiser or to his luscious, made-for-sex body.

Maybe there was more to it than just the thought of a night of sex. The profound sadness lurking behind Bruiser's well-rehearsed smile intrigued her. And despite her denial, that glimpse of vulnerability sucked her in more than his six-pack abs and gorgeous face.

Bruiser's SUV was already sitting in the parking lot when she pulled in and parked her old F-150 next to it. Mac dug through her purse for her feeble collection of makeup and applied a little lipstick and blush. Then she brushed out her hair and frowned. Confined to a ponytail all day, her hair had funny waves in it, flat in some places and sticking up in others. Well, it was the best she could do on short notice.

She hopped out of her truck and restrained herself from running inside. Instead she sauntered, as if she hadn't a care in the world, just as Kelsie had taught her.

Bruiser glanced up, those twinkling eyes sliding down her body and back up like a lover's caress. Mac shivered and as she started to slide into the opposite side of the booth Bruiser shook his head and patted the spot next to him. Mac hesitated briefly then sat down on his side. He slid closer, their thighs touching, and rested his arm across the back of the booth, rubbing her shoulder with his strong fingers.

"Miss me?" He grinned at full wattage, as if really happy to see her.

"Like an ice storm on a Seattle freeway."

"Good. I missed you, too." Insults didn't deter Bruiser. He glanced around. "No Craig tonight?"

"No, he's going back over some leads." Mac refused to give into the guilt.

Bruiser frowned. "Is that all he ever does?"

"Pretty much twenty-four-seven, and I do mean that. He doesn't sleep much. Finding out what happened to Will is his life."

"I think that's sad." Looking down, Bruiser toyed with his coaster. After a few moments, he looked up. "You know, I'll do that for you if it'll help."

"Do what?"

"Come on to Trudy. See what I can find out. I draw the line at getting naked with her though." His grin returned. "There's only one female I'm interested in getting naked with right now, and she's sitting next to me."

"You're toying with me." Mac *so* wanted that to be true.

"Oh, yeah, and I'd like to do so much more." One corner of his mouth kicked up in his trademark, lopsided grin, as he cocked his head at her, while that stubborn lock of blond hair fell across his forehead.

Their gazes caught and held. A tremor rumbled from her toes to the tips of her newly highlighted hair, with the epicenter right between her legs.

Bruiser wound several strands of her hair around his index finger. He brought them up to his nose and inhaled. "Your hair smells damn good."

"And you look damn good." Lately the man had this more-than-a-five-o'clock shadow thing going on, and it was sexy as hell. She'd never been much for facial hair, but Bruiser could have hair on his shoulders and back, and she'd still find him bone-jumpingly drool-worthy.

They ordered dinner and huddled together in their little dark corner like two lovers, or at least would-be lovers. Mac sipped cheap wine. She'd never acquired a taste for the expensive stuff. Give her white zin or chilled red any day. Bruiser sucked down a microbrew and soon they were debating the merits of 3-4 defenses versus 4-3, whether or not Zach had enough gas left in his tank for another season, and the odds on Tyler molding the young offense into a cohesive unit.

They talked so much that they didn't even notice the place had emptied out and the staff watched them with undisguised annoyance. Bruiser dropped a big bill on the table and grabbed Mac's hand. "So my place or yours?"

"Mine is closer."

"As long as your dad stays far away."

"He will. He thinks I'm sick. He's never been good at playing the role of nursemaid."

"So you lied to him?"

"Fibbed. For the greater good."

Bruiser threw back his head and laughed as they crossed the parking lot. "Mac, you'd better watch it. You're getting more and more like me every day."

"That's a scary thought."

"Yeah, one of me is enough. Even I admit that."

"I don't think you're nearly as bad as you pretend to be."

"Now don't go giving me a conscience. That's never been part of the deal."

"You volunteered to chat up Trudy."

"Yeah, well, momentary lapse from my selfish reality. Plus, if it helps get me in your pants, then game on."

"You don't fool me, Bruce Mackey. Under that pretty-boy exterior is a real person and a genuinely nice guy."

"You'll never hear that from me." Bruiser's jaw tightened, making that cleft in his chin even more pronounced. He stared straight ahead, his gaze distant and his expression closed. She'd hit a sore spot, but damned if she knew what.

In a matter of seconds, the pretty boy was back in character. "If being a nice guy gets you horizontal, I can manage that." He grinned at her, but Mac wasn't fooled. She'd seen something deeper, more than just the surface stuff he showed to the world.

He stopped beside her car, then flattened her against the driver's side door and gave her a deep, sexy kiss full of promise and expectations before he pulled back. "See you in a few."

Mac gasped for breath and clutched the door handle. He'd sucked the oxygen right out of her lungs and left her gasping for air and longing for dirty sex.

Well, two could play this game, and she had a small head start.

As soon as she pulled into her driveway, she raced into the house, ran to her room and locked the door, knowing he'd be right behind her.

Mac threw on the revealing, little pink sundress Lavender had given her and adjusted it for maximum cleavage. She slid off her panties and threw them in a hamper. Running a brush through her hair, she fluffed it up, took a deep breath, and entered the living room.

Bruiser stood near her mantle, staring at the pictures. He turned, holding one in his hand and studying it intently. "Your brothers?" he asked without looking up.

"Yes, Will's on the right and Clint is on the left."

Bruiser studied the photo for a moment more, then glanced up and opened his mouth to comment but the words came out in an unintelligible stutter that sounded something like, "Holy shit. You look stunning."

Mac's face turned fifty shades of red. She stared everywhere but at him. "Thank you. Lavender gave me this dress." Moving next to him, she took the picture from his hand and put it back on the mantle before he dropped it.

"That dress looks like Lavender."

"What's that mean?"

"Girlie and sexy. You do it justice." His sexy smile hit her in her most vulnerable places.

"You think I'm sexy?"

"Honey, you are smokin' hot."

Mac grinned at him, feeling naughty. "I'm not wearing underwear."

Bruiser swallowed and cleared his throat. "None?" he croaked. His gaze fell to her chest, where her nipples were showing off for him.

"None."

That crooked smile of his made another appearance. "What if I told you I wasn't either?"

"You aren't?"

He shrugged. "Maybe. Maybe not. You'll need to find out for yourself." He stalked toward her and she slipped away from him just as he reached for her. With a half scream, half laugh, she skirted around the couch away from him.

"Awww, so this is how it's going to be." He sprinted for her, careening around the couch like a man used to running and dodging for a living.

Mac faked one way then leapt the other, but Bruiser wasn't fooled in the least. He grabbed her around the waist with one arm and tossed her onto the couch, shocking her with his brute strength.

She shouldn't have been surprised, not the way he ripped through defensive lines as if they were a peewee football team.

He straddled her and grabbed her hands in one of his big hands, holding them over her head. "Don't mess with the master, darlin', you don't stand a chance."

"Maybe I don't want to stand a chance. Maybe I—"

"Too much talking." He bent down and covered her mouth with his mouth while his stubble scraped across her chin and cheeks. She didn't care one damn bit. Instead, she wriggled under him, pressing her hips against his, rubbing up and down, needing to know she could make him as crazy as he made her, and judging by his reaction, she did.

Payback was a bitch, and Bruiser's mouth laid waste to every shred of rational thought as his lips journeyed down her neck. He nibbled on her collarbone with little bites all along the sensitive skin. With his free hand, he yanked down the stretchy bodice of her dress, freeing her breasts.

Mac froze, worried she might be too small for his taste, but his sharp intake of breath and a slow shudder dispelled those doubts. His eyes drank her in like an alcoholic during last call in a bar on Saturday night. "You're beautiful," he said with such reverence, she couldn't remember ever feeling so admired.

He bent his head and took a nipple in his mouth, laving it with his tongue, while he plucked the other nipple with his fingers. Mac whimpered as Bruiser sucked, sucked harder, released, sucked again.

Their eyes met and he smiled, not one of his practiced seductive smiles, but a warm, genuine smile that said he was enjoying himself and her. He sucked on her nipples until they were sensitive and sore, a good sore.

Bruiser sat back, released her hands, and unbuttoned his shirt, tossing it aside. It was Mac's turn to gasp. She'd seen him shirtless before plenty of times, but not up close and personal, not within touching distance. And touch him she did, running her fingers across the ridges of his hard, well-defined abs, up to his firm pecs, and around his broad, muscular shoulders. God, he felt good, like an oasis in the middle of the Sahara.

He sucked in a breath as she stroked his muscles, giving her confidence that he needed her touch as much as she needed his. Then he lifted himself off her and shucked his pants in one practiced motion—he was commando—like he'd done this a million times, most likely with countless women.

Mac pushed those thoughts away and concentrated on Bruiser with his incredible body. Bruiser with the laughing blue eyes and devil-may-care attitude. Bruiser, the guy who lived life to its fullest yet carried a painful secret. Despite the women he'd been with in the past, tonight he was hers and hers alone. She may never get this opportunity again, and she'd damn well take advantage of it.

Judging by the campfire blazing in Bruiser's eyes, he felt the same. "I fucking want you. Bad. I've been thinking about this since I picked you up that evening for the barbecue." He fished a condom out of his pants pocket, ripped it open with his teeth, and sheathed his magnificent cock faster than it took Tyler Harris to throw a ball downfield.

The barbecue? As much as she tried to convince herself that Bruiser was attracted to the real her, the reality stung. He'd never paid one bit of attention to her until she'd worn a slinky dress, revealed some leg and boobs, and all-in-all made him see her as a woman. She wanted to be a woman for him, but she also wanted to be more than someone he took at face value.

Bruiser plunked his fine naked ass on the couch next to her, and Mac threw her self-pity out the window. Tonight was about the physical, nothing else—the pure physical pleasure of two bodies doing what nature designed, and nature had definitely designed Bruiser's body for sex.

Mac pulled her skirt up to her waist, rewarded by Bruiser's slow grin. The couch cushion dipped as he turned his body toward her, threw a leg over her thighs, and straddled her again, his usually laughing eyes deadly serious and intense, the sexiest thing in the world to see. His impressive erection rubbed against her stomach. She ran her hands up his forearms and clutched his hard biceps.

He closed his eyes for a moment and swallowed. The veins stood out on his neck, and his magnificent body shuddered. "I can't last through much foreplay."

"Just watching you all night was foreplay."

"Are you telling me you're primed and ready for action?"

"Like a well-tuned machine."

"Honey, you're no machine. You're one hundred percent American woman in every sense of the word. Tough. Sensitive. Driven. And passionate." His eyes rolled back in his head, as she gripped his dick and squeezed, guiding him toward that spot that longed for him with an ache that wouldn't die. Mac stared at him, large and erect, waiting to enter her most intimate spot and give her the ride of her life.

She wanted him to mount up and gallop into the sunset. At least for tonight.

"Fuck me, Bruce," she whispered. Judging by his strangled moan, she got her point across. He braced his arms on either side of her and began to push into her slick, tight opening.

He hesitated, a puzzled expression partially replaced his lust. "Are you okay? You're so damn tight."

"I thought men liked tight women."

"Oh, fucking hell, yeah." Bruiser's strained smile attested to that fact.

"I'm not exactly the type that sleeps around much. Especially the past three years."

"I don't want to hurt you."

Mac groaned in frustration. "The only way you can hurt me is by treating me like a fragile little princess. I am neither fragile, nor a princess."

He nodded and managed a strained chuckle as his cock pressed against her folds, and he pushed the tip inside. Bruiser took his time, pushing forward, withdrawing slightly, then pushing deeper with each gentle thrust, as if she were a delicate orchid he didn't want to damage. He tortured her with his slow methodical thrusts, until she swore she'd go mad if he didn't just nail her deep and hard.

"Fuck me," she demanded in a throaty voice that didn't sound one bit like her but said everything about the way she felt. Mac wrapped greedy legs around his waist and with quick hands she pulled his face down to hers, her mouth hungry and demanding.

Bruiser shuddered, a sure sign his control had finally snapped. With one hard, deep thrust, he buried his penis inside her. He held himself there for what felt like a lifetime that would never be long enough. Then his thrusts came harder, each one so deep he touched her womb and her soul.

Together they established a rhythm. Bruiser drove deep and high inside her, stripping off her protective layers until only her core essence remained. Mac's hips rose to meet each thrust. His eyes held hers captive, and she became his willing slave. She buried her fingers in his silky gold hair. He traced kisses along her neck, pausing at times to suck hard. He didn't just mark her once, he was branding her neck, her collarbones, and her breasts—breasts that still tingled from his mouth and lips.

Bruiser's thrusts came faster, his mouth rougher. His body quivered as he buried himself deep one final time. Sweat beaded his forehead and glistened on his tanned skin. He threw his head back and called out her name as he found his release. Mac went with him and they soared through time and space. They existed together, as if their separate souls had melded into one where nothing was hidden from the other.

Mac wanted to stay in this place, clutching him, listening to his raspy breathing laboring in her ear, feeling his sweaty body sliding against hers while his soul intertwined with hers.

She had brought him to this and she reveled in the knowledge of a dream come true.

But dreams never lasted forever.

Slowly they floated back to earth to land lightly on terra firma, arms around each other, holding on as if their next heartbeat depended on the other.

Maybe it did. At least in this moment.

* * * * *

Fucking hell. What just happened?

Bruiser woke up on Mac's bed, their legs entwined, her head on his chest, his arms tight around her.

He breathed in the scent of her hair. She smelled like the flowers that bloomed outside Jacks' HQ every spring, the very flowers Mac so lovingly took care of. She sure as hell had taken care of him. Holy shit on a firecracker, he'd been blown to pieces and put back together, only it felt like some of the old pieces had been discarded, replaced by new ones. He wasn't altogether comfortable with the result.

What the fuck had he just done to himself? And to her? Could they go back to being friends after being lovers? What about his one-week rule? They'd had one night together, and Bruiser didn't think it would be enough. He wasn't even sure a week would do it.

A little voice he usually kept silenced whispered that rules were made to be broken. Yet Mac didn't fit his plans. She didn't further his goals, not like a Hollywood starlet or a rock diva would. Mac would never get him face time with the press. Hell, she'd avoid it. But Bruiser needed that face time. Brice, his bold, daredevil twin, would've expected nothing less from his one-time quieter twin. After all, Bruiser was living for both of them now.

Even worse, he'd fallen asleep with her in his arms. Bruiser didn't cuddle. He got the deed done, once or several times, depending if his dick was up to it, then he got the hell out of there.

He rarely took women home or stayed over at their place —too personal, plus it gave them a foot in the door to demand more than he could give.

He tried to extricate himself, but Mac held on tighter, muttering something in her sleep that sounded like, "No, don't go."

Well, crap. He was torn between his normal M.O. and a desire for more. Plus, his dick wanted a vote in this election, and it wanted Mac.

Bruiser rolled onto his back, and Mac cuddled in the crook of his arm. Morning sun peeked through the blinds and cast a golden light across the bed, like sleeping with an angel. He didn't deserve an angel.

Feeling spooked, he managed to pull away and crawl out from under the sheets without waking her as his brain did a quick recap of last night's activities. He'd banged her how many times? Good thing he'd grabbed a six-pack of condoms.

Mac hadn't disappointed him. That passion and fire she put into everything she did she also put into sex—no holding back.

Usually Bruiser chose women who were like him, women who used him for their own agendas. He had no fucking clue what to do with a woman who didn't fit his usual mold.

Bruiser walked down the short hallway, past the cat sunning himself in a pool of sunlight that ran across the couch. He found his jeans, pulled them on, and continued to the neat and tidy kitchen. He paused and looked around, taking some time to assess Mac's home.

Besides being neat and tidy, the house was decorated in natural tones with glossy hardwood floors, comfortable, overstuffed leather furniture and antiques. Various exotic-looking houseplants thrived in different parts of the room while a garden window in the kitchen held flowering plants displaying vibrant splashes of color.

Mac was quite a decorator. Another thing about her he'd have never imagined.

The kitchen had been remodeled with cherry cabinets and granite countertops. It was a kitchen Bruiser would like to cook in, if he cooked. He easily found the coffee and made a pot, impressed with how organized the kitchen cabinets were. Somehow this tidiness didn't fit his picture of Mac with her hair flying every which way, dirt smudged on her cheeks, and mud on her work boots. Except that was the old Mac, the one he thought he knew. This new Mac dressed neatly, had highlights in her hair, and dirt didn't seem to stick to her like it once did.

He found the girlie Mac sexy, and the natural Mac hotter than hell. She had something none of those other women had. They couldn't come close to duplicating her inner beauty.

Bruiser poured a cup of coffee and stared into the backyard at the array of colors and plants artfully arranged around a deep green lawn. Hell, he didn't even have a lawn. He had a condo. He walked outside with his steaming coffee cup and sprawled in a lawn chair. It was a bit nippy, but the sun warmed him right up, promising a nice day in the making.

The French door opened and Mac stepped outside, coffee mug in hand, dressed in a baggy sweatshirt and worn jeans. She looked every bit the old Mac except for a few subtle differences.

He ached inside, wishing that of all the things in his world that changed on a regular basis, Mac didn't have to be one of them.

"Beautiful morning," she said.

"Sure is. I was admiring your yard and your house."

For a moment she looked away as a cloud passed over her fresh-scrubbed features. "It didn't always look like this."

"Really? How did it look?"

"I moved in four years ago after Grandma died. She'd pretty much kept everything original."

"You didn't do all this work yourself, did you?" Not that it would surprise him. More than once she'd fixed some piece of equipment at the HQ when no one else could.

He flinched when he saw her sad smile.

"I did a lot of it, but Will did most of the carpentry work and plumbing. He could do anything with his hands. Very talented."

"I don't have a handyman bone in my body." Bruiser snorted as he recalled his recent attempt at fixing a leak that ended up costing him about fifteen-hundred dollars after he flooded the apartment below.

"Why doesn't that surprise me?"

He heard the unspoken words, or thought he did: pretty is as pretty does. Man candy with no other talents other than running hard with a football in his hands and screwing women.

Or maybe those were his family's words ringing in his ears, always nagging him, underneath it all accusing him of being the one who lived while the favored son died. He endured the digs from his mother at various family events, the guilt heaped on him because his brother couldn't be there to celebrate with them. His father just plain avoided him because he was constant reminder of Brice.

"Are you okay?"

Bruiser jerked back to reality. "Sorry. I was just thinking."

"About us?"

Unexpected pain sliced through him. There was no *us*. And there couldn't be for a dozen fucked-up reasons, including the biggest one—him.

"Not that we have anything going or that I expect anything. I enjoyed last night, that's all. I mean, it was great fun. Really great fun, nothing more." She finished her statement in flood of nervous words.

"Uh, yeah, right." He felt even more guilt at the strained look on Mac's face.

"I'd make you breakfast but my dad should be here in the next twenty minutes."

In other words, get the hell out of here. So much for a little morning delight. Bruiser downed the rest of his coffee and nodded at Mac. "I enjoyed myself."

"So did I. Maybe we could—" She hesitated.

"—do it again sometime? Yeah, I'd like that. Sometime soon. Maybe tonight?" The words came out in a rush he couldn't seem to stop.

Her eyes lit up, and he knew he'd made another big mistake. Women didn't do recreational sex well, no matter how much they claimed to the contrary.

She grinned at him. "We'll be back around nine or so. Is that too late?"

"It's never too late." Bruiser nodded, even as he was mentally kicking himself in the shins. "I'll be here with pizza."

He bent down to kiss her, aiming for her cheek, but she turned her head. Instantly his peck on the cheek exploded into a passionate kiss with tongue, lips, exchanging of saliva, and mutual groaning.

He pulled away and straightened, running a hand through this mussed hair. "See ya."

"See ya."

The hope in her voice made him feel like the biggest ass in the world. He wanted this to be just fucking good sex. But to her? Hell, he suspected it was more.

He didn't have the strength to stay away in spite of all the reasons he should.

Chapter 12

Staying in Bounds

As soon as Mac mentioned her father dropping by, Bruiser displayed his running abilities by getting the hell out of there. Not that Mac blamed him. Her father drove everyone away.

Meanwhile, Mac's life flipped upside down and turned inside out. She suspected spending time with Bruiser did that to a woman, but for her it was more than that, which was both good and bad.

She wandered back into the kitchen for more coffee. She didn't know what she wanted from her life anymore. Last night had redefined sex for her. She'd never imagined the physical act could touch her so deeply, make her so out-of-her head insane, and raise the bar to what was probably an impossible height.

And Bruiser, how had it affected him? Just another night in the bedroom? He'd move on while she stayed in the same place, crushing on a guy who would never return her affection. And what exactly was the extent of said affection?

Wearily, Mac sipped her Tully's and savored the warm, sunny morning. Colors seemed more vivid, the birds' songs sounded more melodic, and her roses' sweet scent more fragrant. She sat back and tried to relax, to push her troubled thoughts away and just let herself enjoy the peaceful atmosphere.

A few minutes later, her peace was interrupted. Her father came through the back door, a folder of papers under his arm. So much for peace and relaxation. The man looked worse than her cat after a fight with the tomcat next door. He grunted a hello then ignored her, spreading the papers all over her patio table. Craig sat down and rifled through them, even though by now every detail should be committed to memory.

Mac fixed breakfast and placed the plate in front of him. "Eat, Dad."

"I will. Later." He scribbled notes on a yellow notepad, not even bothering to look up.

"Why don't we take a break and do something fun? How about a Mariners game? They're playing at home today. We used to go all the time." Mac held her breath, waiting for his answer.

Her father glanced up, dark circles under his eyes, sadness etched into every line of his face. "Will loved the Mariners. Damn good baseball player, that brother of yours. I still think he could've played in the majors."

Mac fought a surge of jealousy then felt like a bitch for it. It was always about Will. Never anyone else. God, she missed the father Craig used to be. "So let's go to the game. We can get tickets at the stadium box office. Let's honor Will's memory by doing something Will loved to do."

For a moment her tactic almost worked, but Craig's shoulders returned to their perpetual slump. He rubbed his bloodshot eyes. "Too much to do," he mumbled.

Frustration built inside her to the breaking point. "How much longer are you going to live like this, Dad?"

He stared at her, his expression oddly blank. Then he shrugged. "Dunno."

"What if we never find the answers, never find his body? Will wouldn't want to see you wasting away like this."

"You're building a case to desert me, aren't you? Just like Clint did."

"Clint has a family, Dad."

"Yeah, well, he could give his dear old dad and his brother *some* of his time, at least once a month, but that's too much for him. And now you're going to abandon me. Abandon Will."

"No, I'd never do that, Dad. I want the answers as much as you, but maybe we need balance." Guilt engulfed her, pulled her under with its cold, vengeful hand, magnified by the growing fear that her father teetered on the verge of an emotional breakdown.

"Maybe we need to try harder to find Will. The answers are here, somewhere. I can feel it. If only Bruiser could get close to Trudy."

Mac frowned, not liking that option at all. The tightening of her gut couldn't be anything but jealousy, and she had no right to be possessive of Bruiser. They didn't have exclusive relationship, or even really a relationship at all. "I don't think that's a good idea."

"Bruiser might be the break we need."

"I'm not asking Bruiser to do that for us."

"I'll talk to him. I can convince him."

"I don't want you to bug him." Mac sighed. Her father hadn't picked up on the subtle signals from a few nights ago or today that his daughter might have more than a passing interest in Bruiser.

And why was she surprised?

Mac studied the once robust, athletic man. He'd lost at least fifty pounds, become a skeleton of his former self, and aged twenty years in the last three. It broke her heart, but she couldn't do a damn thing to save him no matter how hard she tried.

Maybe you need to save yourself first.

Craig's chair scraped across the concrete patio. He stood and walked into the house. Suspicious, Mac followed him. Her father walked to the window that faced Will's old house. He grabbed the binoculars she kept for bird watching. Standing off to one side, he pushed the binoculars through the slats in the blinds.

"What's she doing out there?" Her father's voice shook with the fierce determination Mac only heard when he talked about Will or Sonja.

Mac peeked through the blinds. "She's toying with you. It's not the first time she's done that. Ignore her. She loves to tweak you. She knows you're watching."

"She might slip up."

"She hasn't yet. She's smarter than you give her credit for."

"She's lucky, not smart. Sooner or later her luck has to run out."

Mac sighed and flopped down on the couch, flipping to the Mariners pre-game show. "The M's have won their last seven in a row. They're only two games out of first place in their division."

"Hmmm."

Mac watched the game alone. Her father never touched his food. Eventually he left, carrying his folder of evidence with him, leaving Mac to her thoughts, which bounced among Bruiser, her father, the scholarship, and her current job.

Some people get all the luck, and currently Mac and her father weren't on that exclusive list.

* * * * *

Bruiser lived by a few simple rules, one of which was not to get involved in other people's business. Tell that to the part of him that pulled into an empty spot next to the diner's back door. Seemed like his rules were shot to shit lately.

It'd been a few nights since he'd slept with Mac. Somehow he'd stayed away, making excuses and forcing himself to put some distance between himself and one night of mind-blowing sex with a woman he couldn't stop thinking about.

This supposedly casual fling with Mac was turning into anything but casual, and his distance remedy didn't heal his sickness. If anything, his desire for Mac bordered on epidemic.

He prayed Trudy wasn't working tonight. He could ask where she was, have one beer and leave.

Opening the door, he entered the dark bar, pausing for his eyes to adjust. Trudy stood behind the counter mixing drinks. When she saw him, a slow, calculating smile crossed her face, reminding him of Mac's cat when it sized him up from its perch on the top of her headboard.

He didn't trust either Trudy or the cat, and he suspected the feeling was mutual. Yet earning Trudy's trust should be an easy feat for a man gifted with his persuasive abilities and charm. Most likely, he'd get the info if he was willing to take it to the limit— only he wasn't sure he could. Not after being buried inside Mac.

Bruiser slid onto the barstool closest to Trudy and ignored the curious stares of the other patrons. He pulled his baseball cap further over his forehead. Perhaps between that and the two-day beard he'd be unrecognizable.

She slid her gaze appreciatively over the muscles in his arms. "So you're slummin' with the common folk. Must be a slow day."

Bruiser offered her a slow half smile, the one ladies told him dripped with sex appeal. "Yeah, I'm a little bored." He caught her quick glance behind him, obviously checking to see if he was alone. Without asking what he wanted, she popped the top on a microbrew and slid it across the counter. Bruiser took a long pull then met her gaze.

"You remembered."

"I always remember what my customers drink, especially ones that look like you."

Bruiser held his beer bottle up in a salute.

"So what's the deal with you and Mac?" Trudy's shrewd gaze didn't seem to miss a thing, a definite challenge to his powers of persuasion.

"No deal. Just know each other through work. Never met her dad until the other night." At least that much was true. He leaned forward, faked interest he didn't feel, forced his gaze to roam over the curves revealed by her tight, low-cut shirt. Her nipples stood out against the fabric. Normally, that would've turned him on, but instead it repulsed him.

"He's a crazy-assed old man."

"You think?" Bruiser fought the urge to rip her a new one, even though what she said was probably true. "No shit."

"He stalked Sonja like she's some common criminal and he's a fucking FBI agent."

"Is she a common criminal?" The minute the words escaped, he regretted them.

Trudy's eyes narrowed to little slits. "You sure they didn't put you up to this?"

Bruiser scrambled to do damage control. "Why the hell would I do something for them? I barely know either of them."

She scowled and suspicion played across her features.

"Aw, come on. Surely, you've heard enough about me to know I'm in it for myself. What do *they* have to offer me?"

Trudy nodded slowly, as if the truth finally dawned on her. "Yeah, I can believe that. Fucking with Mac would be like being with your brother."

Bruiser bit the side of his cheek until he tasted blood. Hell, Mac had more sex appeal in her genuine smile than Trudy had in her entire fake body and made-up face. But now was not the time to defend Mac's honor. "Yeah, she's like one of the guys."

"But I'm not." Trudy moved closer to him, toyed with the collar of his shirt. Bruiser held his breath, trying not to cringe. One of the patrons yelled across the room for another beer.

"Hey, hold onto your shorts. I'll be right there." Trudy shot the man a murderous look, then ran a red-tipped fingernail across Bruiser's chin and gave him a come-fuck-me looks as she poured her patron a drink.

Bruiser let out his breath as soon as Trudy and her perfume moved out of his space. *Fuck. Damn. Hell.* He'd pretty much have to fuck the woman to get any information out of her. Possibly more than once.

He didn't know if he could do that. Not that she was bad looking, and she had a nice body even if a little overdone, but hell, what would Mac say?

And why did he care what Mac said? He *was* doing this for her after all. She *should* say thank you. Yeah, right, like any decent woman alive would thank him for stooping that low.

Trudy came back to the bar and leaned across the counter, making sure that her boobs just about fell out of her tight shirt. Bruiser glanced down and found the entire spectacle boring. What the hell was wrong with him? One night with Mac, and he couldn't appreciate another woman, especially one with assets like Trudy's on display?

Taking a deep breath and begging forgiveness, Bruiser stuck to his script. "Mac's a piece of work. How well do you know her?"

Trudy eyed him with enough street-smart wariness to alert him that he hadn't reeled her in yet. "Not well, just what her sister-in-law has told me." She slid up next to him, her perfume preceding her, and rubbed the back of his neck. Bruiser stiffened for a moment then willed himself to relax.

"Yeah, from what I heard from the guys on the team it's sorta tragic, but after all the years, time to move on, don't you think?" Bruiser pasted an innocent expression on his face.

Trudy chewed on her lower lip for a moment. A slow, malicious smile crossed her face. He'd never done innocent well, but Trudy apparently bought his act. She leaned down and spoke in a throaty whisper. "They'll never find him."

"Is that speculation or fact?"

"Maybe a little of both." She crooked a finger at him, drawing him closer. "But I can guarantee he's never coming back."

"I assumed as much." He shrugged one shoulder as if he didn't care one way or the other. "Dead?"

She glanced around the room. Satisfied no one was paying them any attention, she turned back to Bruiser. "I might know more, but you want the info, you gotta pay."

Bruiser tried to smile, but his face hurt. He suspected the expression stuck on his face was somewhere between a grimace and a maniacal grin. "The answers don't really matter to me."

She raised both eyebrows. "I close about midnight. What are you doing later?" She ran a finger across his lips, down his chin, throat, and to the collar of his shirt. "One night with you could have me telling *all* my secrets."

The Bruiser of even a week ago would've met her later without a second thought. It was just sex, and Bruiser loved sex as much as the next man. But a night with Mac had fucked up his self-centered priorities and left him unsure of his direction. He needed time to contemplate his next move and determine how far he was willing to go for answers that might give Mac and her dad some closure.

He slapped his forehead in mock dismay. "Oh, crap. I forgot. I need to help my sister with something tonight. How about a rain check?"

"I'm here every night this week."

His acting skills were getting pretty good. "Great, I'll be back." Before he could screw things up, Bruiser paid and hustled out of there.

Instead of heading home—the smart thing to do—he headed for Mac's house.

Fifteen minutes later, he broke the remaining promises he'd made to himself since his divorce and rapped on Mac's door.

* * * * *

Mac woke from a sound sleep to someone pounding on her front door. She sprang up from the bed, heart in her throat, not even bothering with a bathrobe over her nightshirt. Middle of the night news was never good.

She ran for the door, stubbing her toe on the coffee table in the process and hopping the rest of the way on one foot. Throwing open the door, she fully expected her father in some state of insanity, but the muscular blond man standing on her porch was *definitely* not her father.

"Bruiser?"

One corner of his mouth tipped up, and he cocked his head sideways. "Were you expecting someone else? You're killing my ego, darlin'." He clutched his hands to his chest, and Mac laughed in spite of herself.

"Uh, no, I just wasn't expecting you." Her heart did a cartwheel up and down her spine.

"Can I come in?" Bruiser smiled again, not so cocky this time. His apparent uncertainty was winning her over, sucker that she was.

"Uh, I don't think this is a good idea." She knew how this would end if she let him in the door.

"I just spent the last hour at the bar where Trudy works."

"You did? Did she say anything?"

"Let me in. I don't want to talk about it out here." He glanced around as if expecting paparazzi hiding in the bushes.

Mac let him in and bolted the door. Bruiser sat on the couch and she sat next to him, too anxious about possible news to worry about them sitting too close.

"What did she say?"

Bruiser took her hands and squeezed them. "Mac, I—are you sure you want to hear this?"

"Are you kidding? I've been waiting three years to hear this." Mac leaned forward, gripping his hands like a lifeline.

Bruiser heaved a deep sigh. "I asked her what happened to your brother. She said you'll never find him."

Even though she'd suspected as much, had prepared herself for bad news for the past three years, hearing the actual words relayed from someone with probable insider knowledge made her stomach drop to the basement of her house. "Did she say how she knew that?"

"I asked if she knew something or if she was speculating. She said a little of both."

"That's the most we've ever gotten out of her." Mac stared at their hands with fingers intertwined together.

"Are you okay?" The genuine concern in his voice almost undid her.

Mac nodded, not trusting her voice.

"I can get more information depending on how far I'm willing to go."

Mac frowned and held his hands tighter. "It's not worth it. Don't compromise yourself."

"Not worth it to finally find out what really happened to Will? Not worth it to make Sonja pay? Not worth it to set you free of your guilt and give you back your life and your father his peace of mind?"

Mac considered his words for a moment, and her answer surprised her. "To me, it's not. I can't ask you to compromise your integrity."

He looked shocked, then pleased. "You think I have integrity?"

"I know you do. You don't fool me one bit, Bruce Mackey."

"Look, I know what it's like to lose someone. You can't change what happened, but I can't imagine not knowing. That would make me crazy."

"How do you know what it's like?" Mac searched his blue-gray eyes for answers but only found that glimmer of pain. "Who did you lose, Bruiser? Your brother?"

He set his jaw, and his eyes froze over like a granite lake. "That subject is off limits."

Mac nodded, feeling crappy that he didn't trust her enough to share his pain. Pulling her hands from his, she rose and walked to the French doors and stared into the night across the wide expanse of lawn.

Sonja and Ben were sitting down by the lake on the beach around their fire pit, laughing and drinking beer with friends, Will's old friends. Her throat constricted, making breathing difficult. If she let it, the bitterness and anger would eat her alive.

Bruiser walked up behind her and put his arms around her waist. He nibbled on her neck. "I want to do it."

"No. Definitely, no." She fought to keep the desperation out of her voice. She looked over her shoulder at his face.

"Why not?" A smile tugged at the corners of his mouth as he turned her around. "Afraid Trudy will damage my integrity?" Bruiser placed his big hands on her hips.

Mac chewed on her lower lip and looked up at him through lowered lashes. "Maybe."

"Don't worry about it. If there's anything of my integrity left to guard, I'll take care of it."

Mac put her hands on his shoulders and tried to push him back. She might as well have been trying to move her house with her bare hands. He swung her around and backed her against the arm of the couch, pressing his erection against her crotch.

She fought for the words that seemed to be diving overboard at an alarming rate, deserting that sinking ship that was her brain. Oh yeah, it had sunk, right down to the wet spot between her legs.

Bruiser pulled at the delicate skin on her collar bone with his teeth.

"You're not nearly as selfish as you pretend to be," Mac panted.

"You think?" He licked his way up her neck to her ear.

"I know."

"That's your fantasy, so you can keep it."

His face was so close to hers she could see a little scar just above his lip. One slight imperfection. It made him more real, more vulnerable.

"Now I want my own fantasy." He picked her up and headed for her bedroom.

One night could be considered a brief fling, but two nights would lead to a third, and another, and another, and then she'd be left with a broken heart and nothing more. Only she didn't give a damn.

Maybe there was a bit of her daredevil brother in her after all.

* * * * *

Bruiser set Mac on her feet, stripped off her oversized T-shirt and tossed her on her bed. A moment later his own clothes dropped to the floor.

She stared up at him, looking incredibly seductive and naïve all at the same time, so much like the old Mac before his teammates' wives had made her over. While the new Mac got his heart thumping and pulse racing, the Mac underneath struck him as a woman he could actually depend on, which would be a first in his life.

"Do you trust me?" He *needed* her trust because he thought, in a weird way, it would help his own inability to trust.

She nodded.

"Give me a minute." He knew exactly what he wanted. Hurrying to the mud room, he grabbed a handful of long zip ties out of a box of heavy-duty lawn bags on the shelf by the back door. Yeah, these would have to do the trick. He strode back into the room, dangling them from his fingers.

Mac lifted her head. Her eyes got big and her eyebrows rose, almost disappearing into her hairline. "What's that for?"

"If you have to ask, I'll need to show you."

"You're not going to use those on me?" She started to get up.

He pushed her back down, his hand just below her breasts, and pinned her to the bed. "A little more control over the lady on the bed while I'm driving her fucking nuts drives me fucking nuts, too."

"You're going to tie me up?" Her mouth formed a big "O" while her eyes danced with *Bring it on*.

"Uh, yeah." Bruce crawled onto the bed. Mac giggled and made a leap for freedom, but she was no match for Bruiser's athletic moves. He pinned her to the bed again, this time straddling her rib cage right snug up against her breasts. He took a moment to appreciate those nice breasts as they rose and fell against his crotch and thighs. Mac squirmed underneath him, making a show of attempting to get free, but not putting much effort into it.

Bruiser grabbed her hands and zip-tied her wrists to the headboard, not tightly enough to cut off the circulation but just enough she couldn't free herself.

She glared at him but not very convincingly. "I still have my legs free. I could do some real damage to you with my knees."

He chuckled and sat back. "Thanks for the warning." Sliding off her, he pulled the tie off her robe. Opening the closet door, he snagged a belt off a raincoat. He turned and stood by the bed, holding the items up for her to see.

"Don't you dare." She licked her lips and writhed on the bed. Yeah, the lady was liking this game despite her protests.

"I don't think you're in a position to make demands." Damn, his dick ached. It was so hard he swore it'd turned to concrete just by his looking at her.

"You're gonna pay for this, buster."

"Promise?" He loved it when a woman threatened him.

She kicked out, grazing his chest with her big toe. He snatched her ankle, keeping free of her other foot and pulled her leg toward the post on the footboard. A couple quick wraps and it was tied. Skirting the bottom of the bed, he managed to grab the other foot despite her wild flailing and kicking, even as she laughed and giggled. He tied the other ankle fast to the opposite post then stood back to survey his handiwork as he stroked his dick.

Spread-eagled and ready for his pleasure, Mac's eyes shot fake daggers through him, even as they danced with pure devilish enjoyment and raging desire. The fight was all for show because they both knew Mac was nobody's slave, and Bruiser wouldn't want her to be.

A fine sheen of sweat glistened on her silky, tanned skin. His gaze slipped down her body, starting with her nipples jutting proudly above those creamy mounds of flesh still bearing his teeth marks from their last encounter, over her flat stomach to the pleasure spot between her spread legs. He liked a woman spread-eagled and open to him. Liked to see her glistening juices, signaling how ready she was for him. In fact he liked every fucking thing about her situation. And his.

Bruiser crawled onto the bottom of the bed. Holding her thighs apart even farther, he dipped his head downward, slid his hands higher, and parted her with his fingers. A lazy smile split across his face.

"Mine. All mine." Oddly enough, he meant it. He wanted to tattoo everything he was all over her body so that when she was with another man she'd smell Bruiser, taste him, see him, feel him. Yeah, that was what he wanted. To ruin her for any other man, so she'd never want anyone but him.

He slipped his tongue inside her, tasting the salty sweetness of her body. She whimpered, arching her back and pressing her hips upward to meet his mouth. He licked her back to front. Sucking on her clit, he pushed a finger inside her, high and deep while he tortured that little nub of pleasure.

Mac wriggled on the bed, making little sounds that made his dick ache. She arched her back and pressed her crotch against his face, while he lapped at her juices, sucked on her clit, and thrust two fingers into her tight snatch. He felt her coming before he heard and saw it.

Satisfied with the results, he waited for her to return reality before he took his own pleasure.

* * * * *

Mac didn't know what death felt like, but she did know what heaven felt like. She might as well have been taking straight shots for the past few hours, as drunk on sex as she was.

"Fuck me," she begged when she was finally able to put two coherent words together.

Rolling a condom over his impressive erection, Bruiser slid up her body until their faces were even. His chest rubbed against hers, his cock rested between her legs—not that rested would be an accurate verb. He kissed her, hard and deep, nothing gentle about it, and she loved it, loved the taste of her on his tongue and lips. Loved how he took charge of her body and her soul.

Bruiser pulled back and looked at her. The strain on his face was as clear as a Seattle summer day. "I really want to fuck you. Hard. Deep. And long. Till you beg for mercy and I give you none. I want you, Mac." He swallowed, and she watched as he visibly wrapped a tight leash around his control. "But I don't want to hurt you. I'm afraid I will because I'm about to lose every ounce of restraint I have."

"Then lose it like a man. I can handle it. I want to handle it."

"A man, huh?" His blue eyes raged with lust and gratitude. "You sure you can handle this man?" He spoke through gritted teeth.

"Positive. Ride me like you've never ridden a woman before."

"Ah, fucking hell." He rose up, holding himself above her with his arms on either side of her shoulders. He entered her with one hard, long thrust and slammed inside her balls-deep. He went in even deeper when it came to her heart.

She wanted more. "Harder. Harder," she yelled, and he obliged, both of them consumed by an animal lust as old as the earth itself, an uncivilized mating ritual of two civilized souls. Over and over he powered into her, taking her sanity and her breath away until the only thing she knew was his name. And she cried out that name as she rocketed out of this reality into another, leaving everything behind and entering uncharted territory. Bruiser was right there with her. She could feel him, not just physically but as an emotional presence deep inside her.

And then she knew the truth of what she'd been denying all along.

This wasn't just about sex.

Chapter 13

Blindsided

Bruiser pedaled the stationary bike faster and faster with the resistance set on high, hoping fatigue would wipe visions of a naked Mac tied to her bed, spread-eagled and vulnerable. Sweat ran down his face, and he swiped it out of his eyes, pushing his damp hair off his forehead. His chest and back were drenched through his T-shirt. His leg muscles cramped, begging for relief, but he pushed harder, relishing the cleansing pain, embracing it, waiting for exhaustion to replace thoughts of one sexy little groundskeeper.

Instead images of Mac played through his mind like the lines of favorite song he couldn't shake. It'd been a week since he'd first slept with Mac—not that he'd slept exactly. Once they'd finished the second round, he'd stolen out of the house while Mac snoozed in a pile of rumpled sheets. At least he'd cut the zip ties first. The last thing he wanted was for her father to find her that way. He almost laughed at the thought. As obsessed as the old man was, he wouldn't bat an eye, if he even noticed. Tragic in a way, but true.

Only that second night, the one that should have been his limit, hadn't been enough, and for the last week Bruiser found himself standing on her doorstep late at night. They fucked each other's brains out until the early morning light, then he dragged himself home for a few hours of sleep, as if not waking up with her in the morning would keep his emotions out of it. To make things worse, he hadn't dealt with Brett either. The entire situation made him feel like a selfish shit, yet he couldn't stay away.

So here he was on a Friday night catching up on the workouts he'd neglected, even though he suspected wild sex with Mac qualified as an adequate replacement.

Bruiser got off the bike, steadied himself on numb legs, and headed for the showers. A desolate weekend stretched out in front of him. Mac promised her father she'd go on an excursion to Oregon to chase down yet another lead, which left him at loose ends.

He could hunt down Trudy, do some sleuthing, or party with some of the guys.

Toweling off, he dressed in front of his locker and pulled on his shoes. He looked up as a shadow crossed in front of him. "Hey, Brett, my man, what's up?"

"How about a drink?" Brett studied him oddly, and a twinge of guilt shot through Bruiser. Had Brett figured out his best buddy had been banging Brett's love interest all week?

"Sure, meet you at O'Malley's." He'd been dreading this moment, but now was the time to come clean.

A few minutes later, they were in a booth at O'Malley's.

"No hot date?" Brett asked him.

"I'm flying solo tonight." Bruiser tilted the beer to his mouth and drained half the bottle, generating a little liquid courage.

Brett squinted at him as if trying to see him in a different light. "I haven't heard about you with any woman for a quite a while now. Going for a round of celibacy? Or did you run out of twenty-something heiresses and movie starlets?"

"Just taking a break. Reenergizing the sex drive."

"Yeah, bullshit. Have you seen Mac lately?" Brett narrowed his eyes, his gaze taking Bruiser's thin story apart.

Bruiser stiffened and measured his words carefully. "I see her mowing the practice field almost every day."

"Yeah, me too." Brett stared at his drink as if it were a crystal ball. "I wish I knew what I did to blow my chance with her."

"Why do you think you did anything?" Guilt tied Bruiser's stomach in knots. What a shit he was.

"Oh, she let me down nice and easy. She told me she didn't want to date me and ruin a good friendship."

"Oh." Bruiser's face felt hot. Thank God it was dark in the bar.

"I think she's seeing someone else. Like Dante, that obnoxious ass. He's been sniffing around her ever since she got her makeover. Didn't give her a second look prior to that."

The hard slap of jealousy fisted his hands. "Dante's been harassing her?"

Brett pursed his lips and frowned at him. "Nothing she can't handle. She ripped him a new one yesterday."

"Good. That ass needs to keep his hands off."

Brett regarded him with even more suspicion. "You wouldn't be— Nah, you and Mac? Never."

Bruiser opened his mouth to lie and deny everything, but he closed it.

"There's something you're not telling me." Brett stared so hard at him that Bruiser wiped his mouth, certain some remnant of the chicken wings he'd been consuming at an alarming rate were on his chin or something.

Bruiser stared at his beer, knowing *GUILTY* might as well be tattooed on his forehead.

"You and Mac?" Brett's face fell, as if he'd just been betrayed by his last friend in the world. Maybe he had.

"I—Uh, it just happened. Nothing we planned on."

"You knew I had a thing for her, and you still went after her?" Brett leaned forward, his hands fisted.

"It didn't happen like that." *Liar.* No, he'd just pursued her, invited himself into her bed, and fucked her brains out. And not just once or twice.

"She's always had a crush on you, and now you're using it to get in her pants. Man, you really are a shallow, selfish asshole." Brett's disgust and disappointment was as loud and clear as the ferry's fog horn on a zero-visibility day.

Bruiser shook his head. "It's not like that." *Yeah, right, idiot, and what is it like?*

"Bullshit. She doesn't understand guys like you. You're just toying with her. She's a novelty to you, but you don't give a shit about her."

Bruiser tried one last time to salvage the best friendship he had. "Brett, I—I didn't mean for it to happen. We're just enjoying each other's company. She knows the score. She's fine with it. Please keep this private. It could jeopardize her chance at that scholarship if Veronica finds out. She wouldn't approve of the two of us."

"I doubt Mac does know the score. And don't worry, I won't tell a soul. Your dirty little secret is safe with me."

"Look, man, I never planned for this to happen, especially for it to end our friendship."

"I trusted you. Saw more in you than most people did. This is what I get for being an idiot. You couldn't even tell me the truth. I bet the whole team knows you've been screwing Mac except me."

"Seriously. No one knows. She hasn't breathed a word to her girlfriends."

"You're a sorry ass. You don't appreciate what you have. If I had a woman like Mac, I'd treat her with the respect she deserves and shout it to the heavens. You hide her and make sure no one knows because it makes it easier for you to move on down the road. And your roads are damn short."

"Brett, I was wrong. I should've told you."

"Yeah, you should have." Brett rose to his feet, his face red and his jaw rigid. "I'd like to beat the crap out of you, but assaulting you isn't worth going to jail."

With that, his only true friend in the world threw a twenty on the table and stomped out of the bar, back stiff, head held high.

Bruiser stared at the door long after it closed behind Brett. He'd screwed up. Again. Every time he got close to someone, he hurt them. He couldn't do a damn thing right except smile and play football. He was a fucking failure as a person, and Mac would be next on his Bruiser-fucked-up list, because that's the way he rolled.

* * * * *

An hour later, Bruiser sat on a barstool in a different bar, doing his penance.

Trudy put up the CLOSED sign and locked the door of the bar. She'd been drinking behind the bar for the past hour and could barely walk, while he'd sipped on the same single bottle of now-warm beer.

She came straight to him and didn't waste a moment. Her fingernails dug painfully into his scalp, her mouth ground against his, while her body did its own grinding. Usually a hot woman in this position got Bruiser in the mood, only tonight it didn't work for him. His dick stayed completely uninvolved, like a disinterested bystander. He kissed the woman back, swallowing his revulsion.

She slid her hands down the back of his jeans and cupped his ass, smashing her hips into his crotch. It wasn't erotic; in fact, it hurt like hell as his balls got squashed by her crazy-assed attempt to have sex fully clothed. A flash of light jerked him backward. She was holding her cell phone out and the camera light was on.

Bruiser pried her body away from his and held her at arm's length. "What the fuck was that for?"

"My friends will never believe I'm with you if I don't give them a picture."

This was not the way to get information out of the woman. Or was it? Bruiser read the lust in her eyes. Hating himself, he slid his hand under her skirt up between her legs, touching her wet panties and rubbing. She pressed back against him. "You want more of that?" he asked.

"Yes, you know I do." Her voice was slurred.

Bile rose in his throat, and he fought the overwhelming need to retch.

"Then give me something. That was the deal. What do you know about Will? Where's his body buried?"

"You'll have to fuck me to find that out."

Bruiser didn't want to, not one bit. Fine time to find his moral compass. "I'm seeing someone."

"So?"

"I don't screw around when I'm in an exclusive relationship."

"Well, I don't give out prime info for nothing."

"You could try helping the family out, you know. You're not friends with Sonja anymore, so why keep her secret?"

"You don't know what she's capable of. I like breathing. It keeps me alive."

"Is that what happened to Will? Did he know something that killed him? Were his wife and his friend embezzling from the business?"

By the way Trudy's lips puckered, that was exactly what happened. "I think you need to either fuck me or leave now."

Bruiser hesitated. He couldn't do this, not even for Mac and her father. He could not fuck this woman. It cheapened whatever he and Mac had, whatever the hell that was. With a quickness that made him legendary on the football field, he grabbed her phone, erased his picture, and walked toward the door.

"Bastard!" She called after him, "You know how to reach me if you change your mind."

"So do you." Bruiser left, conflicted as ever, wanting to do the right thing by Mac and her father, yet not sure what the right thing was.

* * * * *

Monday night Mac sat on her couch next to Bruiser as he surfed sports channels, watching three different baseball games at one time. The scene struck her as so domestic, one repeated by couples across America. Only they weren't a couple. She wasn't sure what they were.

"Do you know what's wrong with Brett?"

"Not sure what you mean." Bruiser's jaw tightened, a definite sign of guilt in her book.

"He's avoiding me, like he's pissed. Do you think it's because I turned down another date with him?" Mac watched him closely. He avoided her gaze, staring at the TV even as a telltale muscle jerked in his strong jaw. "Bruiser, what happened?"

With a sigh, he turned to her. "He knows about us, and he's not happy. He thinks I'll use you and walk away."

"How does he know about us?" She certainly didn't want to be the weekly gossip at Jacks' HQ.

"I didn't say a word. He just figured it out. He won't say anything"

"I'm a big girl. I'll handle my own sex life, thank you. I'm glad he knows. I really am."

"Yeah, I know, but he feels betrayed." Bruiser put his arm around her and pulled her close, and Mac had the distinct feeling it was more to comfort Bruiser than her. Brett's reaction really did bother him.

"I'm sorry. I never meant to hurt him."

"Me neither. I'd give anything to see him find a woman and be happy, but it's out of my control." Bruiser buried his face in her hair, nibbling on her ear lobe.

Mac pushed him away. "Calm down, mister. I need to ask you something before you get too carried away."

He pulled back a little, his expression wary. "Sure, as long as it doesn't have a thing to do with Trudy."

"It doesn't, I promise. I understand there's a huge charity event this weekend. A big deal. I need more time with Veronica. Would you escort me?" Mac knew she was taking a chance. She would get time with Veronica, but was seeing her with Bruiser a help or hindrance?

"You have an invitation?"

"Well, no, but you do. It's a charity that the Jacks—and you—have supported for a long time. The burn foundation."

"Yeah, I know." That muscle ticked harder in his jaw, and suddenly the Mariners seemed to hold more interest than seducing her.

She'd hit that nerve, the same one she'd hit before. "What's the score?"

He blinked a few times and looked at her. "Of what?"

"The game you're so engrossed in?"

"I, uh, don't know."

"You don't have a clue, do you?" Mac socked his arm, trying to steer the conversation from serious to playful. "So what about taking me? I'm not asking for you to declare that we have a relationship, just to take me as a friend."

"Do we have a relationship?" He turned to her, all serious, as his gaze searched hers, as if he'd find the answer somewhere in her eyes.

"A sexual one." She didn't know how else to answer that question.

"Mac," he stared at her, his gaze earnest, "I suck at relationships. The last one I had ended in disaster. I'm not going there again. Not for a long time."

"I understand." Everyone knew Bruiser had been married and that his ex-wife had dumped him for an NFL third-string quarterback. Mac didn't know the details, but obviously the woman had laid waste to Bruiser's heart.

"Actually, you don't. Not really. I'm damaged goods, and there's not a thing you can do to fix me."

"I'm not asking for anything deep." She wanted to reassure him and herself. "This is just a physical thing, and we have to keep it quiet. Veronica won't react favorably to it."

"I haven't told anyone."

And he wouldn't, she thought. He was ashamed to be seen with her as a girlfriend. She didn't fit his image. He didn't have to tell her that. She already knew it. He could use every excuse in the book, but the truth was as obvious as Mountain Morse, the team's all-pro tackle, when he lumbered into the room.

"That doesn't mean I won't take you as a friend. Everyone knows we're buddies."

Oh, lord, is that what they were? Fuck buddies? She'd reduced herself to being this guy's plaything? She thought she had more pride than that, but apparently not.

Bruiser continued, "I'll seat you next to Veronica, and it'll be up to you to impress the hell out of her. I'll help in any way I can."

"It's my last chance, and I appreciate your help." Mac played it cool, just like he did, even though her heart cracked open a little.

"Did you and your dad find out anything on your weekend away?"

Smart man for the swift change of subject. "No. A dead end, a rumor, nothing substantial. Pretty much a waste of time."

"Have you ever considered telling him that you can't keep living your life like this?"

Had she ever? Hell yes, but Bruiser pointing out the obvious irritated her because the statement struck too close to home. She didn't like being reminded of how much time she'd spent searching for her brother, how much of her life she'd given up and how it netted them nothing but pain. "I can't desert my dad. He needs me."

"I'm not telling you to do that. Just start living your life for you, not for someone else."

"Who says I'm not living my life exactly how I want to?" Defensiveness snuck into Mac's tone. The nerve of the man telling her how to live. He should talk.

"Are you? I don't think so. For example, this new look of yours isn't really you."

"How do you know it isn't me? Maybe it is, and I just figured that out." Now he'd really pissed her off. She liked looking more like a woman than a tomboy. Did he really think so little of her that he couldn't fathom she had a woman's wants and needs?

"Believe me, I know. I've spent the better part of my life being someone I'm not." He spoke softly, almost like he didn't want her to hear. He twined his fingers with hers, staring at her hand as if it held the answers to life's questions.

Mac stared at him until he looked up and their gazes held. "You? You seem to be exactly who you want to be—the league pretty boy who exploits his good looks for money any way he can."

Disappointment crossed his strong features, "Things are not always as they seem. What do you think I do with all that money?"

"Spend it on designer clothes and exotic vacations," Mac quipped, in a lame attempt to be funny.

"Yeah, that's me. Superficial right down to my bone marrow." Bruiser pressed his lips together in a flat line. "Maybe I should go." He stood, his body tense and rigid.

Mac's pride didn't allow her to beg him to stay. "Maybe you should. I have to get up early."

Bruiser's scowl said he knew why she was getting up early. Tomorrow was Saturday. Another pointless chasing of tips or hashing over the same clues.

A few minutes later the door shut behind him, and she heard his car drive off, once more leaving her alone with her doubts.

Chapter 14

Out of the Huddle

Saturday night, Bruiser straightened his bow tie, smoothed out his tux jacket and eyed himself with a critical eye in the hallway mirror. He'd avoided Mac for an entire week and been as cranky as a caged grizzly bear, opening himself up for all sorts of ribbing from his teammates in the workout room, which pissed him off all the more. Now he was feeling a rare combination of annoyance and excitement over seeing Mac again.

His cell rang, and he picked it up, half expecting Mac to back out on their date, and hell, it'd been her idea. His idea would've involved never stepping outside her house. He held the phone up to his ear without looking at the number. "Yeah?"

"It's Elliot." The kid sounded tentative, almost scared.

"Hey, bud, how's it going?" Bruiser softened his voice, his irritation melting away.

"I know it's late."

"Nah, it's actually pretty early, but you can call anytime. How are things at your foster parents'?" Elliot had been released from the hospital recently and put in a foster home until his aunt and uncle came back from their mission in South America.

"It's okay, but that's not why I called." The foster parents meant well, but they were too busy, had too many kids, and too little time, leaving Elliot lonely and scared.

"Okay, then what's up?"

"I need to do this. I need to go." Elliot's voice wobbled as if he might cry.

"Go where?" Bruiser felt as if he'd walked into the middle of a conversation he knew nothing about.

"Tonight. To that fancy ball."

Bruiser's mind raced to catch up to this conversation. He'd only mentioned the ball in passing, but Elliot knew some of the burn victims would be attending with parents and staff. "Are you sure you're ready?"

"I don't think I'll ever be ready unless I just do it."

"True." He'd preached that very same mantra to countless kids over the years.

"Could I go with you?"

"Your foster mom isn't going?" Bruiser scratched his head, not sure what the hell was really going on here.

"She's busy. If I think about it much longer I'll chicken out." Elliot's earnest voice struck Bruiser right in the gut. Mac wouldn't mind, and Elliot needed him. He'd let down too many people in his life. He couldn't let down this kid when he needed him most.

"Sure, I'll pick you up. I have to pick up my date first then I'll swing by."

"Oh, you have a date? I'm not causing any issues, am I?"

Bruiser smiled. What kid his age talked like that? "Not unless you hustle my girl." Bruiser choked on the words that slipped out of his mouth. *My girl? Girlfriend?* He'd been hit too many times in the head over the years. He didn't keep a woman around long enough to call her a girlfriend. And he definitely didn't keep them around long enough to be considering the most painful four-letter word in the English language.

"Hey, if she falls for me over you, what can I say? It's the old Elliot charm."

Bruiser had to laugh, thrilled to give Elliot something to be happy about. "I'll be there in about forty-five minutes."

"Great, I'll be waiting."

Several minutes later, Mac's front door opened and a vision of hot, sexy loveliness swam before his eyes. He grabbed the porch railing to steady himself and tugged on the collar of his dress shirt with his free hand. Damn, it was hot all of a sudden.

She smiled at him through lowered lashes. It was so unlike Mac to be shy, but it really flipped his switch. The male part of him loved the skin she showed, from the low neckline of the slinky gold dress to the slit up the side showing a good length of shapely leg. Another deeper part of him was not entirely comfortable with this stranger.

"So what do you think?" Her eyes sparkled, and she whirled around.

"You look—" He tried to think of the words but couldn't. "I'm stunned."

"A good stunned?"

"Oh, yeah."

He got into the car and drove down the street. "You're beautiful with or without the clothes and makeup. I don't want you to feel like you have to change for me or anything else."

"I do if I want to impress Veronica. We both know she's superficial like…" Mac's hand flew to her mouth.

"Like who? Like me?"

"No, that wasn't what I was going to say. Insert any spoiled diva's name."

"Well, thank God you don't think I'm a diva." He should've let it drop, but he couldn't.

She turned on him with mischief in her eyes. "You've been known to be a diva. You're always making sure your hair is perfect when you take your helmet off. The guys think you must carry a mirror everywhere you go."

"True, that," he conceded to an argument he couldn't win. "So…there's one more thing."

She tilted her head in the cutest damn way and studied him. "And that is?"

"I need to pick up someone else also."

"Someone else?" He heard the unmistakable sound of her teeth grinding together. "Don't tell me you double-booked yourself for tonight."

He grinned at her. "That would present some interesting possibilities."

She punched him in the arm, not a wussy girl punch, but one with some power behind it. Actually, it kinda hurt and most likely would leave a bruise.

"Damn, woman, good thing I'm not the quarterback or you'd be explaining to coach what happened to my throwing arm."

Mac snorted like the old Mac. No ladylike snort for this woman. "So who is this person we're picking up?"

Bruiser did a quick rundown of Elliot and his history. "So if you'd treat him like you'd treat anyone, I'd appreciate it. You don't have to avoid the subject, but don't stare either."

"Trust me. I can handle this."

Mac was telling the truth. He sensed it, and it made him appreciate her all the more.

* * * * *

Mac sat in the car as Bruiser went to the front door of the modest ranch house in a rundown neighborhood of lookalike seventies-era houses. Children's toys littered the dandelion-filled front lawn, and rhodies grew wild next to the house, obscuring the windows. Mac noticed stuff like that, but then she was into landscaping.

A few seconds later Bruiser walked out the front door, his arm around a small, scrawny kid in an ill-fitting suit. The kid wore a Jacks baseball cap pulled down over his head and big black-rimmed glasses. Shoulders slumped, the boy kept his head down, and immediately her heart melted for him. When he glanced up, she smiled. He didn't smile back, instead he ducked his head again. Pity overwhelmed her, but she'd be damned if she'd show it. That would be the last thing a kid with his kind of injuries would need.

Bruiser opened the back door and the boy climbed in, but he didn't look at Mac as he strapped himself in.

Bruiser slid into the driver's seat, his expression undecipherable, he half turned to look in the back seat. "Mac, this is Elliot. Elliot, my friend Mac."

"Hi, Elliot. I'm glad you could join us." Mac reached back and offered her hand, but Elliot kept his hands in his lap, fingers clenched. She patted him on the arm instead.

After a tense silence, Elliot looked up at her. Mac was struck by his brilliant blue eyes framed by long lashes and magnified by the thick lenses, set in a face covered with blotchy red burn scars and skin grafts.

He was so small, so vulnerable, and she instantly fell in love with the little boy who'd seen too much tragedy in his short life, a child left behind by those he loved the most. Even though it wasn't his parents' choice to leave, nothing changed the fact that they were gone. Forever. Just like her own mother and Will.

"Are you really glad I joined you?" Elliot spoke quietly.

"Of course I am, and so is Bruiser." Mac smiled, looking him straight in the eyes, past the scars to the part of him that really mattered.

"Yeah, buddy, we're going to have a good time, you'll see." Bruiser started the car and steered it out of the depressing neighborhood.

Elliot turned his attention back to Mac. Distrust shone in his eyes and something more—some of the same shared tragedy she recognized in Bruiser and herself. Oh, God, she wanted to reach for him, wrap him in her arms and make the hurt go away. If only it were that simple.

"So Elliot, what do you like to do for fun?" Mac hoped her question was safe enough.

"I like to read."

"Really? What do you read?" Mac glanced at Bruiser when she heard his chuckle.

"Everything, mostly classics." Elliot almost smiled, and Mac patted herself on the back for finding a subject of interest to him.

"Wow, you like the classics? That's impressive for someone your age."

"My parents had me reading before I started school. I miss them." Elliot swiped a tear that welled in his eye.

"Oh, Elliot. I'm so sorry, honey. I know how it feels to lose someone you love. I lost my mom when I was really young."

Elliot nodded, looking incredibly old and wise for someone so young. "Bruiser gave me a Kindle, and I get to download any book I want on it."

"Maybe you can recommend a few books to me."

He perked up at the suggestion. "I could do that." And just like that, the floodgates opened. Elliot talked their ears off about several different classics, Tom Sawyer being one of his favorites, until they pulled up to valet parking at the hotel hosting the charity auction. He clamped his mouth shut and hunched over, hugging himself.

Bruiser opened the back door for him, while Mac stood off to the side. "Come on, buddy. You'll do fine."

"I'm scared." Elliot didn't look scared, he look terrified and ready to bolt at any time.

"We're here with you every step of the way. You'll have fun because you're with me, and I'm in charge of the fun crowd."

Elliot reached for Bruiser's hand, and Bruiser wrapped the boy's small hand in his big one. His encouraging smile held nothing but kindness and concern.

Mac stood next to them, staring from one to the other. Bruiser obliterated her remaining misconceptions of him as thoroughly as a China teacup run over by a bulldozer.

Elliot looked up at Mac. "Will you hold my hand, too?"

"I will."

Together the three of them walked into the hotel, hand in hand as if they were a family, which was both weird and wonderful.

* * * * *

An hour later, Bruiser stood in the corner of the huge ballroom decorated with all sorts of shiny crap. Several of his teammates debated the merits of play-action versus West Coast offenses. Bruiser only half listened. His gaze kept straying to Mac and Elliot, halfway across the room, holding court with three defensive rookies. He'd never seen the kid smile so much. Mac and the guys carried on an animated conversation with him, obviously including several jokes. Hopefully PG-rated, but Bruiser doubted it. Mac could tell off-color jokes with the best of them.

The rookies paid no mind to Elliot's appearance, but they sure as hell paid attention to Mac's appearance, flirting with her, touching her, pretty much moving in on his territory.

Well, not really his territory, but he didn't like them hassling Mac.

He turned to Zach, not caring that he was interrupting Zach and Harris's current debate. "Hey, get your boys in line. They're pestering Mac."

Zach frowned, looking puzzled. He glanced around the room and spotted the rookies. "She looks like she's having a great time to me."

"Yeah, unlike you." Harris never missed one damn, fucking thing on or off the field. The guy had eyes like a bald eagle bearing down on a mouse in a clearing. "You've been watching her all night long. Like what you see, Bruiser?"

"It's nothing like that. Not a damn thing like that."

Every one of the assholes started laughing at him. Bruiser hated being laughed at as badly as he hated fumbling the ball after a first down. "Fuck you, Harris."

"If that's an invitation, sorry buddy, you're not my type. I prefer Lavender."

Bruiser rolled his eyes while the other guys chuckled, enjoying a good laugh at his expense. Ignoring the idiots' cat calls, he made a beeline for Mac only to have Veronica block his path.

"Going somewhere, Bruce?" Her conniving smile told him more than he needed to know. *She'd* also noticed his preoccupation with Mac.

"Just to check on Mac. Those dipshits are bothering her."

Veronica glanced at Mac, then refocused her sharp gaze on Bruiser. "You came with her, didn't you?"

"Uh, yeah, just friends."

"Then why are you so jealous you're ready to knock some rookies' heads together?" Veronica was as astute as Harris, which didn't give Bruiser much of a chance.

"I'm protective. Like a big brother." He grinned his most innocent grin.

Veronica rolled her perfectly made-up eyes. "And I'm naïve like an Amish girl."

Bruiser chuckled at the thought of Veronica dressed like an Amish woman until the look of death—his—crossed her face. He quickly shut his mouth. He wasn't helping Mac's cause by needling Veronica, so he stepped around her accusations like the minefield they were and directed the conversation to the reason he'd brought Mac here in the first place.

"You should spend some time with Mac. She's well-deserving of that scholarship."

"More than Vince?"

"Definitely more than Vince. You value my opinion, right?" Bruiser looked over Veronica's shoulder. His mouth tightened into a grim line when a rookie defensive back put his arm across Mac's shoulders.

"Not when you're sleeping with her." Veronica's no-bullshit glare tested his acting skills, but his innocent grin didn't seem to earn any points with her.

"Mac and me? She's like a sister."

"Yeah, and I'm like a nun."

"You're full of one-liners tonight. Seem a little tense. Maybe you need to call one of your boy toys and get laid."

"Maybe you need to be laying off—not on—my employees."

"I'm not. I swear." He smiled at her with fake sincerity, shaking his head vigorously.

Veronica squinted at him, obviously not buying his bullshit. "I saved seats at my table for you, Elliot, and your *sister*."

"Come on, Ronnie. Mac deserves that scholarship. No one works harder than she does, and she only has two years left to finish her degree."

Veronica yawned, obviously bored with the subject matter. She waved at some tuxedoed businessman across the room and left Bruiser wondering how big of a hole he'd dug for himself.

And Mac.

But first he had some rookie heads to knock together.

* * * * *

Mac seated herself across from Bruiser and Elliot, surprised when Veronica slid into the chair next to her.

Rather than making Mac the prey of the evening, Veronica actually played nice, which Mac figured might have more to do with the way Bruiser glared at her than any personal interest in Mac.

Bruiser chatted up Veronica and the other guests, always careful to include Elliot, entertaining them with stories of his exploits.

Elliot stared at Bruiser like a kid worshipping his big brother and hung on his every word. She'd never had expected the pretty boy to have such an affinity for kids with disabilities, especially when the camera wasn't on him. Yet as the night wore on, Bruiser protected Elliot while encouraging him to socialize, and nothing about his actions appeared the least bit self-serving.

But what the hell did she know about Bruiser other than he was damn good in bed, had a dead brother he refused to talk about, and loved attention? A public person on the surface, the real Bruiser was as elusive and private as a hermit. She didn't know the Bruiser behind his public mask any more than she knew where her brother's body was buried.

When the program started, Bruiser walked up front and took the podium. He talked knowledgeably about the Cascade Burn Foundation and the important work they were doing. He related an emotional tale of a teenager whose life went from storybook to horror story in a matter of seconds—the long surgeries, the pain, and the shame of being disfigured—followed by a slideshow of kids in various stages of recovery from serious burns.

By the time the pretty boy was done, even tough-guy Zach Murphy—a known tightwad—wiped his eyes and pulled out his wallet as the bidding began for the charity auction.

Bruiser actively bid on several expensive items. He was the highest bidder on a few, but he sure as hell drove up the bids on others. Veronica opened her purse, too, participating in a spirited bidding war with Bruiser and Tyler for Mariners' luxury suite tickets. Bruiser won, but he spent some big bucks to do it—ten times what the tickets were worth.

Afterward, an exhausted Elliot fell asleep in the backseat. Mac waited in the car while Bruiser carefully carried him into his foster family's house. She rubbed a hand over her heart, and a small smile tugged at the corners of her mouth at this glimpse of Bruiser's tender side. When he came back out, she saw a different man. Yeah, she still saw his raw male beauty, handsome face, and muscles on muscles, but she also saw a generous, caring man who looked beyond a child's imperfections and worked to heal his heart. Despite being labeled superficial and shallow, the real Bruiser beyond the slick underwear ads and hard-hitting football player had shattered the mold Mac and everyone else put him in tonight.

The big question was why did he hide this crucial part of who he was? Mac wanted to know, needed to know *that* Bruiser. But to know him like that required their relationship to move to a different level—a level Bruiser had already stated was off-limits.

Bruiser cast a melancholy smile in her direction as he got in the SUV. He pulled out of the driveway and steered toward the freeway. Mac studied his strong profile with that cleft in his chin, those chiseled features so perfect and flawless he could've been carved by a master's hand. But to her the real person, with his flaws and weaknesses, was more beautiful and perfect than his outward appearance.

Bruiser shot a quick glance at her, catching her gawking at him. His mouth kicked up in his half smile. "Awed by my absolute awesomeness again, are you?"

Mac smiled back, picking up the teasing banter. "You're a legend in your own mind."

"Elliot likes you." He sobered a little. Mac got the distinct feeling it was important to him that she got along with Elliot.

"I fell in love with him. He's so damaged, so vulnerable, yet he has a sharp wit older than his years, and he's so brave."

Bruiser nodded. "I fell in love with him, too. Not very many people can look beyond his burns to the real person inside. In fact, aside from the staff at Harborview and the mothers of the kids, I rarely run across a woman strong enough to treat a kid like him with acceptance and without pity. That's really important to those kids."

"I can only imagine how I'd feel." Actually she couldn't begin to imagine how it felt to know people were staring at you everywhere you went.

"I try not to get involved too deeply because at the end of the day, I'm only one small influence in these kids' lives. But Elliot is a different case, and he was from day one. All these other kids have family to support them, but not Elliot. At least not until his aunt and uncle return from their mission. For now the staff, doctors, foster parents, and me—and now you, too—are all he has."

"I'm flattered to be included. I'm not sure I'll be of much help, but I'm here."

"You were more help than you realize. Elliot loved having a beautiful lady on his arm tonight, loved that the rookies were vying for your attention when you were with him. I didn't love it much though."

Mac frowned, attempting to process his words. "Love what?"

"The rookies. I almost bashed a few heads together."

"Why would they bother you?"

Bruiser stared straight ahead, sucking his lower lip into his mouth. "I'm taking Elliot to that Mariners game Saturday. It's a big deal for him to go out in public like this. Would you like to go? He could use the support." He'd changed the topic and didn't answer her question, and she'd really wanted an answer.

"Saturday?"

"Yeah." Bruiser held his breath, as if hoping she'd say yes. "Please, for Elliot. I can tell he really values your company."

Mac was torn, but she'd promised her father she'd spend the day with him. She'd been putting him off a bit lately. "I can't. I promised my dad I'd help him."

"Your dad, again? When do you get time for yourself?" Bruiser's mouth drew into a thin line as he tapped on the steering wheel, the tension in the car as thick as bullshit in a locker room.

"I'm sorry."

"So am I. Elliot will be sad."

Mac really was sorry. She sighed, full of regret and something else. Fear. Fear of the way things were changing. Fear of turning a corner and never being able to go back to blissful ignorance. This Bruiser gave to others, had flaws and weaknesses.

Despite how physically impressive Bruiser might be, the man under the mask was even more irresistible.

Chapter 15

Free Agent

Bruiser slogged through fog as thick as the Puget Sound mudflats. An oppressive haze surrounded him, tightening its grip on his chest until his lungs burned from the effort of breathing. The cloying mud sucked at his feet and pulled him deeper, slowing each step and multiplying the effort it took to move.

Several feel away, Brice lit a match. Laughing, he taunted his brother, waving the match back and forth. Desperately Bruiser shouted a warning to his twin but the words jammed in his throat and strangled him.

Brice grinned and flipped him off. Bruiser fought like a sonofabitch to get to Bry, only he couldn't move, couldn't speak, rendered helpless by the muddy fog.

A flash of light.

A deafening boom.

An ear-splitting scream that never ended, a scream that lived in Bruiser's nightmares and sat on the edge of his conscience mind, ever present.

The entire world exploded, catapulting Brice across the patio, arms and legs flailing. Bruiser broke through the fog, ripped off his shirt, and beat at the blaze engulfing his brother. His twin stared up at him, his mouth twisted in a silent scream as his face melted down to bone and charcoaled sinew. Chaos reigned as Brice's screams melded with Bruiser's and the screams of sirens and neighbors.

The fire sizzled out.

Brice's face rebuilt itself until Bruiser stared into the hollow eyes of Elliot holding a pistol in his small hand.

As if in a trance, Elliot lifted the pistol to his head and pulled the trigger, while Bruiser watched in helpless horror. Bits of brain matter and blood splattered Bruiser's face and clothes. Elliot slumped to the ground, morphing back into Brice, the side of his head blown off and his blood quickly pooling on the concrete. Watching Bruiser with lifeless eyes, Brice sat up, lifted the gun, and aimed it at his twin. Bruiser froze and waited for the end.

"Bruiser! Bruiser! Bruiser!" Mac's voice penetrated the smothering fear and cut through the bad horror flick cycling through his mind. Only it hadn't been a horror flick, and the people involved weren't actors. They were real. The scene had been real.

At least part of it.

Bruiser shot up in bed, chest heaving and body shaking like a rookie quarterback on his first play in the pros. A cold sweat streamed down his face, drenching his hair.

He blinked rapidly and rubbed his eyes. Finally he focused on Mac, alarm splashed on her face.

Mac wrapped him in her arms, and damn, he needed her comfort, needed her warmth, just needed *her*. He held on, breathing in her scent, burying his face in her tousled hair, taking comfort from her nearness.

When his shaking subsided and his heart rate returned to near normal, he drew back, a little sheepish and a lot embarrassed, feeling open and vulnerable.

"Sorry."

"Nothing to be sorry about. You were having a nightmare."

Her concern touched him more deeply than he cared to admit. Rarely had anyone expressed concern over his demons. He'd lived with them for so very long that he just assumed that was the way life was, for him at least.

Bruiser ran a hand through his hair. "Yeah, happens once in a while."

"Is it the same dream every time?" Mac, on her knees beside him, rubbed his shoulders in deep, comforting circles.

"Variations of the same dream." Bruiser relaxed against the headboard and closed his eyes.

Mac slid her naked body across his. She stroked his cheek as she stared into his eyes. God, he could lose himself in those brown eyes. He had lost himself more than once and wanted to again. "Do you want to talk about it?"

No one ever asked him that question. To talk about it meant he'd have to reveal the tragedy and shame he'd lived with since he'd been a kid. He shook his head. "It's nothing. I'll live."

"It was something. You were sweating, tossing around, definitely upset."

"I'll cope."

"Brice is your twin brother."

Bruiser nodded. "How did you know?"

"You were shouting his name. Were you dreaming about his death? Bruiser, what happened to Brice? Why do you carry guilt around like a life sentence?"

Because it was a life sentence for murder. That's how he saw it.

Bruiser gently pushed her off him and stood. "I need to get going." He escaped before Mac could ask any more questions.

* * * * *

That Thursday, Mac rubbed her sweaty palms on her skirt and glanced at the time on her cell phone. She'd been waiting for more than a half hour so far. Vince was still in his interview, which didn't bode well for Mac.

Mac hated wearing a business suit. She couldn't imagine how men endured not just a suit but a constricting tie every day at work. And the shoes—her feet hurt like hell.

She flipped through another magazine without reading it or noticing the pictures until she came across an underwear ad featuring an almost-naked Bruiser and a gorgeous female model with equally minimal clothes. The woman stood behind him, her arms around his waist and her hands under the waistband of his briefs. Bruiser's head was half-turned to look behind him while the model leaned into him. Their lips were only an inch apart. The woman was beyond beautiful, as beautiful as Bruiser. Mac could never compete physically with a woman like that, even if she wanted to. Mac was more interested in competing for his heart, but she was competing with a ghost.

He refused to open up to her, to trust her with his pain, and she couldn't do a damn thing about it. Instead, he withdrew and made himself scarce. She suspected he'd run all his life from those particular demons, and he'd keep running until he worked up the courage to confront them.

The door to Veronica's office opened. Vince came out laughing and chatting with Veronica. He spotted Mac, smirked at her, and nodded at Veronica.

"Thanks so much for your time. Learning from your wisdom is invaluable to me."

Mac resisted the urge to gag, as Veronica smiled broadly as if she believed his sincerity. Mac didn't get it. The guy was a tool. Veronica, a smart, savvy businesswoman, should be able to figure that out.

Veronica turned from Vince to Mac, and her smile faded into a first-class scowl, not exactly a so-happy-to-see-you expression. She glanced at her watch and tapped her foot impatiently. "I'm running behind. Let's make this quick."

Mac bit back a smart retort. It wasn't her fucking fault Veronica was running late.

Veronica ushered her into her swanky office with a view of Lake Washington and pointed at a chair. "Sit down."

Mac sat and waited for the interview to begin. And waited. And waited. Five minutes of uncomfortable silence passed while Veronica stared at her computer screen. Maybe she was looking at Mac's scholarship application, but Mac doubted it. Seething inside, she longed to retaliate for every little insult and slight Veronica had heaved on her over the past few years, but Mac wanted that damn scholarship.

Veronica was once again wielding her power like a narcissistic dictator.

Finally, the woman sat back and speared Mac with a gaze that said she saw everything and didn't like what she saw. "Sleeping with Bruiser is not going to earn this scholarship."

Veronica's blunt words rendered Mac speechless. So that was what this show was all about. What a bitch. A royal, evil bitch.

"Oh, don't look so surprised. Everyone knows he's fucking you. And that's all it is. So don't be so stupid as to think you mean more to him than that."

Mac squared her shoulders and sat up straighter. She returned Veronica's accusatory gaze with one of her own. "I'm here to be interviewed for a scholarship. My personal life is none of your business."

Veronica arched one perfectly shaped black eyebrow. "Everything that happens between my players and staff is my business. If you don't like it, I can replace you quite easily. How hard can it be to mow a field?"

Damn hard, but Mac bit down on the words, leaving them unspoken. She'd like to see Veronica mow perfectly straight lines regardless of the weather. "Could we start the interview? As you pointed out, you're running late."

Veronica actually rolled her eyes. "Fine. Why should I give you this scholarship?"

Mac ran through her rehearsed answers, while Veronica stared at her computer screen, yawned, and then picked up her phone and tapped out a couple text messages.

Mac stopped talking. The bitch had already made her decision. It didn't matter what Mac said or how qualified she was for the scholarship, Veronica didn't give a shit.

"Are you going to devote time to finish your education? You quit once."

"There were extenuating circumstances."

"And are those circumstances gone now?"

"Not exactly." The last nail hit the scholarship coffin.

"Okay, that's all. We'll be in touch." Veronica stood, effectively dismissing Mac. "Oh, and one more thing: stay away from Bruiser. You're not the right image for him."

"Thank you for your time, Ms. Simms."

Veronica snorted. "Don't forget what I said."

Mac wanted so badly to rip into Veronica, but she caught herself in time, snapped her big mouth shut, and escaped with her hope in shreds.

At least she still had her job.

* * * * *

"You need to lose her and fast."

Bruiser glanced up from the weight machine he'd been battling. He wiped the sweat off his forehead and squinted into the bright overhead lights at Veronica. "Excuse me?"

"You heard me. Get rid of Mac." Veronica stood a few feet from him, legs braced apart and hands on her hips, her typical fighting stance.

"Since when do you pick my friends?" Bruiser ignored her concern. Veronica didn't worry him one bit.

"She's not a friend. You're screwing that woman."

"Who I choose to spend time with is none of your fucking business."

"I built you, mister. Don't you forget it. I've been with you every step of the way, getting you great endorsements, helping you with your charity work, and asking nothing in return."

Bruiser laughed. Veronica never did anything that did not benefit her or the team. "I can smell your bullshit a mile away. Our relationship has been mutually beneficial. I use you, you use me. Business partners and nothing else."

"As your business partner, I don't like the message you're sending to your sponsors and your fans if this gets out. Not to mention you shouldn't be banging the staff."

"Since I have no power over Mac and her employment here, I can't see where that's a problem." A muscle twitched in his jaw, and judging by Veronica's shrewd smirk, she noticed.

"Until she sues the team's ass off or someone else does claiming she's getting special privileges."

"Who would do that?"

Veronica stared at him as if he were a dumbshit. "Seriously? Anyone who's passed over for a promotion in favor of Mac."

"And anyone who's applied for the same scholarship."

"There you go; I always knew you were more than a pretty face."

Bruiser almost growled, but Veronica threw back her head and laughed, or more accurately cackled like the wicked witch in the Wizard of Oz.

"So, pretty boy, you understand the problem?" Veronica rarely called him that. She knew how much he hated it, which said a lot, and none of it good.

"There is no problem. Mac and I are just friends. I took her to a few charity events so she could get close to you, that's all."

"Yeah, and you salivated over her like a dog over US prime beef. Bruce, you're naïve if you think anyone with eyes hasn't picked up on the sexual electricity arcing between the two of you."

"Arcing? Seriously?" He laughed.

"Deadly serious. Think about it." Veronica patted him on the shoulder as if he were a pet. Maybe that's all he was to her, a pet who performed tricks for a well-paying audience.

He understood Veronica—usually. Veronica breathed every breath for the team; her entire existence revolved around the team. Team members and staff alike despised Veronica. While Bruiser didn't exactly approve of her methods at times, he understood her dedication to the Jacks. He felt that same dedication to his cause.

People never guessed that underneath Bruiser's polished exterior lurked the sharp mind of a savvy businessman, Veronica knew. She also knew he had an M.B.A. in finance.

People accused him of being greedy and money-hungry, but Bruiser knew his good looks wouldn't last forever so he had to milk every penny possible out of them while he was still marketable. Of course, no one suspected all those pennies didn't go in Bruiser's private bank account but to his secret charity. A charity he started and supported as atonement for his tragic childhood mistake.

Lots of people assumed he'd had a long-standing affair with Veronica, yet they'd actually never slept together. Bruiser just didn't feel it with her any more than she felt it with him.

Nothing like Mac and him.

Mac. What the hell was he going to do about her?

His head said break it off. His dick said no fucking way. And his heart? Bruiser had stopped factoring that piece into a relationship since CeCe stomped all over him and left him bleeding and broken in the aftermath of her affair and their divorce.

He knew better than to get involved again, especially with a woman who couldn't do anything to forward his cause. He couldn't get more donations or publicity by hanging out with Mac, not like he could with a Grammy Award-winning performer or an A-list female actor.

If it were only about Veronica's threats, he'd flip Veronica the bird and go on about his fucking business.

But it wasn't. There was another huge complication. Mac was married to finding her brother. She didn't have room in her life for anything else other than a hookup now and then. Bruiser was married to football and paying his debt because he'd survived and his brother hadn't.

Two damaged hearts with serious baggage didn't bode well for the success of a relationship, if that's what they even had.

* * * * *

Something was wrong. Sure, Mac's interview with Veronica had sucked, but she didn't think that was it. Maybe her radar was working overtime tonight, or maybe she was just paranoid.

Bruiser had showed up late at night, long after she'd given up and gone to bed.

They made love like two people who knew the world could end tomorrow. Afterward, he didn't stick around and cuddle, which he'd done for the past week. Instead he got dressed and came back to sit on the side of the bed. "We really need to be more careful. Veronica's suspicious."

She didn't think this was really about Veronica. More likely his nightmare had revealed too much and he was using the excuse to do damage control.

She decided to play along and see where it went. "Tell me about it. I had a horrible interview with her today."

"Ah, Mac, I'm sorry about that. Really. You denied our relationship, didn't you?"

Mac flipped on the nightstand light and studied him. "What if I didn't?"

Panic crossed his face, which pissed Mac off.

"What if I shout it to the entire world, sell the story of our torrid love affair to a gossip mag or tweet it all over hell and back?"

Bruiser coughed nervously. "You wouldn't do that."

"If I did, would you care if we were out in the open?"

"There's no reason for that. It's not beneficial to either of us."

"Scared?" She needled him, feeling a little used by him and a lot disrespected by Veronica.

"Mac, it'll jeopardize your scholarship." Bruiser folded and unfolded a corner of the bedspread, as if he found it more fascinating that her.

That really ticked her off. "My scholarship is beyond jeopardized. It's dead and buried."

"Aw, Mac, I'm sorry." He reached out to hug her, but she darted away to stand on the opposite side of the bed.

When she caught him eyeing her naked body, she yanked the damn quilt out of his hands and wrapped it around her. "It was a long shot to begin with. I knew it was. I'll just try to save some money to attend night school."

"I could loan you—"

"No, I won't take charity. Not from you, not from anyone."

"I was just trying to help."

"Why help me? It's not like we have a real relationship," Mac hated the bitchiness in her voice but couldn't stop herself.

"There's not time for one. You're searching for your brother and training camp is about to start, not to mention my obligations to my endorsers."

Something snapped inside Mac. "Your endorsers. That's what this is really about. You think word is getting out about us. You don't want to be seen with someone like me. A woman who mows lawns for a living and has dirt under her fingernails."

Bruiser's eyes narrowed, and he fisted his hands. Mac could see the anger vibrating through his body. "Don't ever put yourself down like that. Ever. You don't need to change for me or anyone else. I liked you how you were before."

"You're so full of shit."

"What's that supposed to mean?" Now he appeared good and mad.

"You're acting like this is my fault, when you're the one having an issue with us."

"I'm not having an issue. You are. I can't carry on a relationship with a woman whose dead brother is a huge part of our relationship."

"My brother deserves justice, and my family deserves closure." She was being a bitch, and she knew it, but right now she wanted to make Bruiser disappear. She had a better chance of winning the Powerball without ever buying a ticket than she did of finding her brother alive, yet hearing Bruiser say it with such certainty really didn't work for her. Nor did all this bullshit he was spewing. If he wanted out, he should just say so, but he wasn't going to have her cupcakes and eat them too. Not now. Not at this point.

"I'm sorry. That was insensitive. I mean, I don't know what happened to him, but he's not going to be found alive." He sounded oddly flustered.

"What about your brother? I told you my story, and you don't even trust me enough to tell me about your twin. Why do you have nightmares? Why won't you tell me what happened?"

Bruiser rubbed the back of his neck and refused to look at her. "I told you that subject was off limits."

Mac just shook her head. "If you want to end this *not* relationship, spit it out."

Bruiser stared at the floor, a muscle jerking in his strong jaw. "I don't know. I don't think this will end well, but I don't want to hurt you."

"Oh, the *I don't want to hurt you* speech." Mac's bitter laugh rang through the room.

"Listen, Mac," he met her gaze, "I'm screwed up more than you'll ever know, and you're not far behind. You can't say no to your father and you spend every fucking free minute searching for a brother you'll never find. You don't have time for me or anyone else."

Mac clutched the quilt to herself and glared at him. "Are you telling me to give up on Will? Would you quit looking if you'd lost your brother? Wouldn't you have to know what happened to him? Could you just walk away?"

Bruiser's face fell as if she'd physically hurt him. "You don't know a damn thing about me."

"Because you won't share your life with me. Well, you don't know a damn thing about me either. We were nothing but sex partners. So no regrets. Just get out." Mac pointed toward the door.

The cat stood in the doorway, twitching his tail and regarding them both with equal disdain, as if they were too stupid to see the truth. Maybe Bart knew more than they did.

"Mac, I—" Bruiser held out his hands, palms up.

Mac ignored him and stomped into the bathroom, locking the door behind her. She sank down to the floor and huddled in the corner until she heard him drive off.

Chapter 16

Out of Downs

One week into training camp, Bruiser slumped on a bench in the empty locker room and stared at nothing, contemplating another lonely Friday night. The rookies scattered like geese being chased by a retriever when he hit them up to join him for a drink, while the cagey veterans left the locker room before he could track them down. What the fuck? maybe he hadn't been good company lately.

"You gonna sit here all evening like some pathetic pansy-ass?" Brett walked out of the showers, a towel around his waist. He hadn't spoken to Bruiser except for one-syllable words since he'd learned about Bruiser and Mac.

Bruiser straightened and looked up at his once best buddy. "Haven't got anything better to do." Damn, he hated it when he felt sorry for himself.

"You look like you could use a friend." Brett walked to his locker, tossed his towel aside and started dressing.

"I could. You know of anyone interested in the job?"

Brett chuckled. "Being friends with you *is* a job, all right."

"Yeah, I know. I'm a total ass."

"I wouldn't go that far. Harris has that title all sewn up."

"I'm next in line then." Bruiser had to laugh. One thing they could always agree on was Tyler Harris was an awesome quarterback and a master asshole.

"Harris teaches classes on the twelve steps to being an unrepentant asshole."

"I might have to sign up."

Brett smiled at him. "I'm heading out in the boat, doing a little fishing before dusk, you in?"

Despite his crappy mood, Bruiser couldn't say no to Brett and to fishing. "Hell, yeah."

Within an hour, Bruiser and Brett were sitting in Brett's boat on Lake Washington, fishing lines dangling in the water. They'd run through their usual talk about football—the upcoming season, promising rookies, and how the first week of training camp went.

Then they talked about Elliot and his progress. He was adjusting pretty well to his foster home, going out in public, managing to deal somewhat with the stares and whispers. He'd made some new friends at a summer camp for young burn victims, which Bruiser sponsored every year.

After exhausting those subjects, they sat in a companionable silence for a while. Bruiser relaxed and enjoyed the warm evening. He'd missed Brett. Maybe this day wasn't a total wash.

Finally, he cleared his throat and broke the silence. "You'll be happy to hear that I'm not seeing Mac anymore."

"No shit?" Brett grunted and stared at the blue-black water lapping against the boat.

"No shit." Bruiser tried to swallow the lump in his throat. He felt like crap, couldn't sleep, and had no appetite. The only woman who'd ever made him feel this crappy had been CeCe. He hated feeling like this, hated the regrets and the heartache.

"Well, that makes sense now. You look like shit. It's our first week of training camp, and you haven't been worth a damn. I've seen Girl Scouts tougher than you are."

"I'm a dumbass. A wimpy idiot."

"And an asshole-in-training."

"Damn right," Bruiser laughed. Hell, it felt good to laugh. It'd been a long week.

Brett angled his head and squinted into the sun. "You miss her?"

Bruiser clutched the pole and stared at the tip as if it were a Magic 8 Ball with all the answers to his questions. Only it wasn't. "Yeah, I guess so."

"When did you split?"

"Last week."

"What'd you do to screw that up?"

"I just didn't want to hurt her." It sounded like the lamest excuse ever.

"Yeah, whatever. What really happened?"

"Fuck if I know. I guess I got scared. But she never had enough time for me anyway. She spends all her spare time looking for her brother. Besides, she doesn't understand me." God, he sounded like a whiny ass to his own ears.

"Did you ever give her a chance to understand you?"

Bruiser doubted that he had. "Probably not. She keeps pushing to know about my brother. I don't talk about my brother. Not to family. Not to friends. No one."

"Would you like to talk about him now?"

He opened his mouth to say hell no but shut it again. "Yeah. Yeah, I would." Bruiser's response surprised Bruiser more than it did Brett.

He took a deep breath and began to talk.

* * * * *

Training camp started and Mac worked long hours keeping the grass practice field in perfect shape. One hidden hole or too much water in one spot could make a slippery surface and cause injury to a player and ruin his season, maybe even his career. Mac and the rest of the grounds crew took great pride in the field's durability and appearance.

Her day started after the team left the field, making for late nights. But no matter how many hours she spent at work and how exhausted she was when she came home, Bruiser snuck into her thoughts and her dreams, even though he didn't sneak into her house.

With his absence from her life, she rededicated herself to the search for Will, going after it with single-minded purpose of an alcoholic pursuing his next drink, reminding herself a bit of her father.

Mac caught glimpses of Bruiser on the field with his glistening, tanned, shirtless body and blond hair. On Monday night, he showed up at O'Malley's for the team's night out and sat at the opposite end of the table from Mac, teasing her as usual, like nothing ever happened between them. Maybe to him nothing had. Another day, another woman.

Then she caught him staring at her, and the sadness and regret in his blue-gray eyes haunted her ever since.

Tonight—the first Friday of training camp—she worked until dusk, tired but satisfied with how the turf was holding up. As she walked toward her car, Brett caught up with her. The guy usually studied game film until late at night. Only Zach and Tyler stayed later.

"I'm glad I caught you. Got a few minutes?" Brett asked.

"Sure, I was just heading home."

"How about a drink?"

Mac hesitated, wondering how much Brett knew about her and Bruiser and whether he hoped for a second chance now that Bruiser was out of the picture.

"Hey, just friends, right?" Good thing he was a mind reader.

"Okay, sure." She didn't feel like going home alone tonight, looking across the yard as Will's widow and her new husband had yet another party while her father watched their every move through binoculars.

Mac followed Brett to O'Malley's and sat across from him, making small talk about which rookies and free agents had a chance of making the team. Brett's eyes lit up whenever he talked football. It was a damn shame he wasn't with a team where he'd have a chance of starting, but Harris tied up that job for the foreseeable future.

"I went fishing with Bruiser last week." The sudden change of subject caught Mac off guard. Brett's blue eyes watched her, as if gauging her reaction, not missing a thing.

"Oh, did you catch anything?" She asked, wondering where Brett was going with this.

"Uh." He scratched his head as if he didn't want to answer that.

"Guess not. Do you ever catch any fish?"

"It's the journey, not the destination." Brett smiled at her.

"If you say so. I'll have to take your word for it. Fishing seems like an excuse for guys to laze around on a boat, drink beer and swap tall tales all day."

Brett's half smile said it all. He looked over her shoulder for a moment then back at her. His expression sobered. "Bruiser misses you, Mac."

Mac shook her head, trying to clear it. Surely she didn't hear him correctly. "I thought you didn't like us together."

He shrugged and stared down at the table. "I didn't, but I was wrong. You too were good for each other. Bruiser's been a bigger asshole than Harris for the past two weeks. He's got the rookies shaking in their cleats whenever he comes near. And you—you've been a real bitch, too. All the guys have noticed. They're giving you a wide berth."

"Well, thanks for the compliment." Mac resorted to sarcasm; it was her go-to defense when the shit got too deep to handle. "The team doesn't know about Bruiser and me, do they?"

He shook his head. "Nope, only me, but they sure as hell suspect something's fucked up."

Mac shrugged and raised her hand to order another beer.

"Give him another chance, Mac." Brett finally got to the heart of the matter, and Mac wished she'd gone home instead of accepting his offer for a drink.

"He's the one who walked out, the one who chose to stay away."

"You might need to make the first move."

"Are you kidding? Why would I put myself through that grief again?"

"Because you care about him. He cares about you."

"Did some linebacker slam your head into the ground today or what? Bruiser would never say that."

"Not in words, but I know him."

Mac sighed. Typical Brett. Always putting everyone's feelings ahead of his own. Bruiser and she could learn a thing or three from the unselfish backup quarterback. "I know him, too. It's all about Bruiser. He's an attention slut. Everything he does is carefully calculated to net the most press."

"You don't honestly believe that."

She nodded. She wanted to, oh, how she wanted to. A selfish, egotistical Bruiser was much easier to dislike than the glimpses she'd seen of a completely generous, kind Bruiser. "For example, his work with the burn foundation. He's their sponsor, but you can bet if it didn't net him good press, he'd never do it." She cringed at her own feeble justifications. Bruiser wasn't that guy, and she knew it.

Brett gave her a look that seemed to insinuate that she'd missed the mark. "If you really believe that, you truly don't deserve to be with a good guy like him."

"What do you mean by that?" Now she felt even more like a bitch because Brett spoke the truth.

"Did you know that Bruiser works with child burn victims because of his twin brother?"

"No, I had no idea." Mac's bitch status just upgraded to beyond bitch. She hugged herself tight and stared at her beer as if it held the answers to her problems.

"His twin brother, Brice, was badly burned in an accident."

Mac's hands flew to her mouth. Forget *bitch*—that was too kind of a term for her.

"Brice couldn't deal with his horrendous burns and quality of life, so he shot himself in the head a year later at fourteen years old. Bruiser found him."

"I didn't know." That explained the sadness lurking in Bruiser's eyes and the nightmares—the horrible, horrible nightmares.

"Yeah, well, you of all people should never judge a book by its cover."

She deserved that and more. "Why does he keep his twin a secret?"

"Because he feels responsible for what happened."

"How could he be responsible?"

"Survivor's guilt, maybe. It's not my place to tell you the details. I've said more than I should." Brett looked away, and Mac was certain the Army vet knew a thing or two about survivor's guilt.

"Yeah, I can understand that. I just never imagined Bruiser—"

"No one does. Why do you think he's so good with those kids? Especially Elliot. He's been working with burn victims since college."

Bruiser? Since college? Sure he'd been great with Elliot, and he'd mentioned others and that he tried not to get involved. She'd never guessed the extent of his special mission. Why did he work so hard to play the part of a shallow, pretty boy? It had to have something to do with the pain he lived with every day.

And if anyone understood the pain of losing a sibling, Mac did.

* * * * *

Saturday, Bruiser rushed to Elliot's foster home in response to a frantic phone call from Elliot. No one answered the door at the foster home, but Elliot said he'd be there. Panic rose inside Bruiser as he tried the doorknob and found the door unlocked. Oh, God, no, not again.

The cold hand of fear clutched at his throat, robbing him of oxygen. He froze for a split second, gathered his courage, and prayed to any god who would listen to him.

Bruiser ran to the small bedroom Elliot shared with another kid, fearing the worst as his heart pounded in his ears. The kid sat on the bed, very much alive. Bruiser leaned against the doorway, waiting for his heart rate to slow and his head to stop pounding. Elliot didn't look up, just fiddled with a loose thread on the worn quilt.

Finally trusting himself to speak, Bruiser struggled to keep his voice even and casual. "Hey, buddy. Going somewhere?" He pointed at the duffle bag on Elliot's bed.

The kid stood up, still not looking at him. "My aunt and uncle are back from their mission in South America. She's coming to get me."

"Today?"

"Any minute."

"That's good. You'll be with family." Bruiser hoped like hell they'd give Elliot the love and attention he so desperately needed and at least partially fill the hole left by the death of his parents. Surely, the type of people who spent a year in a third-world country helping those less fortunate could love a physically and emotionally damaged little boy.

"They're not really family. I don't know them. Aunt Ruth was married to my mom's brother. After he died in a logging accident when I was a baby, she married Uncle John. Mom never liked her. Mom said that people like Aunt Ruth and Uncle John are the reason she quit going to church. She called them hypnotists."

"Hypnotists? Oh, you mean, hypocrites."

"Whatever." Elliot looked up, his eyes filled with unshed tears.

"There's nobody else in your family that could take custody?" Bruiser couldn't shake the sick feeling nesting in the pit of his stomach. He wanted to protect Elliot like he hadn't Brice, yet he felt helpless to do so.

"No one." Elliot shook his head and sniffed, looking every bit like he was going to cry. "I want my Mom and Dad."

Bruiser crossed the room and put his arm around the boy, pulling him tight against his side. He'd give anything to take away Elliot's pain, if only he could. "This will be a good thing, you wait and see."

They both looked up as a scowling fat woman waddled into the room. Her polyester pants squeaked as her thighs rubbed together. The woman did a double take when she saw Bruiser, her gaze full of suspicion as if she'd caught him stealing family heirlooms. He tried to smile, but his smile stuck somewhere between his heart and his lips. One look at her and dread rose inside him. Elliot wrapped his arms Bruiser's waist and clung to him.

This woman didn't exactly give off warm and fuzzy vibes. She didn't rush to her nephew and throw her arms around him to comfort, didn't even seem to notice him at first.

When her gaze dropped to the little boy plastered to Bruiser's side, she staggered back a few steps at the sight of Elliot's face and stared, open-mouthed. Her hand went to her heart as if she might faint. Elliot ducked his head and pulled his Jacks ball cap down tight over his face.

The woman looked away and covered her mouth, as if she were going to retch. "Are you ready to go?" She couldn't even look at the kid. Bruiser wanted to grab her and shake her, make her see the scared, lonely kid hiding in this hurt body.

Bruiser stood, tucking Elliot next to him in a purely instinctual protective gesture. "Excuse me, ma'am, I'm a friend. Name's Bruce."

"I'm Ruth Jones, and I'm a very busy woman. I don't have time to stand around here and make small talk with you." She turned her back on them both and headed to the door. "Elliot, let's go."

Elliot glanced at Bruiser, his eyes pleading to be saved. Bruiser faked a smile he sure as hell didn't feel. "It's okay, buddy. I'm sure your aunt's home will be a wonderful one for you." Bullshit and they both knew it. He turned to Ruth. "I'd like to visit."

The fat woman half turned and heaved a put-upon sigh. She dug into her monstrous purse and produced a coffee-stained business card. "Fine. Call me. We'll arrange something as long as you don't expect me to be a taxi service." She still avoided looking at Elliot. "Let's go."

Panic crossed Elliot's face, and he gripped Bruiser's arm. "Can't I stay with you? I won't be any trouble. I'll make my bed, do my homework, and stay out from underfoot."

Bruiser looked down at him and shook his head, feeling like an asshole of the worst kind. "I wish you could, Elliot. I really do."

"Then why can't I?"

Bruiser glanced at the woman tapping her foot near the door. He had a million responses to Elliot's questions and every one of them was selfish. Why couldn't he adopt Elliot? Why couldn't he give a kid a better life than he'd get with this unpleasant witch?

"Please," Elliot begged.

"Look, I'll see what I can do. For now you'll need to go with your Aunt Ruth."

Elliot's shoulders slumped and his entire body sagged. "Okay." He looked toward the door, his aunt already out of sight, hesitated, and shot an accusing glare at Bruiser. "You said everything would be all right."

"It will." Bruiser put his hands on Elliot's shoulders and squeezed, feeling as if he might cry himself.

"Promise?" Elliot stared up at him with earnest, trusting eyes, as if he truly believed Bruiser could fix this fucking mess.

"Yeah, I promise. I do."

Bruiser watched Elliot shuffle from the room and wondered how the hell he would ever be able to keep a promise like that.

Chapter 17

Coaching Strategies

On a rare day off, Mac stared in the mirror as Shanna trimmed her hair with confident precision. It'd been almost a week since her talk with Brett, and she'd been torn between ducking and hiding and facing Bruiser and his secrets head on. First, she needed more info, and Shanna was the one to give it to her.

"I didn't know Bruce had a twin brother."

Shanna's scissors stopped in mid-snip. Mac caught her surprised expression in the mirror. "Bruce told you about Brice?"

"No, a friend of his did."

"Figures. I've never known him to talk about it. None of us do. Our family is weird like that." Shanna tugged on the hair on both sides of Mac's face to make sure it was even.

"Why is that?" Mac pushed it, having no doubt Shanna would nail her if she stepped over the line.

Shanna shrugged and picked up the curling iron. "We're experts at denial."

"Especially Bruiser." Mac planted the bait and waited for Shanna to bite.

"Look, I don't talk about my brother to just anyone. He might seem like a public person, but he's not, not one damn bit. He lets people see what he wants them to see and no more. But I think you're different than his usual girlfriends."

Mac opened her mouth to dispute the statement but Shanna stopped her cold. "Hear me out. You're good for him. You ground him, and God knows he needs that. He's ten times smarter than those bimbos he dates, but you're his equal." Shanna studied her in the mirror, tapping her scissors on the chair.

"What happened to his twin? I know he was in an accident and then—"

Shanna held up a hand to stop her. "We don't talk about the *accident*. If you want to know, he'll have to tell you. But I will say Bruce lives the life he believes Brice would have lived, as if Bruce doesn't deserve to live his life for himself."

"What do you mean?"

"Growing up, Bruiser was the quiet, studious one. Brice was the daredevil, attention seeker, and athlete of the family. Not that Bruce wasn't athletic—of course he was, but not like Brice. Brice overshadowed everything Bruce did. Our parents never hid the fact that Brice was their favorite. After Brice's accident, Dad couldn't deal with Brice's injuries, nor could he look at Bruce because he was a constant reminder of what Brice used to be. So Dad left. And Mom, well, she blamed Bruce—not directly, but she has her ways. She reminds us every chance she gets of Brice's absence in our life. I think she tortures Bruce for living because she doesn't know how else to deal with the grief."

"That's awful." Mac couldn't imagine a parent holding such guilt over a child's head. Or maybe she could. Maybe in a way her father did that same thing.

"Yeah, it took me a long time to forgive Mom and Dad. They're superficial people; their lives and their livelihoods depend on appearances. Neither of them could bear looking at Brice. He did look pretty hideous, the stuff of nightmares, but he was their kid."

Mac wiped an unexpected tear from her eye, getting a yank on her hair in return.

"Don't move," Shanna chastised Mac. "Anyway, Bruce found Brice after he'd shot himself. After that it was weird. Bruce took on his twin's personality. He became Brice, but it didn't matter to our father, and Mom just buried herself in the business. I think it was too painful to look at Bruce and see the mirror image of the son she'd lost."

"Are you saying that Bruiser has been his brother all these years?"

"I'm saying that he's been the person he imagined Brice would be for so long that I don't think he knows how to be Bruce anymore."

"Wow." Mac couldn't seem to wrap her head around how screwed up his whole situation was. Her heart was breaking for him.

"He hates doing all those endorsements, especially the modeling. I mean, he despises modeling. But every penny he makes on endorsements goes to his charity for burn victims."

"I assumed he spent it on designer clothes and stuff." When she thought about it she realized with all the money he made he had to be doing something with it besides buying clothes. She'd bought right into the image he's sold to everyone.

Shanna laughed. "Bruce is a tight-assed bastard. He hoards money. Most of his clothes come via the endorsements or he gets them on sale, or they're last year's designs. He wears them so well no one notices."

Mac shook her head in amazement. "I never knew."

"No one knows. He needs to maintain his man-about-town persona."

"He has terrible nightmares."

Shanna locked eyes with her in the mirror. "And you know this how?"

Mac's face turned bright red. "I—uh—well—"

"Hey, don't fret it. I know how he is with women. Never met one yet that could resist him when he turned on that boyish charm."

Mac hated being just one of his many women. Brett was wrong. Bruiser couldn't miss her. Maybe the sex, but not her.

"Funny, I thought you might be different. That's why we invited you to Sunday dinner. You're real, and Bruce needs a real woman, not some piece of arm candy without a brain in her fucking head. He's so damn gun-shy when it comes to women."

"Gun-shy?"

"His divorce. Surely you know about that one?"

"I know he's divorced and the marriage didn't last long."

"I never liked the bitch. Let me put it this way—she was looking for a man who'd be somebody, so she latched onto him in college. She was smart, clever, and devious. He never saw through her. Totally fell for her. They married their senior year, lived in student housing, and she worked two menial jobs, which she thought were beneath her. When she caught the team quarterback's eye, they had an affair.

Bruce didn't find out until his QB buddy went higher in the draft and signed a bigger contract. She threw Bruce to the curb and never looked back. It devastated him. He was so busy finishing his degree he didn't see it coming."

"Bruiser has a degree?" She'd known he played college ball, but she figured he got drafted into the pros and left school.

"Yeah, in business and finance. He graduated with honors."

Mac shook her head. She felt shell shocked. She hadn't a fucking clue. Everything she thought she knew about him was a misconception.

And just maybe there was one more. Maybe he was a man with the ability to commit long term.

Who the hell was she kidding? The guy carried more baggage than the cargo hold of a Boeing 787, and the last thing he needed was a commitment to a woman who had her own cargo hold full of matched luggage.

* * * * *

Beady little blue eyes bored into Bruiser's back as he sat at the bar. He could feel them. He swung around and came face to face with the team's asshole quarterback. When the jerk continued to stare without saying a fucking thing, he turned his back on Harris again and faced the bar, but the quarterback's laser-sharp gaze still seared his skin as if he held a blowtorch.

Bruiser whipped around again. "What?"

Tyler shot him his trademark smirk, an expression he'd honed over the years. "You are such a fucking tool."

"You would know." Bruiser would never understand what Lavender saw in this guy.

"Hey, I make it my business to know anything that might remotely affect the team. You've been moping around like a pansy-ass about to turn in his man card because of some female."

"You don't know a damn thing about me."

Harris's cronies gathered around the bar, pulling barstools from other locations. So much for a quiet night to think things over.

"Are you fucking kidding me?" Harris threw back his head and laughed so hard Bruiser swore he'd snort up a lung. Finally, wiping his eyes, Harris got a hold of himself. "What would we know about that, right guys?"

Derek seemed to find this hilariously funny, too, along with Zach. Brett half smiled and buried his head in the bar menu, which after all this time frequenting this place, he should have memorized.

Bruiser didn't get it, not one bit. Other than they were annoying the hell out of him. "I don't know what you mean."

"One word, dumb shit. Mac." Tyler's superior smirk pissed Bruiser off, but then Tyler loved to piss people off, it was part of his M.O. If he knew he got under Bruiser's skin, he'd burrow in deeper and heckle Bruiser until hell froze over.

"Mac?" Bruiser played dumb. He was blond, after all.

"Yeah, you've fallen harder than a kicker trying to throw a block on a lineman." Zach snorted beer through his nose. After a coughing fit, he quickly wiped his nose with a napkin. Kelsie *had* taught him a thing or two.

"I don't *fall* for women—not Mac, not anybody." They knew about Mac?

The three idiots shared a private look and burst into another fit of annoying laughter, while Brett's pinched expression made him look constipated.

"Yeah," Harris said. "That's why you're as shit-faced cranky as Lavender when I took away her Nordstrom's credit card."

Bruiser exercised epic denial. "It's not about Mac. Not really." And it wasn't, at least not in total.

Another fit of laughter, then the idiots grinned like a pack of hyenas after a wounded antelope. These assholes were seriously pissing Bruiser off.

"Yeah, sure, then who's it about?" Harris challenged.

"Elliot." Bruiser deflected the Mac questions to a safer subject though just as equally troubling. Thinking about the kid's circumstances made Bruiser sick to his stomach. He'd been visiting Elliot regularly. The boy's Aunt Ruth made no bones about how much the kid inconvenienced her and her brood of "normal" children. All the while, she played the martyr role to the hilt for her church friends. After all, she had taken in this difficult orphaned child of a former sister-in-law.

Bruiser disliked the woman and her husband. They didn't want Elliot but appearances were everything to them. After all, what would people think if they sent the kid back to the foster care system? Bruiser researched a possible guardianship, but The Joneses were adamant that his situation didn't fit Elliot's needs. He grudgingly had to admit they were right to a point.

"Is Elliot the kid from the burn unit?" Derek's smile faded and his brows drew together. Even Tyler's glee over needling Bruiser turned off faster than the power in a Maple Valley thunderstorm.

"His aunt showed up and took him home a week ago. She's a real bitch. Can't even look at him she's so horrified by his burns. Her husband is a fat, lazy slob who sees Elliot as his personal slave so he doesn't have to get out of his La-Z-boy. Elliot wants to live with me."

Four pairs of eyes stared at him as if he'd announced he was hanging up his cleats to take up quilting.

"Crazy, I know," Bruiser admitted.

"I don't think that's crazy. You have lots you could offer someone like him." Of course Derek would say that. Derek saw the best in everyone.

"Even if I tried, no one would give me a guardianship. I'm single, gone a lot, and not in a stable home, or so the aunt says."

"That's what you needed Freddie's number for?" Harris asked. Freddie was Harris's take-no-prisoners attorney sister.

"Yeah, I asked her to look into my options." Which hadn't been very encouraging. The aunt and uncle hadn't done anything to lose custody. They fed and clothed Elliot, kept him clean, and he showed no signs of any physical abuse. Essentially, he had what he needed except for love, and the courts only considered the observable elements of caring for a child. Apparently love couldn't be measured. Bruiser knew better.

And he had promised.

"She'll help if anyone can. Man, I'm scared as hell of my sister."

"So far, the bitch aunt isn't having any of it. She doesn't want the kid. I think it's all about getting her hands on the insurance money from the accident, which should be put in trust for Elliot until he turns eighteen. Plus, their entire social life revolves around their church, and they have this image to uphold. How would it look if they relinquished this orphaned child to a known playboy bachelor with a reputation for partying?"

"You could solve the money concerns by offering them some kind of stipend for their trouble." Harris always worked the angles on any problem.

"Yeah, if the only problem was greed, it'd be simple. I'd donate to their church, which is as good as putting money in their pockets since the uncle is the pastor. I'm sure they'd like to send the kid packing, but how would they justify it as a selfless act? Especially to such an inappropriate choice as me? After all, and I quote, 'my life is not stable.'"

"Marriage shows stability." All heads turned toward Zach.

Marriage-phobic Harris had the same horrified expression Bruiser suspected was on his own face.

Zach shrugged. "Well, I would know."

"You think I should get a wife just so I can get custody of Elliot?" Bruiser rubbed his temples as his brain beat itself against his skull, giving a new meaning to the word headache.

"Yeah, if Elliot means that much to you. Marriages have been made over less than that," Zach said.

Bruiser shrugged, conceding that point. Hell, for him love didn't work the first time around, why should it be a valid reason for marriage this time? Not that there'd be a *this time*.

"I'm a great believer in marry first, and she'll fall in love with you later."

Derek and Harris gaped at Zach like he'd just suggested they join a knitting circle at the senior citizen center.

"Ignore him; he's a moron," Harris snorted. "Marriage is just a piece of paper, doesn't mean a fucking thing."

Derek rolled his eyes and gave his cousin a disgusted look. "Yeah, really? How's that working for you? Rachel tells me Lavender's getting restless. You might just find an arrow in your heart one morning or an empty bed."

"Or both." Zach grinned, as if the thought conjured up some interesting possibilities. "You could try living with a decent woman, but I'm guessing this aunt would consider that a sin. So it's marriage or take your chances."

Brett, who'd been quiet during this entire crazy conversation, finally spoke. "I could see you and Mac together. I think you might have staying power."

Bruiser turned to look at his friend like he'd just proclaimed all football be a non-contact sport. "I've been down the aisle once. No way am I going down that devil's path again, even with Mac. Especially with Mac. There has to be another way."

He looked to each one of his teammates. Every single asshole wore a stupefied expression on his face, except Harris, and he was nodding. This was not good to be on the same side as Harris. What did that say for Bruiser and his judgment? The only place Harris displayed good judgment was on the football field and by picking Lavender.

"Mac's had a crush on you for the last couple years. Everyone knows it. Plus, she'd make a great mother." Derek warmed to Zach's crazy-assed idea.

Bruiser rubbed the back of his neck and stared hard at nothing. Mac? A crush on him? He'd suspected it the past few months, but for a few years? The thought seemed outrageous.

"Yeah, and she'd be devoted. She'd never cheat. She's not that type." Brett added.

Bruiser wanted to pound his head against the wall, but it already hurt like hell. "Sure, she'd be a great mother if she didn't spend every spare minute looking for a brother she will probably never find."

"That's her father playing on her guilt. It's tragic how good people do dumb-shit things and are completely oblivious as to how much they're screwing up their kids," Brett said.

Not one to keep his mouth shut, Zach offered more uninvited advice. "You could ask her. The worst she can do is spit in your face."

If they thought that was the worst thing Mac could do, they didn't know Mac very well. Bruiser liked to keep his privates intact and functioning, not to mention his heart, though it'd already taken a beating because of one little blonde groundskeeper.

* * * * *

Almost a month had passed since Mac and Bruiser did their version of breaking up, which essentially meant they didn't sleep together anymore. Their affair had been short, sweet, and hot, but Mac took some comfort in knowing she lasted longer than any of Bruiser's other relationships in the past three or four years.

Mac still hung out on Monday nights at O'Malley's with the team, along with Bruiser, both of them playing the part of friends without benefits. She missed him more than she'd ever admit, and not just the sex. She missed those blue-gray eyes that could light up the darkest world and make her believe if only for a short while everything would be fine. She missed his quick wit and his storytelling abilities. She missed the gentle, generous soul who worked with burn victims and made their lives that much better.

She just flat out *missed* him, but she doubted she was even a blip on his radar.

After all, a new football season lurked just around the corner, and Bruiser loved his football.

The team was deep into training camp after winning its first two preseason games, led mostly by Brett and the defense. Tyler never played much in preseason; his arm was too valuable to risk. Brett lived for preseason and actual playing time in a game situation. Bruiser—as usual—immersed himself in football to the exclusion of all else.

Like Mac didn't know *that* story. Her father became more rabid than ever to find her brother, spending money he didn't have on private detectives, going places he couldn't afford to go, and looking so rough he'd been mistaken for a homeless person more than once.

More to keep busy than because of any optimism, Mac spent nights and weekends poring over old evidence and hunting down new clues, yet nothing wiped Bruiser's teasing smile from her memory. She could still feel his skin against hers and his lips on her lips.

Late Friday night, Mac still couldn't get Bruiser out of her mind. She walked down the hallway near the locker room on her way to her car. Bruiser burst around the corner and slammed into her, ramming her into the wall and knocking the wind out of her. Before she could sink to the floor, he grabbed her waist and hauled her to him. For a moment, she leaned into him, savoring the feel of his hard body, breathing in his freshly scrubbed scent, and forgetting her best intentions as she drowned in those warm blue-gray eyes. And they were warm tonight. Very warm. He felt so right, so strong, so confident.

And yet he was so wrong for her.

"Whoa, there. Keep that up, and we'll put you on defense, sweetheart. Not that I don't mind. Not at all." He slipped into his charming act so easily Mac wondered who he'd been practicing it on lately.

Bruiser gazed down at her with his sexy half smile and laughing eyes. Lord help her, she wanted to taste him, lick him, and get him naked, not necessarily in that order.

He set her back on her feet. "You okay, babe?"

"I think so." She wasn't okay. She was way beyond okay and nudging toward the screwed-up end of the scale.

He eyed her with concern gentling his eyes as he absently rubbed his stubble. "You're here late tonight."

An obvious observation, but she kept her sarcasm under wraps. "We can't take care of the turf when you're on it. Besides, I could say the same of you. Practice ended hours ago."

"That's how dedicated I am." He grinned his full-blown panty-dropper smile. "I'll walk you to your car." Bruiser held open the door for her and walked beside her to the parking lot.

They'd almost reached her car when Vince sauntered up. "Hey, Bruiser. You guys are looking good this year." The jerk ignored Mac as if she were an insignificant speck of dirt on the asphalt. As usual.

"As long as we stay healthy." Bruiser turned to walk away, taking Mac by the arm and steering her the last few steps to her car.

Vince called to Mac, faking sympathy. "I'm sorry about the scholarship, Mac. Maybe next time."

Mac stopped in her tracks and spun around. "What do you know about the scholarship?"

Vince's hand flew to his mouth in an unconvincing display of contrition. "Oh, no, I'm sorry. Veronica didn't tell you?"

"Tell me what?" But she already knew.

"I was awarded the scholarship." He delivered the gut punch and then smugly nodded at Bruiser and strutted off.

"Asshole," Bruiser muttered. "Mac, I'm sorry. Really sorry." He stared at her, tucking one stray blonde strand behind her ear in a gentle gesture that nearly undid her.

"Not as sorry as I am." A sob rose past her throat. She hiccupped. Oh, fuck, she wasn't going to cry, was she? She rarely cried, even over her brother. She just didn't cry.

"Come on, sweetheart, let me buy you dinner." Bruiser's truly sympathetic gaze melted her heart.

She hesitated. It was a stupid, foolish idea, but she didn't want to go home alone. Or even worse, to go home and find her father there spying on the neighbors. He'd been spending more and more time in the evenings at her house watching Sonja and Ben, who'd been much more active in their garden lately, almost like they were taunting Craig.

"Okay." She ignored the little voice telling her this was *so* not a good idea as she climbed into his car.

They found a dark corner booth in O'Malley's. She didn't complain when he slid next to her, put his arm across the back of the booth, and his muscled thigh pressed hers.

She sniffed and rubbed her eyes. He handed her a napkin. "I really wanted that scholarship."

"I know, honey, I know." He hugged her close to him, tucking her under his arm, with the same possessiveness he gave a football as he busted his way through defenders.

Mac turned her head and buried her face in his broad shoulder. It seemed the most natural thing to do. She sniffled again. The pathetic whimpering sound escaping from her constricted throat sounded like an abandoned puppy.

The lost scholarship was the last straw. All the anguish she'd suppressed over the past three years bubbled up and swamped her.

Bruiser held her to him as she sobbed into his chest, unable to staunch the flood of tears. Her breathing came in staccato gasps of pure sorrow. Nothing had gone right in her life since Will disappeared—except Bruiser. And that hadn't lasted. Sure, he was here now, but only because he was one of the good guys, and he wouldn't desert a blubbering woman.

When she lifted her head, he dabbed gently at her tear-stained cheeks with a napkin. Despite his gentle smile, his eyes shone with fierce determination, as if he'd slay dragons for her—or even the Pittsburgh Steelers defensive line. It'd been so long since anyone worried about her well-being that she almost lost it again. A wet splotch on his shirt gave evidence to the extent of her tears.

"What am I going to do?" Her voice sounded weak and plaintive. God, she hated weak women, and she'd become one herself.

"The best you can with the hand you've been dealt, and I'd put my money on you any day." Straightening in the booth, he looped his arm loosely around her shoulders, his hip pressed against hers. She laid her head on his shoulder.

"Thank you." Along with the gratitude, desire wrapped its tentacles around her rib cage. Her body signaled its interest, and her brain, as usual where Bruiser was concerned, took a vacation.

"I'm truly sorry, Mac. Especially for my part in this."

"Your part? You had a part?" What did he mean? She twisted around and placed her hands on his shoulders and searched his face.

"Yeah, when Veronica suspected that you and I had something going, and she didn't like it one bit. I think your association with me hurt you more than helped you."

Mac sighed. "Is that why you broke it off?" If there might be a ray of hope in this crappy dark cloud hanging over her, it would be that Bruiser didn't really want to end their affair, but that he'd done it for her.

"Yeah, that was part of it, along with not liking to talk about my brother." He gave her a lopsided smile. "We were damn good together. You know that?"

"Yes, we are." Mac chewed on her lower lip, then just blurted it out. "Come home with me tonight."

"I was hoping like hell you'd ask." His slow, sexy smile drove home how happy he was.

"Where is this going?"

"Fuck if I know. Let's just go with it."

Mac nodded. Maybe she was crazy, but she was ready to take the journey with Bruiser. After all, some of the best road trips happened when she'd didn't know where she was going until she got there.

Chapter 18

Puzzled

Bruiser pulled his car behind Mac's in the driveway. He had to stop for gas, so she beat him home by about five minutes. The front door was open, and he invited himself inside. Mac stood by the kitchen counter staring at an envelope in her hand. As Bruiser came up behind her, he caught the Lumberjacks' return address on the letter.

Oh, crap.

Mac's hand trembled, and Bruiser squeezed her shoulder to steady her. She stared at the envelope long and hard.

"Are you going to open it?" He sent up a silent plea that Vince, the jerk bastard, didn't know a damn thing.

Mac ripped the flap off the envelope and read the letter. By the crestfallen look on her face, no such luck. The letter fluttered from her fingers to the floor.

Bruiser held her to him. "I'm sorry."

Mac sniffed again and leaned against his chest. Bruiser kissed her hair, inhaling the intoxicatingly fresh scent of her. Pure Mac, forever engrained in his mind.

"This is just not my day." She tried to laugh, but failed. Together they stood in silence staring out across the backyard, both lost in private thoughts.

Finally, Mac turned to face him. She wrapped her arms around his neck. Despite the remnants of tears on her cheeks, she managed a smile just for him, one that snuggled close to his heart and made him feel special, not for the superficial reasons everyone saw, but for the person inside.

He pulled her close, holding her tight against him and lost his heart and soul gazing into those deep coffee-brown eyes of hers. She felt right, a rightness that went beyond mere lust and, despite some of the more obvious differences, fit him better than a custom-made tuxedo or an old pair of favorite faded blue jeans.

Picking her up, he carried her outside to the back patio. He figured bed could wait. She'd feel better out in the yard she took such good care of, with the crickets chirping and frogs croaking and the sound of a breeze rustling bows of cedar trees.

Mac didn't question his intent, just clung to him, trusting him.

He wanted to be that man for her, the one who stood beside her through all the good and bad things life threw at them, the one who fought tooth and nail for her, the one who gave her everything and got more from the giving than the receiving.

But he couldn't give her everything. He couldn't solve her brother's mystery any more than he could change Elliot's situation. Maybe for a while tonight they could both pretend he could be that guy who could make everything okay—even if it was an illusion.

He laid Mac on the chaise lounge with the overstuffed cushion covered in bright Hawaiian flowers. Glancing around the dark patio and out at the tall fence he doubted anyone would be able to see them. At this point he didn't really give a shit anyway. He just wanted Mac to fill the piece of him that went missing whenever she wasn't around and to be her missing piece in turn.

The only way he knew how to do that was with his body because his glib tongue deserted him when the stakes were too high. Words weren't adequate, words he couldn't say or even think.

So he turned off his mind and gave in to his heart.

* * * * *

Mac gazed up at Bruiser standing over her, looking like a lost little boy carrying the weight of the world on his shoulders. She knew the extent of that weight after conversations with Shanna and Brett, but she wasn't going to say anything. More than anything she wanted him to trust her enough to reveal his secrets himself.

He'd given her comfort tonight, and she'd do her best to reciprocate. "Let me take the lead this time." Mac stood and pointed to the lounge chair.

Bruiser didn't argue. He stripped off his clothes, rolled on a condom, and lay on the chaise lounge, his tanned, ripped body visible in the moonlight. Damn, he was a fine specimen, from those blue-gray eyes, the muscles rippling in broad shoulders, down to his flat, ridged stomach and strong thighs. The man even had sexy feet.

Mac tugged her T-shirt over her head and her bra followed. She shimmied out of her jeans and underwear. Straddling the narrow lounge chair, she lowered herself onto him, sitting back on her haunches and resting her ass on his stomach. His erect penis pressed against one butt cheek. Mac groaned as his muscular chest pressed against her breasts, her nipples hyper-sensitized. She arched her back, pressing her crotch into his, but not letting him penetrate, not yet. Tonight wasn't about wild animal lust, tonight was something gentle and fragile like a rare and delicate orchid blooming for the first time.

She leaned down, planting her palms on his chest, and gently kissed each corner of his mouth, inhaling his minty breath, and reveling in the controlled power underneath her thighs. She sucked on his lower lip and slipped her tongue inside his mouth, slow and easy, taking her time, tasting, exploring, cherishing.

He held still, his hands resting on her hips, his eyes closed. His tongue mated with hers, but nothing else on him moved but for the not-so steady rise and fall of his chest under her palms and his wildly beating heart. The deeper the kiss, the more sanity escaped her, but sanity was highly overrated anyway.

Mac raised her head and studied his strong features. His incredibly long lashes feathered across his cheekbones. His eyes opened, deceptively lazy, yet alert.

"Make love to me, Mac," he whispered as the words flitted off in the breeze, carried on an angel's wings like a promise given and a promise received.

Mac raised her hips and lowered herself back down on his waiting cock. Bruiser watched with hooded eyes. She sheathed him inside her, deeper and deeper until her crotch pressed against his. Hands braced on his shoulders, she threw back her head and closed her eyes, savoring the fullness of him, the hardness held inside her wet softness. She changed the angle of his hips to feel him higher inside her and wiggled on top of him, only to draw a guttural groan from the man.

He gripped her hips and raised her up, slowing lowering her back down, continuing the erotic, slow torture until their last shreds of sanity were obliterated by one final deep eternal thrust which bound them together in ways neither could imagine or prevent.

Bruiser's body convulsed with hers as their releases came in pulses of pleasure, wringing every last bit of energy from them until she collapsed against him, body to body, soul to soul, heart to heart.

Bruiser filled in all her missing puzzle pieces, those empty spots waiting for the right person to come along and complete the beautiful picture hidden in all the bits of joy and tragedy that make up a life.

Now that she'd found those missing pieces, Mac didn't want to give them up.

Chapter 19

Back and Forth

Elliot glanced up at Mac and Bruiser. They'd rescued him for the evening from the "Hippos"—his secret name for his aunt and uncle. He didn't really care that they were both grossly overweight, but he did care that they were hypocrites, parading him out when guests came over to illustrate what good people they were to take in this hideously scarred orphan.

That's what he heard them call him when they thought he'd gone to bed.

Bruiser told him that appearances didn't matter to good people, so Elliot figured that ruled out the Hippos as good people. Aunt Ruth couldn't even look at him. When she talked to him, she stared at the floor or over his head.

Mac and Bruiser looked at him with love, not horror or pity. They also really *looked* at each other, thinking he probably wouldn't notice. They'd been giving each other looks all night long. Obviously, they were hot for each other, not that he had much personal experience with stuff like that.

Before the crash he'd preferred books and gaming to girls. Now girls screamed and ran away when they saw him, and his burned fingers made it hard to play video games.

After dinner, they played Monopoly. He hadn't played it since his parents were gone. It was tough at first, but Mac and Bruiser made it fun. Elliot bought Boardwalk and Park Place and filled them with hotels. Mac landed on Park Place, and Bruiser landed on

Broadway. It was all over after that. Moneybags Elliot, as they called him, kicked their butts. He was still gloating about that.

The clock ticked closer to nine o'clock, when he had to return to his aunt and uncle's house. His stomach cramped up. Really bad. He must have eaten some rotten pizza or something. Maybe they'd let him stay here if he didn't feel like a car ride.

Elliot hated his cousins' pitying stares, his uncle's indifference, and his aunt's open dislike of him. As far as he could tell, the only reason they had him around was to be their errand boy.

Get me this, Elliot. Get me that, Elliot. Feed the cat, Elliot. Put the dishes in the dishwasher. Elliot, don't go outside and play, you scare the neighbors' little girls.

Bruiser stood up and smiled one of those fake smiles, and Elliot's stomach went into convulsions, or at least it felt like that. "Hey, buddy, it's time to get you back home."

"Can't I stay here?" Elliot hated begging, but he did it anyway.

"Sorry, buddy, we have to get you back just like we promised." Bruiser didn't want to take him back. Elliot could tell. So why did he have to do it? Bruiser could do anything. He was like a superhero. Why couldn't he do this if he wanted to?

Because he doesn't want to?

Elliot lashed out. "I hate it there. They don't want me, and I don't want them. Besides, I don't feel good." Elliot held his stomach and rocked back and forth on the couch, wailing and moaning like he'd seen the kid do on *Two and Half Men* reruns.

A quick look passed between Mac and Bruiser, but Elliot couldn't figure out what the heck they were trying to tell each other without speaking the words. Maybe he'd overdone the stomachache because they didn't seem to be overly concerned, and they were usually the concerned type. Maybe too much moaning and wailing. It'd worked on TV.

"We'll do something after the game on Sunday. Mac's going to pick you up. You can watch in the suite with her."

"That's five days away." He didn't like football much, but he liked being with Mac and Bruiser and all of Bruiser's teammates, especially Tyler. Tyler slipped him really awesome gourmet chocolates when no one was watching.

"Yeah, I know. But hang in there. The time will pass faster than you can imagine."

Elliot thought that was a whole lot of bull. After all, Bruiser didn't live in the Hippo house with kids who called him Baby Frankenstein.

"Maybe I could just stay over tonight."

"Elliot, you have to go home." Bruiser's voice got stern, like he was starting to lose patience, not that he ever did with Elliot, but Bruiser liked to make it sound like that.

"That's not my home. I don't have a home anymore." A lump clogged his throat at the memory of the old two-story home with the big front porch that his mother and father had lovingly restored until it was a showplace. He bit back a sob because he didn't want them to see him behaving like a pussy. He'd already been a whiner.

"Why can't I live here? Don't you want me?"

"Elliot, it's not that easy. They're your relatives."

"You can do anything. And you promised you'd—" Elliot stopped when he saw the mad look on Bruiser's face. If he gave them too much grief, they'd go away, like everyone else he'd ever loved, and he'd be left with nothing. He glanced at Mac, who'd been pretty quiet. She smiled at him like she liked him and was sorry they had to take him home.

Elliot heaved a dramatic sigh—another tactic he'd learned on *Two and a Half Men*. "Okay." He gathered up his stuff and steeled himself for the end of the evening and his return to the Hippos' wallow. His mother had been neat and tidy, but this dump he lived in now had crap everywhere, and it stunk. His uncle gave him weird looks that scared Elliot, even though he wasn't sure why.

He really hated it, and he knew he'd have to do something about it because he couldn't keep living there.

* * * * *

Bruiser sat in the car and stared at the door as Elliot disappeared into the house. He shook his head in frustration, hating this helpless feeling. He kept his face turned toward the driver's-side window so Mac wouldn't see how much Elliot's return home affected him.

He'd spent almost every night with Mac for the past few weeks. Neither of them had actually addressed what their relationship was or wasn't. Other than sleeping together, he been buried with training camp and games, while she worked late hours and continued her brother search.

"That was tough," Mac said.

"Tell me about it. It's getting tougher every time." Bruiser put the car in gear and pulled away from the curb. "I hate leaving him here. It's gotta suck being with people who don't want you around and treat you like you're less than human."

Bruiser had to do something. Elliot considered him his hero, and what kind of hero had he turned out to be? The kid needed him, and now the chance to make some of his past wrongs right was dumped in his lap. He didn't save Brice, but he could pay it forward and save Elliot. Somehow.

"Yeah, I wish there was something we could do." Mac sounded sincere and Bruiser jumped on it before he wussed out, a little drunk with emotion, rather than common sense.

"Do you? Really?"

Something in Bruiser's tone had Mac looking wary. "Uh, yeah, I think so."

Marry her, idiot. It'd work well for all of you. You'd pay for Mac's school. She'd be there for Elliot. And you'd have a ready-made family.

Problem was, he'd never wanted a family of any kind. He didn't spend time with the one he had; why get a new, needier, one? *Because you're lonely and something's missing and it might well be them.*

Marriage had been a crazy-assed idea when his moronic teammates brought it up, yet an engagement to a nice girl—not some model or movie star—might convince Aunt Ruth to give him the guardianship, in trade for a generous amount of money, of course. Bruiser knew her type. In fact, he pretended to be her type, the type that did everything for appearance's sake. Ruth Jones wanted to look like a pillar of her church by taking in this poor, disfigured orphan. Bruiser just wanted to repay a debt and do the right thing for Elliot.

Steeling himself for Mac's reaction, he jumped in with both of his big feet. "Elliot wants me to become his legal guardian. I told him I'd try."

Mac started to laugh as if she thought he had to be joking, which he found somewhat insulting. She sobered quickly at the look on his face. "You think you can manage an eleven-year-old by yourself?"

"Not necessarily by myself."

Mac regarded him warily, as if he'd just told her he had a bomb in hidden in the car.

Bruiser stared straight ahead, driving the speed limit for once. "The Joneses don't want Elliot, but they have an image to maintain with John's church. Ruth can look like a self-sacrificing hero if she allows Elliot to live with the right couple, a couple with the means to take care of Elliot and his physical issues."

"Who is this couple?"

Bruiser took a deep breath and slowly let it out. "The guys think you and I should raise him."

Mac's head snapped in his direction. "What?"

Bruiser needed both hands and all his attention on this subject so he glided into an empty bank parking lot and shut off the engine. He turned to Mac and took her hands in his.

"I know it sounds insane, but they think together we'd do a fine job of raising Elliot."

"Define 'together.'" Mac tried to pull her hands from his, but he wasn't about to let go.

Moment of truth time. "You know—*together* together."

"Like ring on my finger together?" Mac seemed to be having a hard time wrapping her head around the concept.

"Uh, yeah, like married."

"Are you drunk? Should you be driving?"

"I am *not* drunk."

"Then you've lost your mind. You and me? Married?"

Bruiser found that somewhat hurtful. He wouldn't be *that* bad of a husband. "Well, yeah. I mean we're good friends, we like to do the same things and I think we're compatible, especially in bed."

"But marriage?" Mac shook her head in total denial. "Have those idiots been sniffing too many cleaning products or gone off their meds or something?"

"I know it sounds like the stupidest idea in the world, but—" Did it ever. Bruiser couldn't believe he'd even proposed it, yet once he had, he charged for the end zone, ignoring every linebacker in his way.

"It doesn't just sound like it, it is the stupidest." Mac shook her head and yanked her hands from his, hugging herself like she always did when she was feeling vulnerable and upset. Vulnerable was good. He could work with that, play on it, because this "stupid" idea was gaining traction in his mind.

"Think about it, Mac. We could be good together, and we'd be helping a kid out who really needs our help."

"You're not serious about this, are you? Bruiser, I would do almost anything to help Elliot, but not that. You and I have different priorities. Right now, mine is finding my brother so my family can have some closure and so my dad doesn't end up in a mental hospital. Even if it weren't, I wouldn't marry you."

"Why not?"

"Because I don't know who you are and neither do you."

"What's that supposed to mean?"

Mac grew quiet and started fidgeting. Bruiser narrowed his eyes and stared hard at her. "What are you trying to say?" he pushed her, not letting her off the hook.

She looked him straight in the eyes with that determined expression that meant trouble. "Your sister told me about Brice."

Anger welled up inside Bruiser. For a minute he couldn't speak. "Shanna should learn to keep her mouth shut." Now that fucking pissed him off. His sister had no right.

Mac blinked and stared at him as if he'd gone even more insane than when he proposed marriage. "I'm glad she did. I understand you more now."

"I don't need you to understand me or try to psychoanalyze me."

"Bruiser, why are you living someone else's life? Why are you being someone you aren't?"

Bruiser gripped the steering wheel, more furious than he probably had a right to be. "Because I should've been the one who died, dammit!"

"That's like me saying I should've been the one who disappeared."

"You don't know." He looked up at her, his world caving in on him. All those carefully constructed walls to keep out the demons started to crumble.

"What don't I know, Bruiser?" She grabbed his hand and held it tightly.

"I gave him those matches and cigarettes." Saying the words strangled him. He couldn't bear seeing the sympathy on Mac's face because all he felt was self-loathing.

"You were a kid. Stuff happens. It's unfortunate, but you can't live your life for someone else." She squeezed his hand, and he took some strength from her touch.

"Have you looked in a mirror lately?"

Mac blinked as if unable to process his words. "What?"

"Yeah, you. Chasing after every imagined clue about your brother, allowing your father to dictate your present and future, and giving up your life for someone who most likely will never be found. When does it stop?" Bruiser lashed out with this uncontrollable need to make her hurt as much as he did.

Mac stared a hole right through him. Oh, he was a hero all right. A real stand-up guy. Sure he'd managed to deflect her questions about him, but at what price to her?

"If your brother were missing, and you didn't know what happened to him, at what point would you consider it time to give up the search?" Mac glared at him, the challenge in her brown eyes.

Bruiser mulled that over, guessing that she didn't expect an answer but hell-bent on giving her one anyway. An honest one she damn well wouldn't appreciate. "The question is when do you consider it time to get on with your life? To live the life you deserve to live? You didn't ask for this. Why should you be punished for it?"

"Hey, neither did you. We both do what we have to do. How much of your brother's life are you living? Do you even like football?"

Now that was a low blow, one of the lowest. He pulled his hand from hers. "What have you seen out of me that gives you the impression that I'm less than one hundred percent dedicated to the game?"

"Nothing, and I won't because you're that type of person. Whatever you do—love it or hate it—you do it with everything you have, which is why you proposed this crazy idea of marriage in the first place."

"You're right. It is crazy, and I'm sorry I even brought it up." Bruiser pulled out of the parking lot. They drove in silence to Mac's house. He dropped her off and sped away without saying goodbye.

And he felt like a shit for it.

Because part of him knew she was right.

* * * * *

As much as Mac hated weakness and women who cried over every little problem in their lives, she'd been doing a lot of that herself lately. As she stood on her porch and watched Bruiser fishtail down the street, a huge sob shook her body and tears streamed down her face. She pounded her fists against the siding of her house in frustration.

Damn him.

What kind of a screwy proposal had that been, or even worse, had it been one at all? And how pathetic was it that "yes" sat on the tip of her tongue? The urge to do something so completely stupid, reckless, and for herself almost overwhelmed her good sense.

Yet how did this constitute something for herself? In reality it benefitted Bruiser and Elliot, not her.

She'd live in constant fear that the pretty boy would get tired of her and find more attractive ground. She might be able to survive with never having anything but a cursory piece of him as long as they stayed together, but she couldn't live with loving him and losing him. For her it had to be a marriage of love. For him it would be a minor inconvenience toward getting what he wanted, including a built-in babysitter.

Maybe he could grow to love her, a small voice inside her nagged. Yeah, just like I-5 wouldn't be backed up in downtown Seattle on game day.

Mac wiped viciously at the tears running down her cheeks and started to go inside when she heard a noise. Voices were murmuring on the other side of the fence over the unmistakable sound of dirt being shoveled into a wheelbarrow. Mac snuck to the spot in her fence where her father spied on his former daughter-in-law and peeked through the knothole.

They were digging something up, all right. She pressed her face up against the hole and couldn't make out much in the darkness, but thanks to a breeze blowing the sound her direction, she could make out their words.

"We should stop now. She's home." Definitely Sonja's voice.

"She went in the house," Ben said.

"Are you sure? That bitch and her dad are devious."

Ben snorted. "The old man isn't here, and the daughter isn't nearly as nuts as the father."

The shovel clanked against metal. Mac held her breath. The two knelt down and dug at the earth with their hands until Ben pried something free. It wasn't a body. It was a metal box about the size of a safe deposit box.

All of a sudden a hand clamped over her mouth, and she tried to scream but the person held on even tighter as she struggled to free herself.

"Shhh. Mac, it's me." A low voice whispered in her ear.

Bruiser?

"What are you doing here?" she hissed when he took his hand away.

"I came back to apologize for being an idiot." He breathed the words. "What's going on?"

Mac stepped away and let Bruiser peek through the hole, while she moved down further to another gap in the fence, only she tripped over her cat who'd been doing his own lurking in the darkness. She stumbled into the garbage can which slammed to the ground with a loud bang. Bruiser gestured to her to not move and mouthed, "Are you okay?"

Mac nodded. Under a small gap at the bottom of the fence, she could see Sonja and Ben.

Ben pulled out a pistol and pointed it in their direction. All Mac could hear was the beating of her heart. "Is that you, Craig? You chickenshit asshole?"

Bruiser held a finger up to his lips. Mac nodded.

Ben and Sonja froze in place, listening. Without speaking another word, the two scurried into Will's house like rats after cheese. Too bad Mac couldn't find a way to bait the perfect mousetrap.

Bruiser gestured to her to go into the house. Once inside, he turned to her. "What was that all about?"

"I don't know. They dug up a metal box. And Ben had a gun."

"Yeah, I saw. I'd tell the detective on your brother's case, but don't tell your dad. He'd go busting over there and get himself either shot or arrested."

Mac nodded, her eyes filling with tears. Her father wouldn't stop until he found out what was in that box. Heck, maybe it wasn't even related to Will. Though she didn't believe that. Most likely it was. The only reason a person would hide a metal box in their garden would be if it contained something sinister or secretive or both.

Bruiser cupped Mac's tear-stained face in his hands. "I'm sorry, baby. Really, I'm sorry."

Mac sniffed and looked up at him. "So am I."

"Hell, I didn't even make it a few blocks down the street before I turned around and came back."

"I didn't hear you drive up."

"That's because I parked down the street. I wasn't sure if I was going to knock or not, so I pulled over and thought about it. Then I decided to walk to your house to see if the lights were on."

Mac had to giggle. "And you call my dad a stalker."

Bruiser's face actually turned red. "I can't explain it, but something called me back. I just knew I couldn't leave yet. I was worried about you. You shouldn't be spying on those people. Desperate people are dangerous."

"What makes you think they're desperate? They've been able to keep this secret for over three years."

"Their actions had desperation written all over them. Something's changed and they're covering tracks."

"You really think so?"

"Fuck, yes. That guy drew a gun. You and your dad need to stop playing amateur detectives before you get into something you can't get out of."

Mac started to sob. Bruiser pulled her into his arms and held her, stroking her back. His tender touch had her losing all control, and once again she blubbered in his arms, grateful he'd come back even though she knew he'd leave, if not sooner, then later.

* * * * *

Bruiser spent the next few nights at Mac's, even though he grew more irritated by the hour. Her father stayed late, and Mac didn't make him leave. Craig showed no concern over the possible danger he created for his daughter by his constant spying on the neighbors. Oblivious to Mac's discomfort, the man constantly badgered Bruiser to get the truth out of Trudy.

Sonja and Ben made Bruiser nervous. Their strange behavior only compounded his suspicions. Craig didn't help the situation, and Bruiser was within a thread of ripping Mac's dad a new one.

On Saturday evening, Bruiser showed up to find Craig pacing the living room and Mac packing a small suitcase. "Where are you going?"

"Dad needs me to go with him. I guess one of Ben's employees called Dad. Ben and Sonja have been at one of Ben's remote job sites late at night the last couple days."

Bruiser scowled and shot Craig an accusing glare. Craig looked away, refusing to meet his gaze. "You can't go. It's too dangerous."

"Since when do you tell me what to do?"

Bruiser set his jaw, ready for battle. "Since you aren't smart enough to figure out what to do yourself, and your father certainly doesn't have your best interests at heart."

"Don't you criticize my father."

"Your father is behaving irresponsibly because he's obsessed. Do you even know this employee of Ben's? Can you trust him?

What if it's some kind of setup?" He towered over her, using the difference in their height to his advantage.

Mac pushed past him into her bathroom, tossing various stuff into her suitcase. "My father needs closure. I'll see to it that he gets it."

Bruiser stalked after her. "What about Elliot? You were taking him to the game tomorrow."

"I'm sorry. Tell him I can't." She sounded like she was going to cry.

"You tell him." Bruiser didn't cut her any slack. He was pissed.

"I don't have time." Mac shoved her toothpaste and toothbrush along with some other girlie stuff into a plastic bag.

"So that's it?"

"That's it."

"I was thinking we might actually have something, not just an occasional lay. But you won't even give us a chance."

"Keep your voice down. My dad can hear." Mac shushed him like he was a recalcitrant child, which didn't sit well with him.

"Like he'd notice if it doesn't involve Will."

She rounded on him, her eyes blazing. "That was out of line, mister."

Bruiser snorted and crossed his arms over his chest, leaning on the doorframe. "Let the police handle this. You're both in over your heads."

Mac stabbed a finger in the direction of the door. "Get out. Now."

Bruiser locked his jaw and glared at her. He'd fucking had enough. One ghost in his life was one too many. He couldn't handle two. "I won't be back, not unless your priorities shift."

"I'm not shifting my priorities. I'm committed to seeing this through with Dad. You're just pretending we have more than sex because you want something from me; you want Elliot."

"You think that's all this is? Do you think I'm too shallow to have deep feelings?" Her accusations hurt more than he'd ever imagined, yet he'd been accused of being shallow all his life, why should it bother him now?

"I think you're too selfish to see how important this is to me." Mac fisted her hands and stood up straight, looking taller and a bit like an enraged mama bear when someone was messing with her cubs.

"I'm selfish?" Bruiser laughed, a hollow sound that echoed off the walls of the room. "Take a look around you; then let's talk about selfish. Maybe it's easier to live your life in limbo. You never take risks. Hell, you never have to take a chance on anyone but yourself, and you can always come up with a bullshit reason why you aren't available emotionally and physically."

"Finding my brother is not bullshit." Mac's voice raised a few decibels short of shrieking.

"It is if you devote your entire life to it and have nothing left to show for it but regrets. What if you never find him? That's highly possible. How long do you plan on doing this? Another year? Another five years? Another ten years? Another twenty years?"

"However long it takes." Mac walked to the door, holding it open for him.

"Then I guess we have nothing more to say to each other."

"I guess not." He heard a note of regret in her voice, as if someone had let the air out of her anger.

Bruiser walked to the door and paused. "Be careful."

"I will. Good luck at your game." She refused to meet his gaze.

"Thanks."

Bruiser walked to his car. This time he wouldn't be coming back in a few minutes to apologize. He was done.

They'd sung their last song together and there wouldn't be an encore.

Chapter 20

Stopping the Play

Bruiser glanced at the game clock: 6:32 left in the game. 21-14, Jacks ahead and in possession of the ball. He lined up in the backfield and sprinted past Harris toward the sideline. Harris faked a handoff, then tossed the ball on a slant route for a ten-yard gain. Seven plays later, Bruiser took the handoff from Harris, kept his legs churning, and powered five yards into the end zone, taking a couple defenders with him. The rowdy crowd in the stadium went wild. Bruiser grinned, over the hundred-yard mark for the game. Damn good way to start the new season. Helluva lot better than last year. But then last year the team hadn't been running on all cylinders.

Bruiser jogged off the field, pausing long enough to salute the skybox where Elliot sat with Rachel, Kelsie, and Lavender. He sank down on the bench, chest heaving, lungs screaming for oxygen. It was a fucking hot day, and he downed a couple cups of Gatorade, not giving a shit that the sticky liquid ran down his face.

Brett slid next to him on the bench and elbowed him in the side. "Good job."

"Yeah, thanks." Bruiser couldn't stop grinning. Damn, he loved this game.

"Is Mac up there?"

"Uh, no, Elliot is." What a way to deflate his good mood. Mac's absence weighed heavily on him. He'd hoped she'd have a change of heart and show up to surprise him, but she hadn't. He'd put her cute face and sexy little body out of his mind on the field, but elsewhere, he just wasn't that strong. As soon as he jogged off the field, thoughts of her flooded his brain, which pissed him off—a little. Women did not affect him like this. But Mac did.

Brett studied him for a moment, nodded, and joined Harris and the coach huddled over a clipboard while poring over the next set of offensive plays. Bruiser rubbed his face with a towel and guzzled another cup of Gatorade.

On the next play, Murphy nailed San Diego's running back for a loss. The veteran linebacker fell on the fumbled ball. Bruiser leapt to his feet, yelling along with the sold-out crowd. Game over. The Jacks won it, 28-14.

Absolutely damn good way to start a season.

Except for this business with Mac.

Bruiser jogged down the tunnel to the locker room, accepting his teammates' praise with a nod or a high five. A bevy of reporters converged on him as soon as entered the locker room. They loved his interviews. Bruiser fielded their questions with his usual charm, even as he engaged in a fantasy of shoving their microphones down their throats. That in itself gave him pause. In the past, he'd basked in the attention, yet today it irritated him, just like the modeling gigs had lost their luster, too.

They asked the same damn questions over and over, stupid questions, not the questions he'd ask if he'd been in their shoes, and not the questions that he would assume the average viewer would want answered.

Bruiser glanced over their heads to Harris, surrounded by a similar group. The guy soaked up the attention like a sponge, grinning and giving the reporters the amusing, blunt responses they'd come to expect from him. Bruiser used to rival Harris in the quick comebacks department. Not today. His answers sounded stilted and disinterested, especially to his own ears, and even a little impatient.

"Bruiser!" One of the most annoying local reporters shouted at him and brought him back to the present.

"Uh, sorry. What was the question?"

"How did you feel about the fourth and one play where you were dropped for a loss?"

That tight rubber band of control inside Bruiser snapped. "How the fuck did you think I felt? Happy? Pleased? You fucking idiot. The team trusted me to get a first down, and I missed the hole. And you're asking me how I felt? I felt fucking pissed." Bruiser snapped a towel in the direction of the reporters, and they quickly backed up.

"I'm done answering questions. Get these fucking things out of my face." The words spewed from his mouth like an evangelist preaching hellfire and brimstone. Instead of carefully measuring his responses and always being the perfect interviewee, he'd shocked them all by saying what he thought for once.

The reporters scurried away. The news stories wouldn't be singing his praises for his hundred-yard day but instead chastising him for losing his temper. They'd blow it all out of proportion and rumors would fly. He'd either be on drugs, ready to quit the game, or having a fight with his girlfriend.

Bruiser froze. Well, shit, maybe he was having a fight with his girlfriend.

He escaped to the privacy of the showers. So far the assholes didn't follow the team into the showers, though he expected that day would come. He stood under the warm water, waiting for it to wash away his frustration and anger. But it didn't. When he finally returned to the locker room only a few of the guys lingered, one of whom was Harris, and his laser-blue eyes were trained on Bruiser like a stinger missile honing in on its target. Bruiser buried his head in his locker.

"A little testy for a guy who's predicted to have a record-breaking season." Harris said in his ear.

"Yeah," Bruiser stood and toweled off his wet hair.

"It's not like you to lose it with those assholes. Something pissing you off?"

"Just them."

Harris studied him with eyes that made rookies pee their pants and veterans take a step back. "Bullshit. You've been on edge all day. Not your businesslike self."

"I got the job done, didn't I?" Bruiser snapped.

Harris blinked a few times, almost smiled. "Yeah. Can't complain."

"Damn straight."

Harris's eyes grew bigger and a sly smiled crawled across his face. "It's Mac."

"How would you know?"

"Because the only person who can tie me in the knots like that is Lavender. It's always a woman. But not just any woman. *The* woman."

"I've got a lot of stuff on my mind."

"Take my advice. Make it easy on yourself and her. Admit defeat, quit making excuses, and go after her."

"Spoken like a man who's been there."

"Definitely a man who's been there." Harris grinned, pulled his shirt on and buttoned it, and slapped Bruiser on the back. "Good game."

The quarterback sauntered from the locker room, looking every inch like a man in control of his destiny. Yet he'd admitted defeat and given in to a woman. Only Bruiser's problem wasn't like that.

This wasn't a battle of wills with Mac. This was a matter of her misplaced priorities and strong guilt overriding her life. And

Bruiser knew all about those two things, which made them kindred spirits and an impossible match.

* * * * *

The Jacks won their first game, and Mac missed it. And for what? Another wild goose chase that came to nothing. Ben's former employee admitted he'd just been trying to cause trouble for Ben. Mac wasted a weekend on another dead-end lead. Now she was back at work and glad to be away from her father's scheming and obsessing for at least a day.

She put away the gardening tools in the storage shed. She glanced up as Jed approached. His guarded, businesslike expression scared the crap out of her.

"Mac, I need to see you in my office when you're finished here." Jed refused to look her in the eye.

"If this is about the scholarship, I already know."

"It's not." Jed walked away.

"Okay, I'll be right there." Mac's internal emergency broadcast system slammed into full disaster mode. Running to the bathroom, she washed her hands, splashed water on her face, and walked to the gallows of her boss's office filled with more dread than a free agent with a poor training camp performance. Call it a sixth sense; she knew the news wasn't good, not even close. Mac ran through the scenarios in her mind. Finally, she bit the bullet and knocked on Jed's door in the maintenance area.

"Come in," he called.

Mac entered the room and sat in the folding chair next to Jed's messy desk. One pile of paper leaned precariously, just waiting for the air conditioner to kick on and send it fluttering across the room like birds scattering when a hungry tomcat shows up.

"So what's up?" Mac clutched her hands in her lap and faked a casual smile.

Jed didn't smile. In fact, he squirmed like a man about to deliver some very distasteful news, and Mac was the recipient.

"Jed?" Her smile stuck on her face, almost painfully.

"Mac, this is hard for me." God, he still wouldn't look her in the eye.

"Then just do it." Mac ground her teeth together and waited for the worst.

"We have to cut a full-time person."

She dug her fingernails into her hands. "No," she whispered.

"You're our newest hire."

"But I need this job. I really like working here. It's my dream job."

"Mac, don't make this any harder than it is." He shuffled some papers on the desk, looked at them as if he were reading them. Mac suspected he didn't see them at all.

"You think it's hard on you? I have bills to pay."

"Mac, calm down. You'll get unemployment, of course." Finally, the coward glanced up, regret and sadness etched into every line on his craggy face. This wasn't much easier for him.

"But you guys need me. I take care of the gardens in front of the building. I make sure the inside plants are healthy. Remember the philodendron? It almost died until I came along and nursed it back to health."

Jed pursed his lips and said nothing.

"Jed, tell me the truth."

"Well, we're hiring some temp staff, interns from the college." He tried to smile. "I'm so sorry, Mac."

Mac forced another smile when all she wanted to do was cry—which had become way too much of a habit lately. "It's okay, Jed. I'll be fine."

He stood, dismissing her. "Are you sure?"

"I'm certain." Mac bolted out the door before he saw how fine she wasn't. Avoiding a group of players jaw-jacking at the end of the hall, she took a detour, and ran like hell for her car.

Once inside the metal sanctuary, she gripped the steering wheel and stared straight ahead, gulping in deep breaths of air and fighting back the panic. She couldn't pay her bills on unemployment. She'd lose her house. Her father would expect her to do detective work twenty-four seven. She'd probably be able to get a job on a landscaping crew, but most of those jobs ended in the fall, and fall would be here in another month.

Mac drove home, fighting back the lump in her throat every step of the way.

She was so screwed. And worst of all, she didn't even have Bruiser's broad shoulder to cry on.

*****

Bruiser was just about to leave Jacks' HQ when Brett waved him down. He rolled down his window. "Miss me already? We just spent the last several hours together."

"Fuck you." Brett glanced behind him then leaned in the window. "I just heard that Mac got laid off."

"What? Why would they do that? She works her ass off for this place." Anger and guilt spread through Bruiser like a wildfire in a dry grass field. This had to do with him. He knew it did.

"Uh, can we say Veronica?"

"Well, shit." When Bruiser got his hands on that woman, he'd have more than a few words with her.

Brett straightened. "Exactly. Well, I thought you'd want to know."

"Yeah, thanks." Shaking his head, Bruiser rubbed his chest with one hand, the other rested on the steering wheel. The tightness in his chest gripped him harder.

As Brett nodded and backed away, Bruiser peeled out, leaving his friend eating his dust. This was partially his fault, and he knew it, making Mac one more person in his life he'd let down. Determination squeezed out the guilt because guilt did no one any good at this point. One way or another, he was going to fix this and keep his promise to Elliot. He would not disappoint the two most important people in his life.

Most important? Elliot, yes, he could honestly say that. But Mac? He sucked in a quick breath and shook his head, but denial wasn't working so well for him right now.

Bruiser took the exit to Mac's house. He might not be welcome, but hell, he'd do it anyway. Her father certainly didn't pay attention to his daughter, and she'd need a friend right about now. He ignored the small fact that they were through, he told her he'd never come back, and that he was a major wuss where she was concerned.

Craig's truck sat in her driveway, but he didn't see Mac's F-150. Bruiser jogged up to the front door and knocked. Her father came to the door, binoculars in one hand and looking worse than ever.

"Is Mac here?"

"I haven't seen her. I've been here all day."

"Have you talked to her?" Bruiser couldn't keep the annoyance out of his voice. This guy needed to be her father for once.

"No, not since last night."

"She lost her job today. I'm trying to find her."

"Damn, what happened?" To his credit, Craig put down the binoculars and actually pulled off a concerned-father expression. Whether it was genuine or not, Bruiser didn't have a fucking clue.

"Layoffs. They're cutting back on permanent staff and hiring college interns for half the price."

Craig rubbed his hands over his face and sighed. He dropped into a chair and gazed up at Bruiser, his eyes bloodshot. The sadness etched into his face made him look much older than his years. "I hope I didn't cause this."

Time to have a come-to-Jesus meeting with Mr. Hernandez. "I'm sure it didn't help with you calling her at work, expecting her to leave at a moment's notice to chase after some red herring."

"I need her help."

"You need to let her have a life." Bruiser crossed his arms over his chest and glared at Mac's father, not cutting the man any slack.

"I have to find out what happened to Will."

Bruiser glanced out the window, across the lawn to the neighbors' house. "And if you never do, how long will you keep this up?"

Craig frowned and stared at his hands clasped around the binoculars. "I don't know."

"Look, Craig, I understand how it feels to lose someone you love. In your case, it's even worse because you don't know what happened, but at some point Mac has a right to a life, rather than dedicating it to chasing every rumor and using every spare minute looking for a ghost. What about college? What about a family? Would Will have wanted her to give up everything for him?"

"No," Craig said so quietly that Bruiser barely heard him. "I just don't think I can do it alone." The man's voice cracked, and Bruiser's irritation subsided. He wished like hell he could heal this poor man's life and Mac's. Only he couldn't.

Unless—

Trudy.

Bruiser shoved those thoughts to the back of his mind.

"Is that fair to her? You're using guilt to manipulate her into helping you."

Craig shrugged. "I guess I have been."

"If you want to dedicate your life to the search, that's up to you, but you shouldn't expect Mac to do it. Hell, be a father for once and think about your daughter's well-being instead of fixating on a son who is no longer here. Do what's best for Mac."

Craig said nothing. His shoulders sagged, his entire body that of a broken man.

"Do you have any idea where Mac might have gone?"

"I don't know."

Of course Craig wouldn't know. He didn't know anything about Mac because he hadn't paid any attention to her these past three years. "Well, thanks. I'll find her."

"If you do, would you have her call me?"

"Yeah, I will." Bruiser glanced back out the window again. "Why don't you go home and get something to eat? You're not going to see anything they don't want you to see."

Craig shrugged but made no attempt to move.

"And start being the father Mac needs. Get some professional help if you can't do it on your own."

Craig nodded.

Bruiser hoped like hell that Craig considered his words.

* * * * *

Mac stood in front of the nondescript condo in Kirkland near Lake Washington. She'd never been to his place before, which was a little weird considering how long they'd been seeing each other, but he'd never invited her. She expected Bruiser to live in that sleek new high-rise on the water, but it was an older condo, still nice, still with a view, but definitely not high-end. It shouldn't surprise her after what his sister had said.

Why the hell she'd come here, she didn't know.

After driving around endlessly, trying not to think about her bleak future, she'd ended up at Bruiser's condo, a place she'd never been to before but had the address for. But Bruiser wasn't home. She stared at her silent cell phone, which she'd switched off hours ago. She didn't make an attempt to turn it back on, not that anyone would be calling except for her father with news of his latest harebrained scheme.

The She-Wolves would be with their guys. There wasn't anyone else. She had hit rock bottom. She needed Bruiser.

It was getting late and Bruiser still wasn't home. He'd probably hooked up with some beautiful woman Mac could never compete with. Of course she'd given up the right to do so after she'd pretty much set him straight about his ludicrous marriage suggestion. As much as she'd like to help Elliot, she couldn't sell her soul to that particular devil. In exchange for what? A wedding ring? A stable home? A college education? A lifetime in a marriage with a man she adored—most likely loved—but who didn't love her?

She must have dozed off because the next thing she knew she was startled awake by someone rapping on her driver's side window. Bruiser's handsome face was illuminated by the street lamp next to her car.

Mac rolled down the window. "Hi."

"I've been looking all over hell and back for you." His brow was furrowed with worry and his blue eyes shone with concern.

"I was here, waiting for you." She loved that he'd been looking for her. It gave her those warm fuzzies. It gave her hope.

"No shit?" He almost laughed. "Come on, let's go in."

"This was a bad idea. I'd better go home."

"You've been waiting here for me and now you want to go home? How about a cup of coffee?"

A cup of coffee sounded good, but it'd be followed by a half gallon of sex. "I'd better not. It's late and you have practice tomorrow."

Bruiser glanced at his Rolex. "It's only ten. I can spare you an hour."

"Okay." Willpower was overrated anyway.

He took her hand and led her into his roomy condo. Inside the entry was a huge open-plan living, dining, and kitchen area, upgraded with granite countertops and dark cabinets. The ultra-sleek and modern furniture was all beige, with pillows for a splash of color. Even though it wasn't her style, it was actually comfortable. Typical man: a huge flatscreen dominated one wall, while through the huge wall of windows, the waters of Lake Washington glittered in the distance.

Bruiser pulled her into his arms and held her close, stroking her hair. "I heard about your job."

Mac resisted the urge to bury her head in his chest and let go of the pain and fear. Instead, she stiffened in his arms. This was not a good idea. In fact, it was a stupid-assed one to the nth degree.

"I'm glad you came. You know I'll always be here for you." His soft, gentle voice washed over her, relaxing her a little. He stroked her back, his touch gentle yet strong. As if he could be strong for her.

"Yes, I know."

"Everything will be okay, Mac. You'll see."

Easy for him to say. He made more than seven million a year. "I know. I'm tough. I'll get through it." She put her palms on his chest and stepped away. "Coming here was a stupid idea."

Bruiser frowned. "Then why did you come here?"

"I don't know." Oh, God, she was going to cry in front of this man again. He must think she spent half her time crying.

He stood a few feet from her, his hands shoved in his pockets, tapping one foot, as if he couldn't stand not doing something. Bruiser was a fixer, but he couldn't fix this. No one could. Not even her.

"Mac," he took a step forward.

She held out her hands to stop him. "I'd better leave. I'm just prolonging the inevitable."

"What's the *inevitable*?"

"The end—again—of our—uh—affair, whatever you want to call it."

"We don't have to end it."

"I do. For my own good, I need to end it."

"Why? Why can't we stay together?"

"As what?"

"Well, the guys had that one idea."

"To get custody of Elliot, not because you wanted to spend the rest of your life with me." Mac rubbed her hands over her face and squeezed her eyes shut for a moment.

When she opened her eyes Bruiser met her gaze, his jaw tight and his eyes hard. "Maybe I do. Maybe I want that. Did you think I'd marry you and then screw around?"

Mac shrugged and looked away, unable to hold his gaze. She picked up a small vase and pretended to study it.

"Well, I'm not wired like that, despite what you might think."

"I don't know what to think. Why would you be willing to spend the rest of your life with a woman you didn't love?" Mac held her breath, praying he might throw her a bone, give her a reason to hope, to believe they might actually have something.

His expression was unreadable. "You're a friend. We like a lot of the same things. We have a lot in common."

"But do you love me?"

Bruiser frowned and stared at his feet. "I don't know. Love is one of those things I've never been good at defining."

But he hadn't said no, and Mac wanted to say yes to this crazy idea. How could she swallow her pride and agree to an arrangement based on practicality and not love? "It won't work."

"Mac, I married once because I thought I was in love. We had nothing in common outside of the bedroom, and obviously that wasn't enough for her. So as I see it, we have a better chance than CeCe and I did."

Mac shook her head. "I can't do it. Even for Elliot."

"I'll pay for your college."

"Now you're bribing me again." She managed a smile.

He gave her one of those sexy Bruiser grins. "Damn right. Anything it takes."

"Just not this. I'm so sorry. I really want you to get custody of Elliot. Really I do. But not this way."

"Think about it. Don't close your mind to the possibilities. We're damn good in bed, you know."

"That's not enough." Mac shook her head. "I'm going to leave now."

Bruiser didn't protest.

Mac, her mind churning, drove back to her lonely house and the company of her cat.

Chapter 21

Baggage Claim

A few days later, Mac sat with Kelsie in Eugenio's, a small Italian restaurant near the Kirkland waterfront. Eugenio's boasted the best lasagna in the area, but it might was well have been sawdust for as much interest as Mac had in her food.

Kelsie gushed about her life with Zach, and Mac felt a twinge of jealousy. She wanted what Kelsie had, yet she knew Zach and Kelsie's relationship hadn't started out that way. Mac, who wasn't prone to nervousness, couldn't quite broach the reason she'd invited Kelsie here. As dinner wound down, and Kelsie kept glancing at her watch, Mac knew she'd better get a set of balls soon or miss her opportunity. She'd never been good with girl talk and spilling her guts.

Kelsie paused, took a deep breath and studied Mac. "I'm sorry, I must be boring you. It's too bad the other girls couldn't make it."

"Actually, I didn't invite them."

"Oh, really?" Kelsie, ever the lady, folded her hands in her lap and waited. A slight smile graced her beautiful, flawless face.

Mac would never look that good if she spent millions on a makeover and plastic surgery. "I thought we could spend a little time getting to know each other."

"Well, that's nice." Kelsie's tone might have been polite but her expression was shrewd. "What would you like to know, specifically, that the other girls can't hear?"

Leave it to Kelsie to manage to nicely cut through the bullshit.

"I wanted to talk to you in confidence about the circumstances of your marriage."

"Okay." Mac could almost see Kelsie's guard going up. "Why are you interested?"

Mac needed to give Kelsie more if she was going to get any useful answers. "This has to do with Bruiser. He wants me to marry him."

"Oh, Mac, that's wonderful. Do you need help planning the wedding?" Kelsie smiled like the beauty queen she'd been, genuinely happy for Mac.

"Not exactly. This would be a marriage based on need, not love."

Kelsie's face puckered in confusion.

"He needs a wife in order to get guardianship of Elliot. And I need his money for a college education."

"Ah." Kelsie nodded and smiled, relaxing back into her chair. "I get it now. A marriage of convenience. That's why you came to me."

"Uh, yeah. I hope you don't mind."

"Not at all, it's common knowledge among our friends that my marriage started as a business proposition that was mutually beneficial to both of us."

"Business partners with benefits."

"Exactly." Kelsie laughed. Even her laugh was classy and feminine. If she wasn't so nice, Mac would be totally insecure around her. "So what are the parameters? Is there a time frame? Does it include benefits?"

"I'm sure it would since we're utilizing those benefits right now. And no time frame that I'm aware of. In fact, he made it sound permanent."

"So what's the issue?"

"What about love?"

"Ah, love. Do you love him?"

Mac opened her mouth to answer but Kelsie held up a hand to stop her. "Give me the truth of what's in your heart, not some rehearsed garbage."

Mac gave Kelsie the truth. "I've had a crush on Bruiser ever since he joined the Jacks, even before I started working there. We got to be friends, and even though I wanted more, he didn't see me that way."

"And now?"

"Now I'm sure he sees me as a friend *and* a sex partner."

"That's a good start. Zach and I didn't even have that, and now we're madly in love with each other." Kelsie's eyes sparkled just mentioning Zach's name.

"We're the reverse of you and Zach. Bruiser is the beautiful one in the relationship."

"Now, Mac, don't sell yourself short. You look fantastic. You have that girl-next-door beauty and that inner glow."

"Thanks." Mac ducked her head, feeling oddly embarrassed and pleased at the same time.

"So when is the wedding?" Kelsie's wheels were turning, obviously a mile ahead on the wedding plans.

"I told him no."

"And why did you do that?"

"Because he doesn't love me."

"Think about it. You'll have more than a lot of marriages starting out. Besides, who says he doesn't love you?"

"He's never said he does."

"I didn't know I loved Zach or that he loved me. Yet I think we did marry for love. We just didn't recognize it for what it was."

Mac mulled over Kelsie's words, then rejected them as ludicrous. Sure, the sex between she and Bruiser scorched right to their souls. They had chemistry, and they had common interests.

But Mac secretly believed in romance and love and all that mushy crap. She wanted a forever love. Maybe her expectations weren't the least bit realistic. Maybe she should lower them.

"Do you guys have mutual goals in life?"

Mac jumped, startled out of her musing. She didn't really have *any* goals anymore. Since neither of them lived their own lives but their versions of what others expected, they were a sorry pair.

So why was she even considering it?

For Elliot?

Or was Elliot a way to justify something she wanted to do for herself?

* * * * *

When Mac pulled in her driveway later that evening, Elliot leapt up from where he'd been sitting on the front porch. He wore a hooded sweatshirt, which had to be too warm for the weather, a baseball cap, and baggy jeans, not the fashionable kind popular with some kids, but ones that were a size too big.

"Elliot? What are you doing here?" Mac glanced around. Bruiser couldn't have brought him. He had flown out yesterday morning to the East Coast for the game—not that she was keeping track of his schedule or anything. He wouldn't be back until late tonight.

"I needed to get out, and Bruiser is gone." Elliot smiled hopefully at her while he fidgeted with a strap on his backpack.

"It's almost eight-thirty. Does your aunt know you're here?" Mac wouldn't be swayed by the kid's attempt to charm her.

Elliot shuffled his feet and stared at the ground. "Uh, not really." Then he glanced up quickly with an engaging grin. "I was bored. I came to see you."

"How did you get here?" Mac unlocked her front door and Elliot followed her in.

"I rode the bus."

"Elliot, you need to call your aunt, then I'm taking you back home."

Elliot plopped down in on the step. "I'm not going. I'll just run away again."

"Please, I can't keep you here."

"Because you don't want to." Elliot sniffled and rubbed what little was left of his nose. Mac handed him a tissue.

"It's not that simple."

"It *is* that simple. Why don't you just marry Bruiser? We can be a family." Elliot perked up and managed a lopsided grin that reminded her oddly of Bruiser.

Mac gave him her best evil eye. "Wherever did you come up with an idea like that?"

Elliot pursed his lips and shrugged, putting on an innocent act. "Just thought it sounded good."

"Did Bruiser put you up to this?"

The kid regarded her with a puzzled frown. "Uh, no, why would he?" He pushed his glasses up higher on his nose.

It was Mac's turn to be flustered. "No reason."

"I heard Aunt Ruth talking to someone on the phone. She said she'd transfer guardianship to Bruiser because he has the means to help me, while they don't, but she needs to make sure that the atmosphere is adequate."

"And that means he needs to be married?"

"Yeah, and settled down. I mean he'd have to stop his modeling and stuff."

"I see." Mac thrust her phone at him.

"Aunt Ruth says modeling half-naked is the devil's work."

Mac nodded, trying not to laugh at the image of Bruiser doing the devil's work complete with pitchfork and pointed tail.

"So why don't you marry him?"

"It's complicated."

"That's what all adults say when it's really pretty easy."

Okay, this conversation needed to end now. Right now. Elliot was essentially a runaway. "Call your aunt. Let her know I'll be bringing you home right away."

"I made a friend at school." Elliot changed the subject so quickly Mac took a moment to catch up.

"Good for you."

"We play chess together."

Mac smiled, happy to see Elliot adjusting well but refusing to fall for his attempt to distract her. "Good, good. Now call her."

Mac went into the kitchen and waited for Elliot to finish his call then she picked up her car keys. "Let's go."

"She's mean to me. My uncle stares at me really funny, and not just because of how I look."

Mac hesitated, the hair rising on the back of her neck. "How does he stare at you?"

"Just—weird. I can't really explain it. Like he thinks I'm a sinner he has to save."

Mac hoped like hell that's all it was.

A lone tear ran down Elliot's cheek. "I miss my mom and dad. Mom always read to me at night from the classics, and Dad helped me with my science projects. These people don't believe in reading anything but the Bible."

"Well, the Bible is a good book." Mac was trying hard to be positive.

"So are a lot of other books."

"What did your aunt say on the phone?"

"They didn't know I was gone, but now that they do I think I'm in trouble."

"I'm sure you are. Elliot, you can't run off like that. Promise you won't do it again."

"If you'll you marry Bruiser."

"That's blackmail."

Elliot nodded, a slight grin on his splotchy face. "Will you?"

"I'll think about it." Mac sighed. "Come on, let's go."

Elliot threw his arms around her and hugged her. She hugged him back, as the clever little boy burrowed deeper into her heart.

"I love you, Mac." He grinned at her and skipped ahead to the car, happier than she'd ever seen him, singing a song that sounded suspiciously like "Love and Marriage."

Elliot loved her, Bruiser wanted to marry her, and she was currently unemployed. She needed to find a way to dig herself out of this complicated hole. It *was* complicated. Wasn't it?

* * * * *

Bruiser stared at the ceiling of the hotel room. He couldn't sleep. Normally he slept pretty well until a nightmare woke him up. Tonight, he couldn't even fall asleep.

"Hey, your thrashing around is fucking keeping me awake." Brett called from the next bed.

"Since when? You'd sleep through a nuclear attack."

"Yeah, well, not tonight." Brett sounded as cranky as Bruiser's Great Aunt Alma without her morning shot of bourbon. "Worried about the game?"

"I wish that's all it was," Bruiser admitted.

"Then what is it? Mac?"

"How'd you know?"

"I'm psychic, what the hell do you think? You dumbass, you're in love with her."

"What?" Bruiser shot up in bed and gave his buddy his best eat-shit-and-die glower, only it was wasted due to the darkness of the room. He slumped back against the headboard.

"You heard me. You've been a jerk to deal with lately. Since you've been hanging around the film room into the evening, I can only guess you're not spending nights in Mac's bed, and no one else's, for that matter. Haven't seen you in one gossip magazine in a few months."

Bruiser laced his fingers together behind his head and stared at the ceiling. "I'm trying to be good to get custody of Elliot."

"Hmm. Is that all?"

"Of course that's all." Bruiser got up and paced the room in his boxers. "Isn't that enough to stress a guy out?"

Brett sat back against the pillows, rubbed his eyes, and yawned. "You're pretty damn transparent."

"Since when?"

"Since I've gotten to know you so well. You have feelings for Mac, and she does for you. Hell, I'd be thrilled if that was happening to me."

"I wish it *was* happening to you. I'm all wrong for her."

"She doesn't think so. If she did, she'd kick you to the curb for good."

"She did." Bruiser stopped and stared out the window at the Boston skyline.

"Bullshit. Nah, it's just one of those female things where they play hard to get and want you to prove your devotion. That sort of crap."

"You think?" Bruiser turned to eye the lump on the bed.

"Hell, I'm not the expert you are but, yeah, I think so."

"I'm far from an expert on relationships. Sex is a different story."

"Yeah, I get that, but the team has had a lot of guys getting hitched in the past couple years, and they seem disgustingly happy."

"Except Harris."

"Harris is a law unto himself. He might not be wearing a wedding ring, but he's sure as hell wearing a ball and chain."

"Pussy-whipped."

"You'll never see that with me."

"Me neither."

Brett laughed. "Buddy, you're already on your way. The second you give power to a woman to set your moods, the moment your happiness depends on her happiness, then, you, my man, are screwed."

"Fuck you."

Brett laughed.

"Hey, your time will come."

"Never. I'm not the marrying type. Too much baggage for any decent woman."

Bruiser wondered what kind of baggage Brett might be referring to, but he never asked and Brett never volunteered. That was the way their friendship went.

Besides, Bruiser had his own baggage to worry about, baggage that needed to be stowed somewhere so he could get on with his life.

Chapter 22

Zone Blitz

Returning home from dropping off Elliot, Mac caught movement in her backyard. Gripping a baseball bat, she slipped out her side door and stayed in the shadows of her house, heart pounding so loudly she couldn't believe the intruder didn't hear her.

Just as she stalked to within a few feet of the skulking figure, whose shape looked remarkably like her father's, the man climbed on top of a stool and lowered himself over the fence into the neighbors' backyard. Mac stood on tiptoes and looked over the fence.

"Dad, what are you doing?" she hissed.

Craig held his hand up to his mouth. "Shh."

"Get out of their yard."

"I saw them leave."

"They could be back any minute. Where'd you park your car?"

"Down the street. Shh. We don't need to announce our intentions to the rest of the neighborhood, especially nosy old Mrs. Rockhurst."

"Mrs. Rockhurst has been invaluable in keeping us apprised of what's happening over here. She's as nosy as you are."

"Not that invaluable, or they'd be arrested."

"Get out of their yard, *now*, or I'll call the police on you myself."

Her father shook his head. Mac leaned the bat against the fence. With a sigh, she climbed the fence to retrieve the stubborn man, even though she didn't know what good it would do other than get them both arrested for trespassing.

In one hand her dad held a shovel, in the other a flashlight.

"What are you planning on doing? You have a restraining order. You can't be here."

"That bitch killed my son. I have a right to know. If the law won't handle it, I will."

"Dad, they could have dumped Will's body in the woods or the sound. Somewhere we'll never find it."

Craig turned to her. "We will find it or die trying."

Mac frowned. She didn't want to do this the rest of her life, she really didn't. She wanted more. She wanted—

Bruiser. And Elliot. A family.

If only they could make it work, but the odds were not good as long as her father obsessed over his missing son.

"Get out of their yard." She grabbed his arm and pulled. "Come back to the house with me."

They both froze as a car came down the street and turned into Mac's driveway. She looked through a crack in the fence. Thank God it was Bruiser, though she had no idea what he was doing here this late at night. The team plane must have just gotten back after a heart-wrenching 14-10 loss to New England.

While Mac's heart did a little waltz right up to Bruiser, she almost forgot her body was standing in her former sister-in-law-turned-murder-suspect's backyard.

She ran back to the fence and called to him.

Bruiser peered over the top board. "What are you two doing?"

"I'm trying to get Dad out of their yard before the police show up and arrest him."

Bruiser vaulted over the five-foot fence like it was nothing, the epitome of athleticism and grace. "Come on, Craig, we need to get you out of here."

"They're gone and won't be back for a long time."

"What if they have motion cameras?" Bruiser suggested.

Both Mac and her father turned as one to stare at the back of the house. Sure enough, there was a camera mounted above the back door and another over the patio area.

"Crap," Mac spoke under her breath. "Let's get out of here and hope we're out of camera range."

"Not until I've had a chance to do some digging."

Bruiser grabbed Craig's arm. "Not tonight, old man." He pulled Craig along, not taking no for an answer.

Mac grabbed his other arm, and they literally dragged him to the gate, only to find it padlocked. "Double crap," Mac cursed.

"I'll get us out of here. Let me get a ladder." Back over the fence Bruiser went. A few minutes later they stood on the lawn in Mac's side yard, breathing heavily, just as a police cruiser, lights flashing, pulled into the neighbors' driveway followed by Sonja's car.

"Busted." Mac groaned. She turned to Bruiser. "Wait in the house. They can't see you out here. It'll be all over the papers. This is our problem, not yours."

Bruiser hesitated.

"Don't be a hero, Bruiser. Go inside," Craig insisted, looking more than a little sheepish.

Bruiser glanced again at the patrol car now sitting in the driveway. The officer was talking to Sonja and her husband; then he turned to Mac's house.

"Get inside. Please."

"Okay, but if you need me, I'm here."

Mac had no idea why he was here. He'd saved her ass and possibly her father's by getting them out of the backyard before the police came, but he'd shown up here for a reason.

She hoped she was that reason.

* * * * *

With one exception, Bruiser had never been a guy to back down from a fight or run from a problem. He faced his problems head on, but Mac's father needed face up to reality. Bruiser just hoped Craig didn't drag Mac down with him. Still, he felt like a coward as he watched the entire thing play out in Mac's driveway through the slats in her blinds.

After a short conversation with Mac and her father while Sonja and Ben looked on, the officer cuffed Craig, put him in the back of the patrol car and drove off. Sonja and Ben cast a last threatening glare at Mac and returned to their house.

Bruiser met her at the front door and wrapped her in his arms. She melted into his body, clinging to him. He held her tight, burrowing his fingers in her hair, intoxicated by her fresh scent and the feel of her sexy body against his.

"You okay?" He spoke into her hair.

Mac pulled back, and Bruiser loosened his hold. She looked up at him, her gaze oddly resigned. He'd expected to see tears. Instead he saw defeat. "They arrested him for violating the no-contact order and trespassing. It was inevitable. I'm surprised it didn't happen sooner."

"He needs help. He's out of control."

"Tell that to him." Mac's voice took on a monotone he'd never heard from her. Weariness lined her face and she had dark circles under her eyes. Her makeup had long ago worn off. Even like this, she was still the most beautiful girl in the world, and he wanted to make her smile again.

"Do you need bail money?"

"I can't ask you for that." She fisted her hands in his shirt and gazed up at him. He liked how she clung to him, as if he gave her comfort.

"Sure you can. We're friends, aren't we?"

"I guess." She frowned, as if he'd disappointed her, and nodded. "I'll take a loan. I don't have many other options. And God knows Dad doesn't have any money."

"You got it." Bruiser slanted a grin at her, hoping his signature smile would loosen her up a little. She was wound tighter than his sister on a bad hair day.

"I'm surprised to see you here."

"I couldn't stay away." He nuzzled her, burying his face in her hair and inhaling her scent.

Mac pushed away from him, and he let her go, even though his arms felt empty without her. She moved into the kitchen, effectively putting the counter between them—her own personal barrier. Bruiser understood barriers, and the emotional barriers Mac put up were proving a challenge to tear down, while Bruiser's were about as stable as a rotten picket fence.

Bruiser slid onto a barstool in front of the kitchen counter and took the beer she offered him. He lifted it to his mouth, hesitated, and set the bottle down. "I guess I shouldn't be drinking this if we're going to the police station. How about a rain check?"

"After we get Dad home and tucked in for the night in his own bed?"

"Yeah."

Her smile lit up his life, warmed his heart, and made his day. After the team's loss earlier, he needed to come home and see that smile.

Home?

God, how he'd missed that brilliant, sassy smile of hers in the night that he'd been away. How he'd missed *her*. He tried to recall if he'd ever missed a woman as much as Mac, or obsessed over a woman as much as Mac, or when he'd been tied up in such knots over a woman as much as Mac. Not even his ex-wife did it to him like Mac did.

That realization hit him in the gut like a sucker punch from a prizefighter.

Maybe his marriage proposal had more to do with him than with Elliot. He fought for balance; Mac made him so dizzy he didn't know which end of the field to run toward.

"What the hell was your dad doing?" He leaned forward, chin resting in his hands.

"Trying to find evidence." Mac sighed and poured them both a cup of strong Tully's.

Bruiser laughed. "What's he expecting to find?"

Mac glanced in the direction of Sonja's house and swallowed. "My brother."

Bruiser processed that comment. "Why?"

She met his gaze. "Dad thinks he's in the garden, compost for the tomatoes."

"Seriously?"

"Damn serious. He says you don't get tomatoes that look like hers without some incredible fertilizer."

"Dead bodies make good fertilizer?" Bruiser rubbed his stomach. He felt a little queasy, and he wasn't a squeamish type of guy.

"The best, and to think I've eaten her tomatoes back when we were still speaking, asked her how she managed to have such a great crop, what her secret was. She just laughed."

"Oh, God."

"Yeah, no kidding." Mac leaned against the counter, looking a little green herself.

Bruiser stood up and walked to the window. He could just make out the garden in the distance. "Good place to hide a body."

"Especially considering when Will went missing, she'd just started digging it up to plant it. The police never had enough evidence for a search warrant."

Bruiser swallowed and wondered how Mac could live in this house knowing what might have happened next door. "I guess we should get your dad."

Mac nodded and Bruiser took her hand as they walked out the door as if they were a real couple.

And perhaps they were.

* * * * *

A few hours later, they were on their way back to Mac's house. Her dad had been bailed out of jail and was home in his bed. Gone was the obsessive gleam in his eyes, replaced by defeat and absolute sorrow. Mac wasn't sure which was worse. She'd never thought she'd be thinking this, but she liked him better when he was fighting. At least it gave him something to live for.

Up until an hour ago, she'd been prepared to tell her father that he couldn't drag her into his schemes again or his endless searches for information. But after seeing the look on his face when they'd picked him up, she didn't know what to do.

Bruiser walked Mac to her front door. She hesitated with her hand on the doorknob, debating on the wisdom of inviting him in. But wisdom was highly overrated.

"Do you want to come in?"

"Always." His smile settled in her heart, while his sexy blue-gray eyes wrote a love story in her dreams.

Love? The for-better or for-worse kind? Was she ready to try for that? Was Bruiser? Elliot had already declared his intentions and made it sound so simple. If only it could be. She was far from sure, yet part of her screamed, *Go for the Hail Mary and take the risk*. Risk was what made life worth living, and she hadn't lived her life in at least three years. She'd been hunting for her brother, who'd be the last person on earth to want this life for her.

Could she take that leap of faith with Bruiser? Was he the right choice?

"What are you thinking?" He put a finger under her chin and lifted her head. His gaze slid over her face, as if memorizing every curve.

"I'm thinking I'd like you to come in the house and finish that beer."

Mac grabbed a beer for each of them and steered Bruiser to the patio. It was a warm, late-summer night, too good to waste by staying inside. They sat together on the love seat.

She lit a few candles on the patio table, strictly to drive away mosquitoes, of course.

"Elliot came over last night." Mac watched Bruiser's reaction in the flickering candlelight.

"Mac, thanks for spending some time with him."

"I didn't exactly invite him. He ran away, but I took him back." Mac repeated the entire conversation with Elliot, leaving out the marriage part.

Bruiser lifted his troubled eyes to her. "What do you think that means about the uncle looking at him funny?"

"Could mean a lot of things besides the worst-case scenario." Mac hated the thought of brave Elliot living with some kind of child molester.

"I need to get him out of that house." Bruiser said with renewed determination. He sat next to her on the small wicker loveseat and took her hand. "What are we going to do?"

"Elliot wants us to get married. Did you put him up to that?"

Bruiser chuckled. "Nope, but he's a smart kid. What do you say? Wanna give it a shot?"

Wanna give it a shot? What kind of marriage proposal was that? It sounded like the kind a man gives to a woman he isn't marrying for love.

Bruiser rushed on, as if he had his foot in the door and was going to bully his way inside. "I think we could make it work if you made our family your priority."

"And give up the search for my brother?"

"At least scale it back for your own good and your father's."

"I don't know if I could do that to him. You saw him tonight. But what about you? Are you going to give up being someone you aren't? Bruce Mackey wasn't the one who died all those years ago. He deserves a life."

"So do you." Bruiser spoke so quietly she barely heard his words.

"I know." She met his gaze and let her guard drop, squeezed his hand and took the risk. "Tell me about the accident." She needed to know that he trusted her. She could work with that, build on it.

For a long time Bruiser stared at the candle flame as if hypnotized, but he didn't let go of her hand. Mac waited, holding her breath.

Without lifting his head, he began to talk in a quiet, unemotional voice. "We were goofing around. Brice was always the charming daredevil, the attention slut, everybody's favorite. I was the quiet one, the thinker, the one who lived in Brice's shadow. So I swiped some of Mom's cigarettes and a lighter. I was showing off with them, letting Brice know I could be a daredevil, too. Brice wouldn't be outdone. He grabbed the cigarettes, stuffed one in his mouth, and lit it. I chased him, and he ran behind the gas barbecue and tipped it over, cracking the gas line. There was a huge explosion. It knocked Brice all the way across the patio, his clothes burst into flames. I ran to him and tried to put the fire out with my sweatshirt. A neighbor heard the screaming and came to help.

"They rushed him to the hospital with second- and third-degree burns, his face all but melted off." Bruiser stopped for a moment, breathing as if he'd just done wind sprints. "He almost died. The doctors induced a coma, did so many operations I lost count. After nine months they finally released him.

"Three months later, on the anniversary of accident, we got into a huge fight. He told me he hated me because every time he looked at me he saw the person he once was. He said I cheated him out of his life. He went into mom's bedroom and shut the door. She kept a pistol under the bed. I'll never forget the sound of that gunshot.

"I ran in there, expecting him to start laughing, teasing me for being such a wuss, but he was on the floor and his blood was everywhere." Bruiser gripped her hand so tightly that it hurt, but Mac didn't care. Pain and sadness shone in his eyes, along with something else. Relief? Relief that he'd finally gotten this childhood secret off his chest?

"So you've been living his life for him?"

Bruiser looked up and nodded. No tears, no anguish, just sorrow and uncertainty.

I'm so sorry." Mac put her hand on his arm, and he leaned his head on her shoulder. He'd told her his deepest pain and it meant the world to her.

"You can see why I've kept it quiet all these years. I felt responsible."

"But you weren't. It was an accident. He made the decision. He blamed you because he was hurting and had to lash out at someone. You'd proven you'd be by his side no matter what so he knew you'd be there, despite the abuse he heaped on you. Shanna said your parents couldn't stand seeing their imperfect son and that they laid a major guilt trip on you."

"Yeah, they did. Brice couldn't deal with his friends shrinking away at the sight of him, strangers staring at him and pointing. None of it. And he didn't have support at home. I tried but I was just a kid. Our mom was a single mother by then and ill-equipped, monetarily and emotionally."

"Guilt is a powerful motivator. I should know. You can't keep blaming yourself. Cut Bruce—the child—some slack. While you're at it, the adult Bruiser should cut himself some slack, too. You're a special person, Bruiser; let the world see it, let them have the privilege of knowing what a generous, caring man you are."

Bruiser shrugged. "I suppose you're right."

"It's time to put Brice to rest and move on."

Bruiser's eyebrows climbed at her suggestion, and she knew exactly what he was thinking—that she should talk.

"And you?" He nailed her with his stormy-sea eyes. "I'm willing to take a risk, make some changes, and create a better person out of tragedy. I just trusted you with my most painful secret, and you aren't offering anything in return."

"My situation isn't the same."

"The guilt is the same, Mac; whether you admit it or not, you're living your life out of guilt, just like I was." Bruiser tucked a strand of hair behind her ear.

"If we could just get an answer to what happened then Dad and I could both get on with our lives."

"I don't want to live with you gone every evening and every weekend, putting yourself in danger, chasing after the next rumor, or hunch, or tip."

"I don't expect you to wait. I just need a little time to figure this all out."

"Where do we go from here?" Bruiser asked.

"I don't know. I want to keep seeing you." Mac studied him, really looked at him. There was something there, something permanent and lasting, a promise in his eyes she'd only dreamed of, yet she was blowing him off.

Tonight if he'd said *I love you* she would have followed him to the ends of the earth, but declarations of love had to be given freely, and neither of them were quite there yet.

Instead, he made love to her so sweetly and tenderly that she couldn't deny the obvious.

Bruiser loved her.

Mac loved Bruiser.

What hell did a woman do with that information?

* * * * *

The Jacks won the next game on Sunday Night Football, and Bruiser ran for his third consecutive hundred-yard game. He invited Elliot to attend but Elliot's uncle wouldn't let him go. *Sunday was for worship, not watching grown men play a violent game.*

On Tuesday evening Bruiser and Mac picked up Elliot, the first time Bruiser had been able to carve out the time in over a week.

The kid was reverting to past behaviors, not wanting to go out in public, pulling into himself, and avoiding contact with strangers.

Bruiser hated to see the changes and knew it came from Elliot's overbearing, self-righteous uncle and judgmental aunt, not to mention the cousins. The good work the mental health and hospital staff had done to improve Elliot's confidence and attitude was unraveling right before Bruiser's eyes, and he intended on doing what he could to sew the ragged edges of Elliot's confidence back together.

Elliot loved to bowl, so Bruiser and Mac took him bowling. Brice had hated bowling, but Bruiser liked it, so this was a step in the right direction for all of them. Bruiser was working on taking Mac's words to heart. He'd done a lot of thinking about his life and knew she was right. He couldn't shrug off years of guilt just like that, but he'd chip away at it a little at a time doing things Bruiser would do, not things Brice would do.

After they picked their bowling balls, they sat down on the plastic chairs and Elliot took the scorer's desk.

"People are staring at me." Elliot pulled his Jacks' baseball cap down farther until you could barely see his eyes.

"No, Elliot, they're staring at Bruiser. He's a big celebrity around these parts. Remember?" Mac tugged on his sleeve and smiled at him.

"Oh, yeah. You're right." He grinned his toothy grin. "Can I go first?"

"Sure, bowl away. Take a few practice shots," Bruiser said and glanced at Mac to find her looking at him with an expression on her face that would've scared the hell out of him if she'd been any other woman. He reached over and took her hand and squeezed it. She squeezed back.

For a moment, the old "time stood still" thing happened. Everyone but Mac faded away. Her thoughts mingled with his, her needs became his needs. Everything that mattered to him revolved around her. God, he was a sap, a *lovesick* sap—because what the hell else could possibly be wrong with him?

"You're Bruiser Mackey, aren't you?" A middle-aged man wearing a Jacks' cap with his wife and two kids diverted Bruiser's attention. The little boys were wearing Jacks jerseys.

Bruiser nodded. He'd been lucky so far that only a few people had ventured into his space and asked for an autograph.

"This must be your family," his wife gushed.

For a moment silence reigned except for the sounds of balls rolling and the crash of the pins. Without glancing their way, he felt Mac and Elliot's eyes on him as they waited to hear what he'd say.

"Yes, this is my family."

"So nice to meet you." Neither the man nor the woman paid much notice to Elliot, for which Bruiser was grateful. He gladly signed the guy's hat and the kids' shirts. After thanking him, the family trundled off, leaving Bruiser with—

His family.

Yes, they were his family. And he'd see to it that it became official.

One way or another.

Chapter 23

Handoff

Bruiser stifled a yawn and stared at nothing. Once he fulfilled his current contractual obligations, he'd never model again.

"Bruce, I need that smoking-sexy look only you can do."

He snapped to attention and totally faked the photo shoot. Hell, he didn't even remember what he was endorsing, other than his shirtless body. God, he hated this shit.

"Come on, one more pose, and we're done."

"Damn right, we're done." Bruiser was crankier than hell, but he'd been like this for two weeks. After what seemed like a few hundred more clicks of the camera, Bruiser got dressed and headed out. His cell chirped, sounding a lot happier than he fucking felt. He hoped like hell it was Mac calling, he could use her brand of therapy.

He glanced at the text message.

I need to talk to you. It was from Trudy.

Bruiser started to call Mac and stopped, not wanting to get her hopes up. He texted Trudy back. *Where to meet you?*

Bar. Soon.

Bruiser stared at the phone, wondering what to do next. He called the one person he knew with a level head and no-nonsense advice. In a few short minutes, he'd filled Brett in on the latest.

"So how far are you willing to go to get this information?"

"I don't know. I can't cheat on Mac, even if it might crack this case."

"You are so hosed."

"Tell me about it."

"Another good man bites the dust for a good woman." Brett laughed, but the sadness lingering in his voice made Bruiser feel like a shit. Once he settled his own problems, he'd put the Terrible Trio to work finding Brett a nice woman. Or maybe they'd become the Formidable Four, since Mac appeared to have joined their little group of strong women.

Bruiser headed for the bar, making it in record time.

His cell continued its merry chirping, and he checked it. Several calls and texts from Mac asking him to call her. He would call her. Later. He needed to take care of Trudy first. Bruiser turned into the parking lot and got out.

Taking a deep breath, he walked into the bar. It was empty of customers, and Trudy looked up as he walked in. She frowned at him, as if he were distasteful medicine she had to take. Interesting. She wasn't happy to see him.

Ignoring her less-than-welcoming glare—she'd invited him after all—he sauntered up to the bar, as if he hadn't a care in the world. He could and would do this for Mac and her father. They deserved to know what happened, and Will needed to be put to rest. Maybe if he poured on the charm, Trudy wouldn't be able to resist. But Trudy seemed agitated. She scrubbed the same spot on the counter with a bar rag over and over.

"So what's up?" He leaned on the bar and took the beer she offered.

After glancing over her shoulder, Trudy got right to the point, not even taking the time to proposition him. "The house is being foreclosed on."

"What house?"

"Ben and Sonja's. They have to be out within the week. They're worried; I think there's incriminating evidence. Like on the property."

"And why are you telling me this now?" Bruiser eyed her with suspicion, fearing he might be walking into a trap.

"I can't sleep. This is really wearing on me." Trudy kept glancing around as if she expected Sonja and Ben to walk in.

Bruiser didn't buy it. Trudy only cared about herself. "What do you get out of this?"

Trudy leaned forward across the bar and grabbed a handful of his shirt. "I'm scared shitless. I think I'm next." Her face was whiter than his away jersey and her lower lip quivered.

"Why did you call me instead of the police?" Bruiser extracted her hands from his shirt and backed out of range.

"I'm afraid. They'll think I helped do it."

"Did you?"

She didn't answer.

"You can ask for immunity before you tell them anything. I'll get you an attorney to help make a deal."

"Will you? Will you go with me? I don't have anyone else. All of my friends are her friends."

Bruiser hesitated. He didn't trust this woman. Her story could be part of a trap. He'd seen firsthand how a female like her could ruin a man's career and reputation. It'd happened too many times to teammates. If she involved him in any kind of scandal, even on the periphery, he could kiss goodbye to his efforts to gain guardianship of Elliot.

Bruiser studied her closely and hoped like hell she wasn't that good of an actor. He nodded, his decision made, for better or worse. He'd take the chance. For Mac and for Elliot he would do this. And for their future.

He pulled out his phone to make a call. "Okay, let's go. I'll drive."

His cell was dead.

* * * * *

Mac paced the floor while Elliot sat huddled in a corner and her father channel-surfed. She tried Bruiser's phone one more time, furious he wasn't returning her calls or text messages. Once again it went straight to voicemail.

The Joneses would be here any moment. She needed Bruiser here now. Mac and her father had just spent several harrowing hours looking for a kid they thought was lost in downtown Seattle.

Elliot had taken a wild bus ride all over town, texting Mac with clues every half hour or so on the cell Bruiser had given him. Like this was some kind of game. Mac and her father were frantic to find him, and Bruiser was AWOL. Mac was pretty pissed at the world in general right now.

Thanks to Craig's incredible sleuthing skills, he tracked Elliot's journey on a bus through different parts of Seattle until Elliot's tracks led right back here to Mac's house. Craig had found the kid hiding in the tool shed in the backyard.

The Joneses claimed they hadn't noticed he was missing until late last night and refused to call the police for reasons Mac didn't understand.

She didn't know whether to hug Elliot or chew his ass out, but she did know she'd had her share of drama lately and was fed up.

"I'm sorry," Elliot mumbled as he hugged himself, looking lost and small.

She stopped pacing in front of the boy. "Did you realize we were scared to death?"

Elliot shrugged and fingered the fabric on his sweat pants.

"You could've been hurt or worse."

"I won't go back there." He stuck out his lower lip, and it quivered. His eyes glistened with tears and something close to fear, effectively deflating Mac's anger.

"Elliot, you have to. They're your legal guardians."

"I want you and Bruiser to be my guardians."

"Things like that take time." Mac sighed with exasperation. God, she would have cut through the red tape if she could, but she couldn't.

"You aren't even trying. Neither of you. You're telling me you are, but you aren't."

"Bruiser has an entire team of attorneys on it."

Elliot rubbed his eyes with his fists and hiccupped. "He stands in my doorway and watches me. I pretend to be asleep, and he goes away. Tonight, he didn't go away, he came in after everyone else had gone to bed. When he pulled back the covers, I grabbed my cell phone and ran." The dam broke and tears streamed down Elliot's blotchy face.

Which totally explained why the Joneses didn't want to call the police.

Mac dropped to her knees and wrapped her arms around Elliot. "Oh, Elliot, I didn't know. Has he touched you?"

Elliot shook his head, sobbing uncontrollably now. "No, and I don't want him to either. Don't make me go back there."

"I won't," she promised. Knowing what she knew now, Elliot would never be going back to the Joneses. She wouldn't allow it, and Bruiser certainly wouldn't. In fact, she'd have her hands full stopping him from killing the asshole. If only she could find Bruiser.

Mac glanced at her watch, frustrated. She needed Bruiser here. He'd know what to do, and how to fix this.

A few minutes later, Mac heard his beast of a vehicle in the driveway. She ran out of the house, ready to rage at him, but something in his weary yet satisfied expression stopped her cold.

"Where've you been? I've been trying to call you."

"I know, I'm sorry. Trudy called, then my cell went dead, and we've been down at the station all night long. I didn't want to wake you and—"

"Trudy? The station?" Mac's mind whirled as she tried to process his words into something that made sense.

"Yeah, she gave the detectives her statement. She's—" Bruiser's words were cut short by a convoy of police cars pulling up next door. Illuminated by the orange light of a rising sun, Mac recognized the lead detective on Will's case as he led uniformed men up the front steps, pounded on the door and yelled for Sonja and Ben to open up. When no one responded, they broke the door down and entered the house.

Mac grabbed Bruiser's arm. "What's happening?"

Elliot walked onto the porch to watch. "Wow, look at all those cop cars."

Bruiser's brow furrowed as he focused on Elliot. "Elliot, what are you doing here?"

"That's why I tried to call you. He ran away."

"I didn't run away. I went on an adventure." Elliot wiped his eyes with his T-shirt and put on a brave face. "Mac says I don't have to go back."

Bruiser looked from one to another with an adorably puzzled frown on his haggard face. He ran his hands through his already rumpled golden hair and sank down on the front steps. "Elliot, we've had this discussion. I can't—"

"He isn't going back." Mac interrupted Bruiser.

"I'm missing the meat of this story, aren't I?" Bruiser held his hand over his mouth as he yawned.

"Here they come," Elliot hid behind Bruiser and grabbed his arm, as the Joneses minivan weaved its way through cop cars and parked across the street.

Mac clutched Bruiser's other arm, talking as fast as she could. "His Uncle has been standing in Elliot's doorway late at night. Elliot fakes like he's asleep. Tonight, after everyone else was asleep, he approached Elliot's bed and pulled back the covers."

Mac didn't have time to say more as Ruth and John crossed the street. Bruiser's face turned hard and formidable. That muscle jerked in his jaw, and he looked ready to beat the crap out of someone—a very fat and pompous someone.

"Don't do anything stupid," Mac hissed as she held his arm.

"Can I castrate the bastard?"

Mac shook her head, even though she'd love to give Bruiser the thumbs-up.

Bruiser balled his hands into fists, spread his legs apart in a fighting stance, and waited for Ruth and John to walk up the sidewalk. He looked more than intimidating.

"Get in the car, Elliot," Ruth ordered, pointing a pudgy finger at Elliot.

"He's not going with you. I'll have my attorney draw up the papers and deliver them next week." Bruiser's deadly quiet voice carried a threatening undercurrent.

John stepped backward a few steps and moved behind his wife, not hard to do since she was as wide as she was tall. What a fucking coward.

The big woman puffed out her chest and snarled at Bruiser. "He's going with us. I'll call the police and report you for kidnapping." She looked down the street. "Even better, I'll go get them right now."

"I'll report your husband for child molestation." Bruiser countered, his voice as frigid as the waters of Puget Sound in the winter.

Mac noticed the woman didn't blink once, which meant this might not be the first accusation she'd heard of this nature.

"I never touched that kid," her husband insisted.

He hadn't, according to Elliot, which meant they may not have a legal leg to stand on.

"You bastard, I'm going to—" Bruiser surged forward, hands fisted.

Mac dove in front of him, knowing she had no hope of stopping him if he didn't want to be stopped. She clutched at his sleeves, "Please, let me handle this. Trust me."

Bruiser nodded tersely but stayed on the balls of his feet like a prizefighter waiting for his opponent to engage.

Mac smiled sweetly at the Joneses even though playing nice curdled her stomach. "We all want what's best for Elliot. Bruiser has the means to take care of Elliot's expensive medical treatments and special needs. He can give Elliot a loving home surrounded by caring people, which is of the utmost importance to both of you."

Ruth relaxed slightly, while her husband coughed and elbowed his wife in the ribs. "We do our best, but it's difficult with the size of our existing family," she said.

"Bruiser is willing to give your church a healthy donation. That should ease your stress level." Bruiser tensed behind Mac. She lifted one foot, stepped back and planted her heel strategically on the top of his foot. He grunted but kept his mouth shut.

"A donation would help," John spoke from behind his wife.

Ruth's fat face pinched together, and her triple chin became more pronounced. "What would the congregation think if we allowed Elliot to live with this—this playboy?"

Her husband rubbed his chin and shrugged.

"You can tell them that those days are over for Bruiser. He's getting married, settling down, building a big house on a farm—a perfect place for a kid to grow up with his younger brothers and sisters, a stable home in the country with loving parents, horses, dogs, cats. Your congregation will be thrilled."

Ruth nodded, warming to the idea and the money. "And we'll be able to afford improvements the church and the parsonage so badly need." She turned to her husband, and they held a subdued conversation.

Bruiser whispered in Mac's ear, his long fingers spanning her waist. "And exactly who am I marrying and creating this Camelot with?"

"Me, of course." Mac turned her face so that their lips were mere inches apart.

"Are you proposing to me, Mackenzie Hernandez?" His eyes sparkled, and one corner of his sexy mouth tipped upward.

"I believe I am."

Bruiser grinned like a kid with a new bike at Christmas and pulled her around to kiss her soundly. He felt so good she forgot about their audience until Elliot tugged on her sleeve. Mac pushed on Bruiser's chest, and he released her, resting his big hands on her hips.

"We'll agree to your terms. Have your attorney call us at her convenience." Ruth said, her lips puckered in disgust as their public display of affection. She hauled on her husband's arm and dragged him to the car.

Next door, the police emerged from the house with Ben and Sonja in handcuffs.

Mac realized her father must have fallen asleep in the easy chair and missed all the drama, but Mac wouldn't have missed it for the world.

Elliot threw his arms around her, and she hugged him back. Bruiser put his arms around both of them and held tight.

Grinning, Elliot glanced up at both of them. "So when am I getting a pony?"

* * * * *

Bruiser stood behind Mac as a backhoe rumbled across the neighbors' huge backyard toward the garden area. Several uniforms and plain-clothes policemen swarmed the area now cordoned off with crime scene tape. Behind them, her father paced back and forth in a lather. Elliot slept in Mac's bedroom, exhausted from his all-night adventure.

"Dad, sit down, you'll have a heart attack." Mac didn't leave her station in front of the window.

Much to Bruiser's shock, Craig slumped into a chair, put his hands up to his face, and started crying, big silent sobs that shook his shoulders and made him gulp for air. The man had never cried, not once during this entire ordeal, but he was now. "It's over, Mac."

"I know, Dad, I know." She patted his shoulder, while Bruiser stood back, feeling helpless. He hated that feeling.

"I'll be all right now. Thank you, Bruiser." Craig actually smiled.

Bruiser smiled back. "You know, Craig. I have a proposition for you. I've been thinking about starting a detective agency to help people find missing family and friends. Maybe you'd like to work for me. You have tons of experience, and I don't have a clue what I'm doing. I've already talked to a retired detective about heading it up. He could train you."

"Can I think about it?" Craig wiped at his eyes.

"Sure, take all the time you need."

"Thank you." Mac grabbed his hand and squeezed it. "He needs a purpose in his life."

Bruiser nodded, he couldn't agree more.

"What did you have to do to get the information out of Trudy?"

"Don't worry. Nothing, really. She thought she might be next on Ben and Sonja's hit list."

Mac almost smiled. "We need to report Elliot's uncle. If he pulled that shit with Elliot he's done it to other kids."

"I'll deal with it as soon as he signs the guardianship over to us."

"Then deal with this, too: I love you, Bruiser Mackey, and I think you love me." Mac held her breath.

One corner of Bruiser's mouth lifted up in a half smile. "You're damn right, honey. I love you." He wrapped his arms around her and pulled her close to him. He kissed her hair and murmured sweet words in her ear, words only meant for her, words he'd never said to another woman and the most honest, heartfelt words he'd ever spoken.

Finally, he lifted his head and laughed. "How do you feel about being Mac Mackey?"

* * * * *

For the next few days, the detectives sifted through the soil in the garden next door until they finally found something. A bone. A human femur. Followed by more bones, then a pelvis. Finally a skull. Dental records confirmed what they all knew.

The metal box dug up earlier by Sonja and Ben held a gun and bullets.

The mystery was finally solved and Mac's brother could be put to rest. Relief washed over her along with deep sadness.

Bruiser stood by her side the entire time.

Chapter 24

Game Over

Bruiser and Mac married three weeks later. Brett was Bruiser's best man, and Kelsie was Mac's maid of honor. Elliot sat in the front row between Zach and Tyler, grinning for all he was worth. Never much for the details when it came to girlie stuff, Mac had stood back and let the She-Wolves handle the wedding planning. They didn't let her down, and Bruiser happily provided the blank check.

Just yesterday, the custody agreement had been signed. Elliot's uncle had been arrested following a tip from Bruiser and a police investigation. Sadly, there'd been other little boys. At least they'd gotten Elliot out of there soon enough.

The Jacks had won two out of their next three games, well on their way to a division title.

Where There's a Will Detective Agency was opening its doors next month. Craig immersed himself in learning the business. He and the grumpy retired detective heading the agency got along great, arguing one minute, best buddies the next. They hired a second retired detective who'd previously worked on Will's case to do part-time legwork.

Mac put her house up for sale. She loved the place but found herself unable to live that close to her brother's murder scene. They found the perfect house on five acres near Rachel and Derek's farm. Since it was vacant, they moved in immediately. Mac went wild purchasing plants and doing the landscaping.

Elliot started in his new school and appeared to be doing well. Bruiser had made a point of taking him to school his first day and enrolling him. The secretaries swooned and principal asked for his autograph. Kids had gathered around Bruiser like he was the second coming. Bruiser promised to come back and speak at an assembly on the importance of looking beneath the surface. He should know that story better than anyone.

Sonja and Ben were charged with first-degree murder, at which point Ben sang like a bird and pointed fingers at Sonja, swearing she was the mastermind, and he'd just been the cleanup guy. After all this time, Mac hadn't expected it to hurt as much as it did, despite her relief to finally know the truth.

At least she had Bruiser to share the pain as they helped each other heal from similar tragedies.

Mac surrounded herself with friends and family, learning how to live like a normal person again. Along with her dad and Elliot, she invited Shanna and Eunice to attend Bruiser's games with her, finding out—much to Bruiser's shock—they were big fans and could recite Bruiser's stats from memory. They critiqued every game, and he tolerated their criticism with as much grace as he could muster.

Mac didn't know what the future held, but she knew Bruiser and Elliot would be in it.

Mac was in love, and Bruiser loved her back.

That was all that mattered in her book.

AUTHOR'S NOTE

I'm a true-crime junkie. For this book, I finally decided to put all those hours of watching true-crime television to use. I've always been fascinated by the families who continue to search for their missing loved ones years after they've disappeared. I've been torn between applauding them and wanting them to move on and live their lives. I especially feel sorry for the brothers, sisters, and children of the missing family members, as it often seems they're forgotten while the family strives to unearth the truth.

    I wanted to know how it felt to be a sibling of a missing person, especially when your parent dedicates his entire life to finding your sibling and expects you to do the same. Such is Mac's story in *Backfield in Motion*.

AUTHOR BIO

An advocate of happy endings, Jami Davenport writes sexy romantic comedies, sports hero romances, and equestrian fiction. Jami lives on a small farm near Puget Sound with her Green Beret-turned-plumber husband, a Newfoundland cross with a tennis ball fetish, a prince disguised as an orange tabby cat, and an opinionated Hanoverian mare.

Jami works in information technology for her day job and is a former high school business teacher and dressage rider. In her spare time, she maintains her small farm and socializes whenever the opportunity presents itself. An avid boater, Jami has spent countless hours in the San Juan Islands, a common setting in her books. In her opinion, it is the most beautiful place on earth.

Did you enjoy this book? Drop us a line and say so! We love to hear from readers, and so do our authors. To connect, visit www.boroughspublishinggroup.com online, send comments directly to info@boroughspublishinggroup.com, or friend us on Facebook and Twitter. And be sure to check back regularly for contests and new releases in your favorite subgenres of romance!

Are you an aspiring writer? Check out www.boroughspublishinggroup.com/submit and see if we can help you make your dreams come true.

CPSIA information can be obtained at www.ICGtesting.com
Printed in the USA
LVOW10s2207191016

509492LV00016B/674/P